P9-DXG-880

THE SUGAR FROSTED NUTSACK

THE SUGAR FROSTED NUTSACK

• • • • • • • • •

A NOVEL

• • • • • • • • •

MARK LEYNER

Little, Brown and Company
New York Boston London

Copyright © 2012 by Mark Leyner

Little, Brown and Company
Hachette Book Group
237 Park Avenue, New York, NY 10017
www.hachettebookgroup.com

First Edition: March 2012

Little, Brown and Company is a division of Hachette Book Group, Inc., and is celebrating its 175th anniversary in 2012. The Little, Brown name and logo are trademarks of Hachette Book Group, Inc.

The publisher is not responsible for websites (or their content) that are not owned by the publisher.

The Hachette Speakers Bureau provides a wide range of authors for speaking events. To find out more, go to www.hachettespeakersbureau.com or call (866) 376-6591.

Ike's "10 Things That I Know for Sure About Women" list was originally published as "What I Know for Sure About Women" in *O, the Oprah Magazine*.

Pages 82 and 87 were inspired by *Theatre in Southeast Asia* by James R. Brandon (Harvard University Press, 1967).

Library of Congress Cataloging-in-Publication Data
Leyner, Mark.
 The sugar frosted nutsack : a novel / Mark Leyner.—1st ed.
    p. cm.
 ISBN 978-0-316-60845-9
1. Butchers—Fiction. 2. Gods—Fiction. 3. Goddesses—Fiction. 4. New Jersey—Fiction. I. Title.
 PS3562.E99S84 2012
 813'.54—dc22
    2011030555

10 9 8 7 6 5 4 3 2 1

RRD-C

Printed in the United States of America

THE SUGAR FROSTED NUTSACK

There was never *nothing*. But before the debut of the Gods, about fourteen billion years ago, things happened without any discernable context. There were no recognizable patterns. It was all incoherent. Isolated, disjointed events would take place, only to be engulfed by an opaque black void, their relative meaning, their *significance,* annulled by the eons of entropic silence that estranged one from the next. A terrarium containing three tiny teenage girls mouthing a lot of high-pitched gibberish (like Mothra's fairies, except for their wasted pallors, acne, big tits, and T-shirts that read "I Don't Do White Guys") would inexplicably materialize, and then, just as inexplicably, disappear. And then millions and millions of years would pass, until, seemingly out of nowhere, there'd be, fleetingly...the smell of fresh rolls. Then several more billion years of inert monotony...and then...a houndstooth pattern EVERY-WHERE for approximately 10^{-37} seconds...followed by, again, the fade to immutable blackness and another eternal interstice...and then, suddenly, what might be cicadas or the chafing sound of some obese jogger's nylon track pants...and then the sepia-tinged photograph from a 1933 *Encyclopedia Britannica* of a man with elephantiasis of the testicles...robots roasting freshly gutted fish at a river's edge...the strobe-like fulgurations of ultraviolet emission nebulae...the unmistakable sound of a koto being plucked...and then a toilet flushing. And this last enigmatic event—the flushing of a toilet—was followed by the most inconceivably long hiatus of them all, a sepulchral interregnum of several trillion years. And, as time went on, it began to seem less and less likely that another event would ever occur. Finally, nothing was taking place but the place. There was a definite room tone—that hum, that hymn to pure ontology—but that was all. And in this interminable void, in this black hyperborean stillness, deep in the farthest flung recesses of empty space, at that vanishing point in the infinite distance where parallel lines ultimately converge...two headlights appeared. And there was the sound, barely audible, of something akin to the *Mister Softee* jingle. Now, of course, it wasn't the *Mister Softee* truck whose headlights, like stars light-years in the distance, were barely visible. And it wasn't the *Mister Softee* jingle per se. It was the beginning of something—a few recursive, foretokening measures of music that were curiously familiar, though unidentifiable, and addictively catchy—something akin to the beginning of "Surry with the Fringe on Top" or "Under My Thumb" or "Tears of a Clown" or "White Wedding." And it repeated ad infinitum as those tiny twinkling headlights became imperceptibly larger and drew incrementally closer over the course of the million trillion years that it took for the Gods to finally arrive.

These drunken Gods had been driven by bus to a place they did not recognize. (It's almost as if they'd been on some sort of "Spring Break," as if they'd "gone wild.") At first, they were like frozen aphids. They were so out of it, as if in a state of suspended animation. It took them several more million years just to come to, to sort of "thaw out." The first God to emerge, momentarily, from the bus was called *El Brazo* ("The Arm"). Also known as *Das Unheimlichste des Unheimlichen* ("The Strangest of the Strange"), he was bare-chested and wore white/Columbia-blue polyester dazzle basketball shorts. He would soon be worshipped as the God of Virility, the God of Urology, the God of Pornography, etc. El Brazo leaned out of the bus and struck a contrapposto pose, his head turned away from the torso, an image endlessly reproduced in paintings, sculptures, temple carvings, coins, maritime flags, postage stamps, movie studio logos, souvenir snow globes, take-out coffee cups, playing cards, cigarette packs, condom wrappers, etc. His pomaded hair swept back into a frothy nape of curls like the wake of a speedboat, he reconnoitered the void with an impassive, take-it-or-leave-it gaze, then scowled dyspeptically, immediately turned around, and returned to the bus, where he sullenly ensconced himself, along with the rest of the Gods, for another 1.6 million years. It's extraordinary that, among these sulking, hungover deities who chose to forever doze and fidget in a bus, there were several with enough joie de vivre to continue beatboxing that hypnotic riff for an eternity—that music that's been so persistently likened to a dance mix of the *Mister Softee* jingle. Perhaps it was a fragment of their alma mater's fight song. They did act, after all, like classmates, as if they'd grown up together in the same small town.

One of the first things the Gods did, once they sobered up and finally vacated that bus, was basically put things in order, make them comprehensible, provide context, institute recognizable patterns. (The Gods imposed coherence and meaning, one suspects, as an act of postbender penance.) And that spot in space where they'd fatefully decamped became consecrated forevermore as the celestial *downtown*, the capital of a very hip, but unforgiving, meritocracy. It was very much the Manhattan Project meets Warhol's Factory. And there was that chilly vibe of militant exclusivity, that cordon sanitaire, that velvet rope which segregated the Gods from everyone and everything else. From the outset, it was clear that these Gods had very rigid opinions about who *could* and who *couldn't* be part of their exclusive little clique. No socialites. No dilettantes. No one who was merely "famous for being famous." Just Gods. But their affect was so labile that, depending on your angle, they'd appear completely different from one instant to the next. It was like those lenticular greeting cards. There they'd be, ostensibly a group of elegantly accoutered eighteenth-century aristocrats, straight out of Watteau's rococo *Fête Galante* paintings, amorously cavorting in some sylvan glade with the lutes and the translucent parasols and the flying cupids...but if you shifted your vantage point ever so slightly, they'd look exactly like the members of some Japanese noise band smoking cigarettes backstage at All Tomorrow's Parties at Kutsher's Hotel in Monticello. One minute they'd have assumed the guise of a bunch of tan, well-heeled, ostentatiously casual CEOs chitchatting at the annual Allen & Company Sun Valley media conference...but then you'd tilt your head a bit, and they'd have metamorphosed into a little army of street urchins with matted hair and yellow eyes scavenging for food in garbage dumps, sucking on bags of glue. And because they were omniscient and so tight-knit, they could be very adolescent and pretentious in the way they flaunted their superiority. It wouldn't be unusual for a God to use Ningdu Chinese, Etruscan, Ket (a moribund language spoken by just five hundred people in central Siberia), Mexican Mafia prison code, Klingon, dolphin echolocation clicks, ant pheromones, and honeybee dance steps—all in one sentence. It's the kind of thing where you'd be like, was that *really* necessary?

Everything we are and know comes from the Gods. From their most phantasmagoric dreams and lurid hallucinations, we derive our mathematics and physics. Even their most offhanded mannerisms and nonchalant, lackadaisical gestures could determine the fundamental physical and temporal structures of our world. There was once a birthday party for the God of Money, *Doc Hickory,* who was also known as *El Mas Gordo* ("The Fattest One"). Exhausted from feasting, El Mas Gordo fell asleep on his stomach across his bed. *Lady Rukia* (the Goddess of Scrabble, Jellied Candies, and Harness

Racing), who'd been lusting after El Mas Gordo the entire
night, crept stealthily into his bedroom, rubbed a squeak-
ing balloon across the bosom of her cashmere sweater, and
then waved it back and forth over his hairy back. The way
the static electricity reconfigured the hair on his back would
become the template for the drift of continental landmasses
on earth. Another great example would be, of course, the
God *Rikidozen,* also known as *Santo Malandro* ("Holy Thug").
Rikidozen was once absently tapping a Sharpie on the lip
of a coffee mug, and the unvarying cadence of that tap-tap-
tap became the basis for the standard 124 beats-per-minute
in house music. The Gods were the original (and ultimate)
bricoleurs. They created almost everything from their own
bodies. From their intestinal gas—their flatus—we get nitrous oxide, which we use today as a dental anesthetic and in
our whipped cream aerosol cans (our "whippits"). From the
silver-white secretions that crystallize in the corners of their
eyes after a night's sleep, we obtain lithium, which we use to
make rechargeable batteries for our cellphones and laptops.
Once the God named *Koji Mizokami* had a small teratoma—
a tumor with hair and teeth—removed from one of his testicles. He took it home and fashioned it into the composer
Béla Bartók. He went outside in order to fling him into the
future. But he wasn't sure into whose uterus (and into what
epoch and milieu) he wanted to jettison the musical genius.
Several Gods happened to be strolling by at that moment.
They were the ones known as *The Pince-Nez 44s* or *Los Vatos
Locos* ("The Crazy Guys"). Frequently, they had completely
off-the-wall suggestions, but sometimes these actually turned

out to be pretty decent ideas. "Why don't you have him born to a family of racist Mormons?" one of them suggested. Mizokami looked down at the wriggling larval Bartók in the palm of his hand. "I'm not at all sure about that," he said, in his languid drawl. And then someone else said, "Maybe it would be funnier if he were Joel Madden and Nicole Richie's son? Or make him a Taliban baby." (Eventually, of course, Mizokami-san decided to hurl Béla Bartók into the womb of a woman in Nagyszentmiklós, Austria-Hungary, in the 1880s.)

Generally, the proprietary realms of the Gods were organized and assigned in a very conscientious, collegial manner. There'd usually be some taxonomic category that would ensure a high degree of structural and/or functional relatedness among the various domains that fell under a particular God's purview. But, occasionally, the link between jurisdictions was so tenuous and slapdash that it smacked of reckless endangerment or criminal negligence. For instance, the giantess *C46*, the Goddess of Clear Thinking (i.e., *lucidity*) was, for a brief period, also the Goddess of Clear Skin! It's said that at the end of a long, grueling day, *Shanice* (the very cute, unfailingly effervescent Goddess who functioned as a sort of traffic manager at meetings) noticed that no one had claimed Clear Skin, and she was like, "C46, since you already do Clear Thinking, how about taking this one?" And everyone was so fried at that point that they all just shrugged and acquiesced. On the first Wednesday of the next month, though, everyone realized that Clear Skin should have obviously gone to the God of Dermatology,

José Fleischman (who was sometimes called *The Jew from Peru*). And, without objection, C46 courteously relinquished the realm to The Jew from Peru (who was also known as *The Valiant One* and *He Who Never Shrinks from Anything Pus-Filled*). The point here is that even these kinds of remedial decisions were almost always made by consensus. But sometimes there were disagreements over turf which would escalate into savage internecine conflicts among the Gods, intractable conflicts with ever-widening ramifications.

El Burbuja, the God of Bubbles—a stubby, pockmarked, severely astigmatic deity—originally just ruled over the realm of inflated globules. At first, everyone assumed he'd be satisfied as a kind of geeky "party God" whose dominion would be limited to basically balloons and champagne. And no one paid much attention when he published an almost impenetrably technical paper in some obscure peer-reviewed journal in which he claimed sovereignty over Anything Enveloping Something Else. He then named himself, in rapid succession, God of Ravioli, God of Kishkes, God of Piñatas, God of Enema Bags, God of Chanel Diamond Forever Bags, God of Balloon Angioplasty, and then God of Balloon Swallowers (the drug smugglers who swallow condoms full of drugs). This then enabled him to proclaim himself God of the Movie *Maria Full of Grace,* which gave him entrée not only into the movie industry but—by simply parsing words in that title—into the music business. He immediately became God of the Song "How Do You Solve a Problem Like Maria" and then claimed the entire Rodgers and Hammerstein music catalogue as his own. This all happened, of course, millions of years before these songs were even written. A shrewd, uncannily prescient, and relentlessly enterprising business-man, El Burbuja quietly parlayed a series of discreet lateral "acquisitions"—kielbasa, snow globes, inflatable bounce houses, boba balls (the tapioca balls used in bubble tea), and soft gel encapsulation—into a vast empire of interlocking realms that included Asian magnesium smelting, automated slot machines, first-person shooter games, social networking websites, and iTunes—again, eons before any of these things existed. If ever there were a God destined to appear on the cover of *Cigar Aficionado* magazine, it would be El Burbuja. Probably the most stunning example of how El Burbuja tire-lessly maneuvered under the radar to expand his empire is when he proclaimed himself God of Those Blue *New York Times* Bags People Use to Pick Up Their Dogs' Shit. The other Gods' initial reaction to this was, predictably, one of complete befuddlement. Who'd want *that?* But El Burbuja was playing many moves ahead of the others. He quickly as-sumed the mantle of God of Dogs, God of New York, and God of Shit. Again, this is before there was ever such a thing as "New York" or "dogs" or even "shit." (The Gods' ex-crement is called "loot drops." It's a slurry of coltan—the metallic ore used today in many cellphones and laptop com-puters.) No one seemed to even notice or particularly care when he took the next logical step and made himself God of Times, because all that really entailed was track and field records and multiplex showtimes (e.g., 11:50 AM, 2:15 PM, 4:45 PM, 7:20 PM, 9:45 PM, 12:15 AM). But then El Burbuja, on a late Friday afternoon before a long holiday weekend—and as he'd been planning to do all along—lopped the "s" off "Times" and became the God of Time. It was a characteristically ingenious, some might say cynical, even unscrupulous, ploy, but once everyone realized that what had appeared to be a proofreading correction was actually a coup of epic proportions, it was too late—they were presented with a fait accompli and had no other choice than to acquiesce. And that is how this unprepossessing, chubby God with the bad skin and the weak eyes parlayed jurisdiction over bags of warm crap into irrefutable control over one of the fundamental dimensions in the universe, thereby making himself one of the most formidable Gods in the whole fucking pantheon! But even though El Burbuja had clearly finagled for himself the vast Realm of Time, the other Gods continued to indulge the astigmatic "Mogul Magoo" (as he came to be called) basically because he was *so* homely and *such* an obsessive workaholic, and they just found his insatiable acquisitiveness sort of... *cute.* They'd say, "Oh, that's just how little Mogul Magoo rolls" or "Oh, that's just Mogul Magoo being Mogul Magoo." (And they knew, of course, that he was destined to become the tutelary divinity of plutocrats and rich, pampered celebrities.) Granted, sometimes the other Gods were like, "Magoo, what the fuck? Relax." But no one ever really felt like begrudging him the fruits of his monomaniacal labor. It was something relatively mundane that caused Magoo to run afoul of the irascible El Brazo, who sometimes referred to Magoo as *Fräulein Luftblase* ("Miss Bubble")—a taunting homophobic slur. Without any fanfare, one day, Magoo had asserted himself as the God of the Breast Implant and God

of the Nutsack. He dutifully submitted his boilerplate rationale: Anything Enveloping Something Else. Just as a bubble
is a globule of water that contains air, the scrotum is a pouch
of skin and muscle that contains the testicles, and the breast
implant is an elastomer-coated sac containing a thick silicone
gel. Ergo, it's perfectly logical and reasonable to conclude
that both spheres fall within my purview. This completely infuriated El Brazo, who, as the God of Urology and the God
of Pornography, considered the nutsack and the breast implant his inviolable domains. The antipathy that developed
between these two Gods (and, subsequently, between Magoo
and the Goddess *La Felina*) would have significant consequences throughout the ages. El Brazo began to routinely,
and very publically, threaten Magoo and his cohorts with liquidation in a sort of Night of the Long Knives. And Magoo
began traveling around with a posse of "Pistoleras"—half a
dozen divine, ax-wielding mercenary vixens who were total
fitness freaks with rock-hard bodies. Each of them had a venomous black mamba snake growing out of the back of her
head, which she'd pull through the size-adjustment cutout on
the back of her baseball cap. And this is the origin of today's
fashion in which women gather their hair into a ponytail or
a braid and allow it to hang through the hole in the backs of
their caps.

The Gods used a drug called "Gravy," also known as *Pozole* ("stew"). Their drug use was heavy and appeared to be
both ritualistic and recreational. At one time, it was considered to be what actually made the Gods deities, and there
was speculation that consumption by human beings might

bestow certain divine qualities on them. Gravy was originally thought to be a smokable version of the Vedic drug
Soma and assumed to be hallucinogenic and derived from
psilocybin mushrooms or *Amanita muscaria* (psychoactive ba-
sidiomycete fungus). Some have speculated that Gravy is a
form of hallucinogenic borscht—a theory endorsed by such
scholars as Mircea Eliade, Georges Dumezil, and University of Chicago Professor of the History of Religions Wendy
Doniger. Today, though, many experts believe that Gravy is
a solvent similar to what's found in glue, paint thinner, and
felt-tip markers. This theory has gained considerable sup-
port among a wide range of prominent people, including
TMZ's Harvey Levin, forensic pathologist Cyril Wecht,
criminal defense attorney Mark Geragos, and professional
beach volleyball player Misty May-Treanor. Before the im-
bibing of Gravy, ritual protocol required the recitation of a
sacred oath, and then the guest would clink his golden chal-
ice against that of his divine host and solemnly ask, "You
gonna shoot that or sip it?" There are about fourteen Weight
Watchers Points in a half-cup serving of the rich hallucinogenic beverage. Smokable Gravy—made by heating liquid
Gravy and baking soda until small pinkish-white precipitates
("rocks") form—is more quickly absorbed into the bloodstream, reaching the brain in about eight seconds. (Side
effects can include: Progeria, Necrotizing Fasciitis, Bovine
Spongiform Encephalopathy, Craniopagus Twins, Elephantiasis of the Testicles, Projectile Anal Hemorrhaging, and
Gangrene of the Eyeballs.)

* * *

Yagyu—a God who was also known as *Dark Cuervo* ("Dark Raven") and *Fast-Cooking Ali* created "Woman's Ass," which was considered his masterpiece. Nothing he'd done before prepared the other Gods for the stunning, unprecedented triumph that was "Woman's Ass." His previous accomplishments had been deliberately banal. He'd created the Platitude, for instance. When the Gods first *came to*— once they'd finally recovered from whatever dissipated spree they'd been on—they came to with a jolt, pulsing with intensity and ambition. They worked nonstop, didn't sleep, their pupils were dilated, they were jittery, quivering with nervous tics, and they talked incessantly—they had this self-indulgent, hyperintellectual diarrhea of the mouth. Like, instead of just muttering "Fuck," a God who cut himself shaving would launch into an anguished soliloquy in the iambic tetrameter of John Milton's *Il Penseroso*. And the simplest, most perfunctory questions, like "Hey, how's it going?" would elicit long, recondite Spinozan disquisitions on "attributes" and "modes" and discursive, inferential perception. Fast-Cooking Ali was a very shy, introspective, solitary individual. So he created a series of stock phrases that more reticent, self-effacing Gods like himself could use in response to the query "Hey, how's it going?" These included "It's going," "Hangin' in there," "Same shit, different day," and "If you want to live, don't come any closer." Fast-Cooking Ali's bromides quickly became part of the standard repertoire, but he pretty much disappeared from the scene and became a recluse and no one after that knew what he was working on or if he was even working on anything. It was said that he was spending his days holed up in a room somewhere, by himself, smoking Gravy, muttering to himself, lost in masturbatory fantasies about loop quantum gravity and supersymmetric particles. And then one day he emerged with "Woman's Ass." El Brazo was the first to see it. "That's so fucking hot! It's genius," he exclaimed, immediately summoning the other Gods. There was considerable discussion about hair—how much, how little (final decision: none on the cheeks, some along the perineum, downy fuzz above the crack)—and the pigmentation of the skin around the anus (final decision: slightly darker for white women). Despite the great acclaim he received for "Woman's Ass," Fast-Cooking Ali dropped out of sight again. Although it would not become public knowledge for millions of years, he had begun a very secret, very intense affair with La Felina, the Goddess of Humility. La Felina would, over the course of time, have many relationships with mortal men. She has a heavy sexual thing for Hasidic and Amish guys, as well as anarcho-primitivists, including Theodore Kaczynski (the Unabomber). Sometimes she wears a Japanese schoolgirl sailor outfit. La Felina hates the rich and she hates celebrities. (She has recently tried to induce a deranged person to stalk and kill the designer Marc Jacobs.) El Brazo is the God who fills our bodies with desires that can never be satisfied. But La Felina is the Goddess responsible for making ugly women more erotic than beautiful women.

The God of Head Trauma (who was also, of course, the

God of Concussions, the God of Dementia, the God of Alcoholic Blackouts, the God of Brainwashing, Implanted Thoughts, and Cultural Amnesia) was called *El Cucho* ("The Old Man"). This was a facetious epithet because El Cucho had a lustrously youthful appearance—a million-watt smile and a streaming surfer-boy mane of blond hair. He wore a tiger-skin loincloth. In the eternal schism between El Brazo and La Felina on one side versus Mogul Magoo and his snake-headed Pistoleras ·on the other, El Cucho (who was also known as "Kid Coma" and "XOXO") was firmly in the El Brazo / La Felina camp. XOXO liked sitting around with circus performers and hockey players and boxers and plying them with drugged sherbet. He liked to mess with people's minds—to make them forget things or put alien ideas in their heads. (Year after year, he was consistently voted both "Most Sadistic" *and* "Friendliest" God by his peers!) Once, he gave Pittsburgh Penguin center Evgeni Malkin a concussion during a game at Mellon Arena, and although Malkin's body (his "mortal husk") lay unconscious on·the ice for about ten human-minutes, XOXO actually "kidnapped" Malkin's soul and took it to his garish hyperborean hermitage miles beneath the earth's surface in what is now Antarctica, where he kept it captive for two and a half God-years. There was a suffocatingly sweet smell at the hermitage, as if Eggnog Febreze was being continuously pumped in through the ventilation system. XOXO served Malkin's soul drugged sherbet, which made Malkin's soul woozy and disinhibited enough that it agreed to be dressed up in a U.S. Marines tank top and PVC diaper briefs. Then the two of them played a card game called snarples, and every so often XOXO would chastely kiss Malkin's soul on the mouth. Then XOXO shampooed and cornrowed Malkin's soul's hair, and, using a sharp periodontal curette, he carved short secret phrases into the furrows on his scalp (like "Puppy Love" and "Book Club" and "New You"). It was creepy. Each time XOXO would kiss him, he'd exhale fervently into his mouth. It was really more like CPR than making out. XOXO's breath was like mentholated Freon. And when Malkin finally came to on the ice at Mellon Arena, he pawed violently at his throat saying over and over again in Russian, "My uvula is frozen!" All Malkin could remember was being given a ticker tape parade. But then he realized with a shudder that it wasn't ticker tape at all but the gossamer scales of his own molting mind that were falling all over the streets of Pittsburgh! XOXO also delighted in abducting legal proofreaders from midtown office buildings in the middle of the night and taking their souls to his remote, sweet-scented hermitage, where he'd keep them captive and toy with them for years. They'd wake up back in their office cubicles thinking they'd lost consciousness from anaphylactic allergic reactions to ingesting peanuts in candy bars they'd gotten out of the vending machines. XOXO had once shown a poem he'd written to Shanice, the irrepressibly chipper Goddess of Management—the adorable one with the awesome organizational skill set—and her reaction was uncharacteristically negative. XOXO had literally asked for it, though. He had explicitly requested that Shanice not give him one of those glib "Oh, it's really great!" responses, but to take her time, read it over carefully, and provide him with a very honest critique. And he told her, furthermore, that the more unsparing the critique was, the more meaningful it would be to him, and that he was only showing the poem to her because he considered her the most trustworthy of all the Gods and he could depend on her, and only her, to be completely candid with him. What Shanice didn't realize at the time—although she would eventually—was that the offering of the poem was a gesture of seduction. Not that the content of the poem was seductive per se—it was not a "love poem" in any sense. The poem depicts a group of businessmen who are returning home from work one evening. On a lark, they diverge from their customary route and end up deep in the woods. They gang up on the "new guy" (someone who'd only recently been transferred to their division), and, in what appears to be a sort of hazing ritual, they tie him to a tree and whip him with his own belt. His pants fall to his ankles, and it's obvious that he's aroused. *But*—as the poem goes on to suggest—he's aroused not by the robust flagellation but because he sees an ineffably beautiful butterfly flit by. Everyone had always considered XOXO to be kind of frivolous. He actively pursued his hobby of snatching hockey players' souls and messing with their minds and what not, but he didn't seem to apply himself diligently to much of anything else. He came across as something of a dilettante and an underachiever. XOXO thought that the poem would show Shanice a more serious side and a more delicately registered sensibility than he was usually given credit for. Shanice had always assumed that

XOXO was unequivocally gay—something confirmed, in her mind, by the homoerotic tenor of the poem. One could certainly discern an element of shame in the poem or at least a desire on the part of the poem's protagonist to displace or mitigate the cause of his arousal. And Shanice did, in fact, discern this strain of discomfort in the poem. She wasn't at all what she seemed either. And, in this way, she had a great deal in common with XOXO. They both felt underestimated by the other Gods. (It was Shanice's sense that the other Gods considered her to be affable and competent, but basically pedestrian.) Anyway, if Shanice had realized at the time that XOXO was offering her the poem to read and critique as a gesture of seduction, she probably would have finessed her evaluation a bit. But she didn't. And it was quite a blow. The incident made things tense between Shanice and XOXO, left them somewhat estranged, and undoubtedly influenced Shanice—whether she was conscious of it or not—to align herself with Mogul Magoo (on whom she soon developed an insane crush). It also left XOXO embittered and implacably hostile to anyone who ever tried to put his or her thoughts and feelings into words. And so XOXO, this resentful poet manqué, became the God who delights in spitefully snatching brilliant thoughts from people's minds and casting them into oblivion. When you're lying in bed, in that hypnagogic state, neither awake nor asleep, and you have a lovely idea that seems to evanesce almost as soon as you're conscious of it—that's XOXO snatching it away. And when you're high and you have an extraordinarily inspired and unprecedented idea and then you wake up the next day and have to glumly acknowledge how banal and derivative it actually was—that's also XOXO's doing. During the night he came down and sabotaged the idea, gutted it—leaving only the banal and derivative. He keeps a vast cache of stolen ideas in his hyperborean hermitage.

Why Do Gods Like Having Sex With Humans So Much?

For them it's a kind of slumming, rough trade, a *nostalgie de la boue* ("nostalgia for the mud"). And many of the Gods—including several of the *major* deities—feel that human beings' finite life expectancies and their comparatively limited intelligence simply make them SUPER-SEXY! These Gods find human existential angst—being aware that death is inevitable, but not knowing, at any given moment, exactly when or how it might occur—to be a total TURN-ON! They paradoxically find those very characteristics that so definitively subordinate human beings to the Gods—mortality, benightedness, and impotence—to be HOT, HOT! HOT!! And the very thought of abjectly defiling themselves—of *wallowing*—in all the pungent excretions and effluvia of the human body maddens them with desire. This is the good news. The bad news is that, for a human, having a sexual/romantic relationship with a God can be a daunting, traumatic, and even tragic experience. You have to be very careful! Gods are self-important. They tend to have ADD. They love to fuck with your head. Because they're immortal, they tend to be late all the time. And because they're omnipotent, they usually exhibit a complete lack of empathy. They are narcissistic and furiously self-absorbed. If they want to have sex with you, it doesn't really matter to them how you're feeling or what you're going through. So don't expect understanding or patience from a God just because you're getting your period or you have to study for your SATs or you're leaving the next day for a tour of duty in Afghanistan. And if a God does seem to evince some concern or betray any vulnerability, you have to be very skeptical because their behavior is frequently insincere and manipulative. And they're supermercurial and you have to always put up with their cryptic moods and petulant fatwas. And they can come and go (i.e., materialize and disappear) so that no one else can see them—which can make you feel very isolated from other people. Mi-Hyun, age twenty-nine, worked at a florist shop. She was *very* pretty. She had a page-boy with cute blunt-cut bangs. One day, *Bosco Hifikepunye,* the God of Miscellany (including Fibromyalgia, Chicken Tenders, Sports Memorabilia, SteamVac Carpet Cleaners, etc., etc.) espied Mi-Hyun as she smoked a Parliament Light outside the florist shop. He couldn't believe how HOT she was! And soon the God and his "Little Flower Girl" were having completely insane sex-a-thons. But, of course, Hifikepunye would arrive and depart invisibly, unbeknownst to anyone but Mi-Hyun. Mi-Hyun's neighbors—the old Dominican ladies—would always tease her: "You're a pretty girl, Mi-Hyun. When are you going to get a boyfriend?" And Mi-Hyun would be like, "I have boyfriend. He visit me every night." "But we never see him," the old ladies would reply. "We never see *anyone* visit you." And soon they started to think that Mi-Hyun was crazy. At first, it didn't really bother Mi-Hyun. She was too happy. The God, Hifikepunye, was GREAT in bed! He'd anoint her clitoris with Witches' Flying Ointment (aka *Lamiarum Unguenta* or "Witches' Unguent"), a mixture of Gravy, belladonna, chimney soot, clove oil, and the fat of an unbaptized child. Once he made her fifty feet tall and put the mummified body of King Tutankhamen into her ass as she came. She liked that so much that he turned Lenin's corpse and Ted Williams's cryonically preserved head into anal sex toys too! These are things that, of course, Mi-Hyun would excitedly tell her co-workers at the florist shop the next morning, but they would just shake their heads and say, "Mi-Hyun, you need to see a psychiatrist." Soon Mi-Hyun was let go from the florist shop. And she became alienated from her neighbors. And, worst of all, the Goddess Lady Rukia (Scrabble, Jellied Candies, Harness Racing), who coveted Hifikepunye and was jealous of his mortal paramour, gave Mi-Hyun periodontal disease so she'd have bad breath and bleeding gums and be less alluring to the God. Sure enough, Hifikepunye lost interest in her and stopped coming around. (One Christmas, he felt guilty and put a winning Pick 6 Lotto number into one of her dreams. But XOXO made her forget it as soon as she woke up.) Heartbroken, lonely, penniless, and now dying from the high levels of bacterial endotoxins that her infected gums had released into her bloodstream, Mi-Hyun lay across the tracks at the West Side Rail Yards one freezing

night and waited for a freight train to end her misery.... She
was picked up by the police and brought to the Emergency
Room at Bellevue Hospital where she was admitted with a
fever of 104 degrees, refractory hypotension, tachypnea, and
a white blood cell count of 14,000 cells/mm^3. She was immediately administered oxygen, fluids, and antibiotics and
transferred to the ICU where she was given an APACHE II
score of 25 and diagnosed with severe sepsis. She was put
on norepinephrine and a continuous infusion of piperacillin-
tazobactam with aminoglycoside. Three weeks later, it was
determined that she was healthy enough to be transferred
to the psychiatric unit. After telling psychiatrists and nurses
about her sexual liaisons with the God Bosco Hifikepunye
and about how he made her fifty feet tall and used Ted Williams's cryonically preserved head as an anal sex toy and
about how XOXO, the God of Dementia and Implanted
Thoughts, had made her forget the winning Pick 6 Lotto
number that Hifikepunye had hidden in her dreams and
about how Lady Rukia, the Goddess of Scrabble and Jellied Candies, in a jealous rage, had given her periodontal
disease that eventually developed into endotoxemia and sepsis...she was diagnosed with paranoid schizophrenia and
put on 15 mg per day of the antipsychotic drug Zyprexa.
When she failed to respond to the medication (i.e., when she
continued to insist upon the veracity of her stories about the
Gods), she was given electroconvulsive therapy four times a
week for the following several months. And although this resulted in severe retrograde amnesia (she no longer has *any*
memories of her parents or her childhood), her memory of

being fifty feet tall and fucking a God remains vividly intact. And this memory, like a single calligraphic stroke on the white page of her erased mind, caused a dreamy smile to permanently settle across the catatonic impassivity of her face. XOXO had ineradicably inscribed the memory in Mi-Hyun's mind at the behest of La Felina (who detests the vain, the rich, the celebrated and champions the humble, the indigent, the anonymous, the unknown and inaccessible, the marginalized, the deranged, the antimodernists, the anarcho-primitivists, the fanatical Luddites, the bedraggled, plump, sweaty working-class women with hairy pussies, etc.). The Gods glorify chosen mortals ("the elect") by having XOXO ineradicably inscribe in their minds the story of the Gods. Now this particular story brings up a very interesting point about the Gods and their complex and often opaque relationships. Why would XOXO ineradicably inscribe into the mind of a mortal woman an amorous memory about Bosco Hifikepunye (who was also sometimes known as *Cara de Papa* ("Potato Face")? After all, wasn't XOXO aligned with the El Brazo / La Felina / Fast-Cooking Ali axis, which generally contended against the Mogul Magoo / Shanice / Lady Rukia / Hifikepunye camp? Yes, but although the Gods' roiling antipathies and interpersonal feuds were genuine and their larger schisms intractable and polarizing, they constituted, in the grand scheme of things, a kind of "play." The Gods disported themselves by endlessly acting out their essential natures, the affirmation of their own wills and the fulfillment of their own desires—this "sport" perpetually reproducing (as if inadvertently) the harsh patterns and eternal recurrences of human life. The settlement of divine differences inevitably results in human collateral damage for which the Gods feel absolutely no responsibility or remorse. But the bonds of kinship among them are indestructible. And their protocol—their lordly code of precedence and etiquette vis-à-vis one another—as inscrutable as it will forever remain to us, is scrupulously observed, without dissent, by them. When, by some unspoken consensus, the Gods determine to glorify a chosen mortal by having XOXO ineradicably inscribe in his or her mind the story of the Gods, it's done, regardless of whomever's proxy or fuck-buddy that mortal might have been. Just as when, by some unspoken consensus, the Gods determined one day that their Belle Époque was over and that it was time to disperse for a while, for each God and Goddess to go his or her own way.

During the Belle Époque—that period of time, about fourteen billion years ago, after the Gods were delivered by bus from some sort of "Spring Break" during which they are said to have "gone wild"—the Gods put things in order, made them comprehensible, provided context, imposed coherence and meaning, i.e., they created the world as we know it today. But although, as it's been said, they abide by a stern, hieratic protocol, these Gods—Rikidozen, Los Vatos Locos, José Fleischman, The Pistoleras, etc.—when viewed from a certain perspective, can seem like harebrained cartoon characters lurching haphazardly from one debacle to another, motivated as much by mischievousness and perversity as anything resembling intent or design. For instance, most of the butt-calls that people make today are the result of bored Gods just fucking around. And a lot of the weird, unexplained things that happen to people in Florida are the work of the Gods. In a Gravy-fueled tantrum one night in a Pensacola Motel 6, the Dwarf Goddess *La Muñeca* ("The Doll") turned her mortal girlfriend Francesca DiPasquale, a Chief Warrant Officer in the U.S. Navy, into a macadamia nut, then a jai alai ball, and then into 100,000 shares of Schering-Plough stock. How credible did Pensacola Chief of Police Ellis Moynihan consider speculation that a lesbian Dwarf Goddess high on a smokable form of hallucinogenic borsht called "Gravy" might have turned the missing DiPasquale into Schering-Plough stock? In other words— was Moynihan one of the *elect,* one of the *illuminati?* Unfortunately, we'll never know. Two weeks after DiPasquale disappeared, Moynihan died of anaphylactic shock from a severe allergic reaction to peanuts in a vending machine candy bar. Strange, isn't it? Moynihan had never previously shown *any* symptoms of even a mild sensitivity to peanuts. In fact, he *loved* peanuts and consumed them in such quantities that his coworkers in the squad room had begun referring to him as *El Hombre Elefante* ("The Elephant Man"). (Although, perhaps, as Desk Sergeant Nate Seabrook confided with a nudge and a wink, that nickname actually derived from the massive plexiform neurofibroma that obscured half of Moynihan's face.) Stranger still—when officers looked frantically for the epinephrine auto-injector in the emergency first-aid kit, they found that someone had replaced it with a whippet, a small cartridge of nitrous oxide (aka "Laughing Gas"). A taunting cosmic joke? Yeah, maybe. But what does this wild oscillation between the sublime (e.g., the creation of musical harmony, the electromagnetic spectrum, prime numbers and the Riemann Zeta Function, etc.) and the gratuitously sadistic (e.g., giving someone a grotesquely disfiguring facial tumor) reveal to us about the Gods? La Muñeca was the Goddess of Architecture—she designed some of the most spectacular of the Gods' hyperborean hermitages, in addition to the huge biomorphic resin and silicone dining table for the Hall of the Slain that's considered as radical today as it was eleven billion years ago when she first impulsively sketched the design on a napkin at a club! Doesn't sabotaging a first-aid kit in a Pensacola, Florida, police station so that someone suffocates to death, someone whose only offense seems to have been suspecting that you turned your girlfriend into a jai alai ball when you were high—doesn't this, in addition to being mind-bogglingly petty and vindictive, seem like a colossal waste of time for the Goddess of Architecture? Well, first of all, a God would contend, you can't waste something of which you have an inexhaustible supply. And secondly, since anything a God does is an expression of that God's essential nature and thus imparts meaning and transfigures the manifold totality of the real, gradations of significance don't exist—everything is equally important.

Think of the sweetest, most wonderful things you've ever experienced in your life...just randomly, off the top of your head...things as ineffably sublime as the beautiful butterfly which aroused the businessman in XOXO's poem....Now, make a list. For instance:

- It's 1960 in Jersey City and you're falling asleep in your mom's lap on a Hudson Boulevard bus to the metronomic cadence of the windshield wipers and the sound of the tires on the rainy street, and sitting all around you are nuns and stooped gray men in fedoras.
- Egg-drop soup and egg rolls at the Jade Restaurant in Journal Square, Jersey City.
- The gurgle of watercoolers and the pungent aroma of legal accordion folders in the supply room at 26 Journal Square.
- Mid-1960s, late afternoon, drinking Yoo-hoo with your dad at the driving range, and then, later that night, sitting in front of the TV with him and the intro for *Combat!* comes on ("*Combat!* Starring Vic Morrow and Rick Jason"), and your dad offers you a stick of Black Jack gum.
- Eating tea sandwiches with your mom at the Bird Cage in Lord & Taylor, in Millburn, New Jersey.
- The first movie scenes that gave you a hard-on: when seaman John Mills (played by Richard Harris) gets flogged with a cat-o'-nine-tails in *Mutiny on the Bounty* (also Harris's O-Kee-Pa suspension initiation ritual in *A Man Called Horse*); and when Candace Hilligoss gets out of the bathtub in *Carnival of Souls* (to creepy organ music), also the scene where Candace Hilligoss tries different stations on the car radio (but can only get creepy organ music), and the scene where Candace Hilligoss takes her clothes off in the dressing room at the department store (to creepy organ music); and also when Martine Carol emerges from her bathtub in *Lucrèce Borgia* (aka *Sins of the Borgias*), and

also, in the same movie, when she's whipped by her brother, Cesare (played by Pedro Armendáriz).

- That moment in the early '90s when there were three made-for-TV movies about Amy Fisher: *The Amy Fisher Story* (Drew Barrymore), *Amy Fisher: My Story* (Noelle Parker), and *Casualties of Love: The Long Island Lolita Story* (Alyssa Milano); and then, soon, Tonya Harding and Jeff Gillooly's "Wedding Video" sex tape came out.

- That total goose bump moment in the Pet Shop Boys song "What Have I Done to Deserve This?" when Dusty Springfield starts to sing ("Since you went away, I've been hanging around / I've been wondering why I'm feeling down").

- In 2004, the long-awaited pedestrian bridge over Kennedy Boulevard (formerly Hudson Boulevard) links the East Campus and the West Campus of St. Peter's College in Jersey City.

- Nice and drunk on Chivas Regal, eating ravioli, first heavy snow falling outside, fat girl at the bar (nice and drunk too) smiles at you.

Each of these numinous moments, these epiphanies, is *of the Gods, a manifestation,* a *Godding (Götterung),* and in each we are able to unmistakably discern the hand of a specific God. Mogul Magoo's fingerprints are all over those egg rolls at the Jade in Journal Square. And, surely, we can identify, in the pedestrian bridge that spans Kennedy Boulevard, linking the two campuses of St. Peter's College, the animating spirit of La Muñeca. And who else could have been behind the unprecedented phenomenon of Amy Fisher and Tonya Harding but La Felina, the fanatical champion of unsublimated passion and base motives, who glories in authentic intensities like lust, jealousy, and vengeance? The Fisher/Harding upheaval seemed to augur an astonishing revolution in the sociology of glamour—the erotic exaltation of the homely, unscrupulous, working-class girl. But it was so short-lived as to actually be a last gasp, because reality entertainment almost immediately reverted to a depressingly predictable perversion of all that, exalting instead the Hilton/Richie/Kardashian axis of "beautiful" celebutantes. This development so infuriated La Felina that, at one point, she was about to unleash a hybrid of Charles Manson and Pol Pot on America to completely purge it of every single "beautiful" celebutante when Fast-Cooking Ali dissuaded her at the very last minute, not because he was against the idea but because they were incredibly late to something, and La Felina—who exalts the physically deformed and the mentally unbalanced and the sans-culottes and the scum of the earth, and who wet her pants during the September Massacres of 1792—decided to shelve the plan for another time.

By some unspoken consensus, the Gods determined one day that their Belle Époque was over and that it was time to disperse for a while, for each God and Goddess to go his or her own way. This was the Diaspora of the Gods. Several stayed in the vicinity of the Gods' original "bus stop," which experts have speculatively situated in the Abell 1835

Galaxy, some 13 billion light-years from Earth, while others place it in the Markarian 421 Galaxy, which is located in the constellation Ursa Major, a mere 360 million light-years away. Some Gods (e.g., El Brazo), of course, moved into Versailles-like coral and onyx palaces and sumptuous frangipani-scented hermitages miles underground in what is now Antarctica. Los Vatos Locos submerged themselves in a peat bog in Denmark for several million years. While some pursued esoteric, purely theoretical existences in strange, impalpable, zero-dimensional realms, others chose drab, quotidian lives (à la Jenny from the block) in small cities in the Midwest. Mogul Magoo, Shanice, and the Pistoleras inhabited the lush mountains of the Gondwana supercontinent. Lady Rukia and Doc Hickory lived on a cul-de-sac in Chula Vista, California. The lovers La Felina and Fast-Cooking Ali—both avatars of humility and self-denial—shrunk themselves down to about three micrometers tall (the size of a typical yeast cell) and lived in the anal scent-gland of a capybara named *Dawson* in the remote Caura forest in southern Venezuela. And then, one day in 1973, by some unspoken consensus, the Gods determined that their Diaspora was over and that they would all reconvene and, from here on in, occupy the top floors of the world's tallest and most opulent skyscraper. Thus began a nomadic period during which the Gods constantly moved, en masse, from what had become the former tallest-building-in-the-world to the latest tallest-building-the-world. So, in the summer of 1973, the Gods and Goddesses all moved into the top floors of the Sears Tower (now known as the Willis

Tower) in Chicago, Illinois. They then relocated, in 1998, to the Petronas Twin Towers in Kuala Lumpur, Malaysia; the Taipei 101 in Taiwan, in 2004; the Shanghai World Financial Center in China, in 2008; and finally, in 2009, the Burj Khalifa in the Business Bay district of Dubai, United Arab Emirates. The Burj Khalifa is 2,717 feet tall. And this is where the Gods currently reside.

The Sugar Frosted Nutsack is the story of a man, a mortal, an unemployed butcher, in fact, who lives in Jersey City, New Jersey, in a two-story brick house that is approximately twenty feet tall. This man is the hero IKE KARTON. The epic ends with Ike's violent death. If only Ike had used for his defense "silence, exile, and cunning." But that isn't Ike. Ike is the Warlord of his Stoop. Ike is a man who is "singled out." A man marked by fate. A man of Gods, attuned to the Gods. A man anathematized by his neighbors. A man beloved by La Felina and Fast-Cooking Ali, and a man whose mind is ineradicably inscribed by XOXO. Ike's brain is riddled with the tiny, meticulous longhand of the mind-fucking God XOXO, whose very name bespeaks life's irreconcilable contradictions, symbolizing both *love* (hugs and kisses) and *war* (the diagramming of football plays).

What will give us goose bumps and make us teary-eyed when, in the end, Ike dies? It's the same thing that gave us goose bumps and made us teary-eyed when we heard Dusty Springfield sing "Since you went away, I've been hanging around / I've been wondering why I'm feeling down" in the song "What Have I Done to Deserve This?" It's the same thing that makes all pop music so heartbreaking. Even when Miley Cyrus sings "So I put my hands up, they're playin' my song / The butterflies fly away / I'm noddin' my head like 'Yeah!' / Movin' my hips like 'Yeah!'" in her song "Party in the U.S.A." It's that chirping mirth against a backdrop of despair, that juxtaposition of blithe optimism against all the crushing brutalities and inadequacies of life. The image of an ineffably beautiful butterfly flitting by the shattered windows of a dilapidated, abandoned factory is not so poignant because it highlights the indomitable life force. To the contrary, the butterfly (and the pop song) is like a PowerPoint cursor; it's there to whet our perception of and strengthen our affinity for what's moribund, for what's always dying before our eyes. Loving the moribund is our way of signaling the dead from this shore: "We are your kinsmen…"

When Ike dies, at the hands of the ATF snipers or Mossad assassins or Interpol agents, or is beset by a swarm of nano-drones (depending on which story you choose to believe), he dies with a metaphysical coquettishness that befits a true hero, greeting his violent demise with silly, sweet, uninhibited laughter. All the Gods are suddenly talking at once; it's this Babel, this incomprehensible cacophony, that just degenerates into white noise. And then it's as if he's stepped into an empty elevator shaft on the top floor of the world's tallest building, and as he plummets down, he whistles the *Mister Softee* jingle—"those recursive, foretokening measures of music; that hypnotic riff"—over and over and over and over again to himself…

A hero.

1.

*What subculture is evinced by **Ike**'s clothes and his shtick, by the non-Semitic contours of his nose and his dick, by the feral fatalism of all his loony tics—like the petit-mal fluttering of his long-lashed lids and the **Mussolini** torticollis of his Schick-nicked neck, and the staring and the glaring and the daring and the hectoring, and the tapping on the table with his aluminum wedding ring, as he hums those tunes from his childhood albums and, after a spasm of **Keith Moon** air-drums, returns to his lewd mandala of Italian breadcrumbs?*

So begins the story of **Ike Karton**, a story variously called throughout history *Ike's Agony, T.G.I.F. (Ten Gods I'd Fuck),* and *The Sugar Frosted Nutsack*. This is a story that's been told, how many times?—over and over and over again, essentially verbatim, with the same insistent, mesmerizing cadences, and the same voodoo tapping of a big clunky ring against some table.

Every new improvisational flourish, every editorial inter-polation and aside, every ex post facto declaration, exegeti-cal commentary and meta-commentary, every cough, sniffle, and hiccough on the part of the rhapsode is officially sub-sumed into the story, and is then required in each subsequent performance. So, for instance, the next time *The Sugar Frosted Nutsack* is recited, the audience will expect that the sentence "Every new improvisational flourish, every editorial interpo-lation and aside, every ex post facto declaration, exegetical commentary and meta-commentary, every cough, sniffle, and hiccough on the part of the rhapsode is officially sub-sumed into the story, and is then required in each subsequent performance" be included in the recitation, and if it's not, they'll feel—and justifiably so—that something vital and in-tegral has been left out.

The audience will, in fact, demand that the sentence "So, for instance, the next time *The Sugar Frosted Nutsack* is recited, the audience will expect that the sentence 'Every new impro-visational flourish, every editorial interpolation and aside, every ex post facto declaration, exegetical commentary and meta-commentary, every cough, sniffle, and hiccough on the part of the rhapsode is officially subsumed into the story, and is then required in each subsequent performance' be included in the recitation, and if it's not, they'll feel—and justifiably so—that something vital and integral has been left out" *also* be included in the recitation. And also the sen-tence that begins "The audience will, in fact, demand that the sentence 'So, for instance, the next time *The Sugar Frosted Nutsack* is recited, the audience will expect that the sentence

"Every new improvisational flourish...,"'" etc. And also the sentence that begins "And also the sentence that begins..." And also the sentence that begins "And also the sentence that begins 'And also the sentence that begins...'" Et cetera, et cetera.

To a critical degree, this infinite recursion of bracketed redundancies is what gives *The Sugar Frosted Nutsack* its peculiarly numinous and incantatory quality. Everything *about* it becomes *it*.

Keep in mind that the original story (what we've gleaned from cave walls, cuneiform on clay tablets, and papyrus fragments) was only one paragraph long, consisting in its entirety of: *What subculture is evinced by **Ike**'s clothes and his shtick, by the non-Semitic contours of his nose and his dick, by the feral fatalism of all his loony tics—like the petit-mal fluttering of his long-lashed lids and the **Mussolini** torticollis of his Schick-nicked neck, and the staring and the glaring and the daring and the hectoring, and the tapping on the table with his aluminum wedding ring, as he hums those tunes from his childhood albums and, after a spasm of **Keith Moon** air-drums, returns to his lewd mandala of Italian breadcrumbs?*

For hundreds, even thousands, of years, this was all there was to the "epic" story of **Ike**, the 5'7" unemployed butcher, incorrigible heretic, and feral dandy who slicked his jet-black hair back with perfumed pomade and dyed his armpit hair a light chestnut color and who was dear to the Gods (themselves ageless, deathless).

Then, sometime circa 700 B.C., the subhead <u>**Ike** Always Keeps It Simple and Sexy</u> was added. And over the ensuing centuries, as this was told and retold, and with the accretion of new material with each successive iteration, the complete story that we all know today as *The Sugar Frosted Nutsack* came into being.

Don't expect soaring "epic" rhetoric from the 5'7" forty-eight-year-old **Ike Karton**. **Ike**'s first extended speech wholly concerns itself with the mundanity of breakfast. ("I can't decide what to have for breakfast today. I don't want something *breakfasty*—that's the problem. You know what I'd really like? A shawarma and a malt. But you can't find good shawarma in this fuckin' town now that it's full of Jews and Freemasons....I'm *serious!* So I'm either gonna have a pastrami and sliced beef tongue with cole slaw and Russian dressing on rye and a Sunkist orange soda, or maybe just a big bowl of Beefaroni and some chocolate milk or something.") He's an unassuming, plain-spoken (albeit delusional and anti-Semitic) man. He speaks with the air of a hero accustomed to—even weary of—fame (even though he's completely unknown outside the small Jersey City neighborhood of attached and identical two-story brick homes where he's considered an unstable and occasionally menacing presence—although it must be added that women overwhelmingly find him extremely charming and sexy, and many suspect that **Ike** playacts his indefensible anti-Semitism only to make himself a more loathsome pariah on his block, i.e., to make himself even *more* charming and sexy).

As you hear this or read it, the God **XOXO** is indelibly inscribing it into your brain. But **XOXO** is a puzzling figure. It's not possible to characterize him as "good" or "bad"— these terms are meaningless when applied to the Gods. He's mischievous—a trickster. Though frequently innocuous or merely "naughty," his meddling can cause enormous inconvenience and suffering, i.e., it can be wicked in its consequences. And it certainly seems as if he often acts under the compulsion of his own ancient grievances—primarily the humiliation he suffered when the Goddess **Shanice** criticized his poem about the businessman who became so terribly aroused when he was flogged in the woods by some of his colleagues. Like some disturbed stenographer, interjecting his own thoughts into the court record, **XOXO** will constantly try to insinuate his own lurid "poetry" into this story. For instance, you will soon come upon the unfortunate passage "Pumping her shiksa ass full of hot Jew jizz." Now that may be an appropriate phrase for some **Philip Roth** novel, but it has no place in *The Sugar Frosted Nutsack*. This is a perfect example of a gratuitous interpolation on the part of **XOXO**. This is **XOXO**—the embittered poet manqué— trying to ruin the book, trying to give the book Tourette's, trying to kidnap the soul of the book and ply it with drugged sherbet. And make no mistake about it—he *will* try to kidnap the soul of the book and ply it with drugged sherbet.

You can actually help preserve the integrity of *The Sugar Frosted Nutsack*. You can help wrest control of the story back from **XOXO**. When you come upon a patently adventitious phrase, one that can, with a reasonable degree of certainty, be attributed to **XOXO**, like "Pumping her shiksa ass full of hot Jew jizz," you can ward off the meddlesome mind-fucking God with the rapid staccato chant of "**Ike**, **Ike**, **Ike**, **Ike**, **Ike**!" It should sound like **Popeye** laughing, or like **Billy Joel** in "Movin' Out (Anthony's Song)"—"But working too hard can give you / A heart attack, ack, ack, ack, ack, ack." It's similar to that moment when, after **Captain Hook** has poisoned **Tinkerbell**, **Peter Pan** asks the audience to clap their hands if they believe in fairies, or when, in *The Tempest*, **Prospero** beseeches the audience, in the play's epilogue, to "Release me from my bands / With the help of your good hands....As you from crimes would pardoned be, / Let your indulgence set me free." But remember, when you chant "**Ike, Ike, Ike, Ike, Ike!**" to fend off the spiteful interpolations of **XOXO**, it absolutely has to sound like **Popeye** laughing or like **Billy Joel** in "Movin' Out (Anthony's Song)," or it won't work.

2.

Each section of *The Sugar Frosted Nutsack* is called a "session." The sessions were produced—over the course of hundreds, even thousands, of years—by nameless, typically blind men high on ecstasy or ketamine, sipping orange soda from a large hollowed-out gourd or a communal bucket or a jerry-can. The brand of orange soda traditionally associated with *The Sugar Frosted Nutsack* is Sunkist.

The first session, the ninety-six-word paragraph beginning with the phrase *"What subculture is evinced by **Ike**'s clothes and his shtick, by the non-Semitic contours of his nose and his dick"* is considered the only original session. Everything else is considered a later addition to, or a corruption of, that original session. But if one were to recite or perform only the original session without all the later additions and corruptions, the audience would feel—and justifiably so—cheated. And they would probably feel completely justified in killing and ritualistically dismembering and cannibalizing the blind, drug-addled bard. At the very least, they'd demand their money back.

Some experts have gone so far as to propose the hypothesis that that "original" ninety-six-word paragraph is itself an addition and a corruption, and that the only true, historically valid version of *The Sugar Frosted Nutsack* (the urtext) is the four-word phrase "The Sugar Frosted Nutsack." They surmise that blind men high on ecstasy, seated in a circle, and sipping orange soda from a jerrycan would chant the words "The Sugar Frosted Nutsack" over and over and over again, for hours upon hours, usually until dawn. As time went on, a stray word or phrase would be appended, resulting, eventually, in the ninety-six-word paragraph now generally accepted as part of the first session, under the subtitle: **Ike** Always Keeps It Simple and Sexy.

The Sugar Frosted Nutsack was never actually "written." A recursive aggregate of excerpts, interpolations, and commentaries, it's been "produced" through layering and augmentation, repetition and redundancy. Composition has tended to more closely resemble the loop-based step sequencing we associate with Detroit techno music than with traditional "writing."

3.

Session One Is All Wrong

You can clearly see in the tabloid style of the First Session, with its boldface names and the breathless, staccato, exclamatory sentences (e.g., *He's wearing a hot little white wifebeater! It works for his body and he goes for it! It exaggerates his ripped torso — those monster pecs and sick, big-ass pipes!*), an attempt to hyperbolize **Ike** and his wife, **Ruthie**, both of whom are unusually reserved people. It's a distorted depiction that makes them appear more glamorous and significantly more scandalous (and inane) than they actually are (were). For instance, the idea that **Ruthie**, in public, would put her hand down the back of her husband's sweatpants and tickle his butt-crack (*Like she's checking his prostate!* cackles the First Session) is absolutely ludicrous. So is the notion of the relatively modest **Ruthie** (*She's an anarcho-primitivist too!*) parading around on her front lawn, wearing a transparent "prairie dress" and no underwear. And so, most egregiously, is the idea that **Ike** would build some garishly obscene statue of the Goddess **La Felina** (*naked, dildo-impaled!*), when it's so much more likely that he'd construct something elegant and self-contained to propitiate the Goddess, something akin to one of **Joseph Cornell**'s enchanting little shadow boxes. But, obviously, generations of blind, spaced-out, Sunkist-swilling bards who—over hundreds, if not thousands, of years—mixed and remixed the First Session felt obliged to pander to an audience which prized the salacious over the subtle and preferred their heroes loony and rotten to the core. Or **XOXO** sabotaged the First Session. (One can't discount, even for a second, the possibility that **XOXO** kidnapped the First Session and plied it with drugged sherbet.) Over the years, a number of experts including **William Arrowsmith**, **Richmond Lattimore**, **Bernard Knox**, and most recently the Dutch classical scholar, expert on circumpolar populations, and milliner **Pym Voorjans**, aka **DJ Doorjamb**, whose wife has a spectacular big-ass ass (courtesy of **Fast-Cooking Ali**), have each provided incisive analyses of one of the most glaring errors in the First Session: **Ike** raising his voice (*"And they're gonna eat my fuckin' Italian breadcrumb mandala!" he screams with mock consternation, then cracks up...*). **Ike** only speaks in a whisper. In point of fact, he is said to be frequently inaudible. **Ike** is reticent and sometimes abjectly bashful. He is so self-effacing that one wonders where his galvanic charisma, his *magnificence*, derive from. Aside from this erroneous characterization of Ike *screaming* in the First Session, there are only two instances in *The Sugar Frosted Nutsack* in which **Ike** actually raises his voice above a whisper: in Session Nine, when he eulogizes his late father and threatens to destroy the synagogue, and in the Final Session when he chants the entirety of *The Sugar Frosted Nutsack* to his half-divine infant grandson, **Colter Dale**—a recitation that, of course, includes this paragraph about the only instances during which **Ike** actually raises his voice above a whisper. Had **Ike** neglected to include this paragraph—if for no other reason than the fact that, as he was chanting, the ATF or the FBI or the British SAS or the Dutch Korps Commandotroepen or (most likely) the Mossad was firing 3-Methylfentanyl (the aerosolized fentanyl derivative that Russian Spetsnaz forces used against Chechen separatists in the 2002 Moscow theater hostage crisis) into his modest, brick, two-story *hermitage* in Jersey City, causing **Ike** to consider, under the circumstances, a slightly abridged version—**Colter Dale** would have felt—and justifiably so—cheated. Also, **Ike** scrupulously eschews the use of profanity, although, unfortunately, you wouldn't know that from the First Session. He would never say, for instance, "my *fuckin'* Italian breadcrumb mandala!" or "you can't find good shawarma in this *fuckin'* town now that it's full of Jews and Freemasons." He can be wrenchingly graphic in his hypersexualized flirtations (even this, though, is invariably delivered in his gentle, barely audible murmur), and his truculent asides to other men can be phantasmagorically violent, but they're always discreetly conveyed *sotto voce* into the ear of his antagonist, and the language, as bellicose as it may be, is never vulgar or profane. **Ike**'s a Taurus and an auto-didact, and his diction tends to be Victorian, actually (think **Matthew Arnold** and **Thomas Hardy**). The "real" **Ike** is such a sweetheart, such a pussycat in a way...although he's capable of unprovoked spasms of explosive violence where you're like:

I cannot believe
He just did that.

4.

We know of the so-called "real" **Ike** that he often speaks poignantly of never ever *ever* wanting to leave Jersey City, of his memories, of...

"...the opaque stillness of its abstract, ashen evenings, in which even a five-year-old child could discern the siren call of his own fate, the homecoming of death itself."

"...dialogue from old movies leaking from the HVAC shafts of abandoned hospitals."

"...the spectacle of sugar melting on the glistening pink flesh of a halved grapefruit (in the background, the white noise of adult conversation)."

"...the gravitas of chivalrous, pensive, amoral men—men who were impossible to spoof (and their disappearance, one by one, from the face of the earth)."

"...the indescribable surprise of finding a cricket asleep amidst silver dollars in a cigar humidor."

"...the *F-Troop* theme song, as you're being mildly molested by a chubby babysitter with big-ass titties chewing Juicy Fruit (and begging your parents for her again)."

"…the thwack of a straight-edge razor on a leather strop, combs refracted in blue liquid, **Jerry Vale** ('Innamorata'), hot lather on the nape of your neck mysteriously eliciting the incipient desire to be whipped by chain-smoking middle-aged women (and/or sweaty Eastern-bloc athletes) in bras & panties."

…of never ever even wanting to venture beyond his three-block enclave of two-story brick homes. But we also know that he lets slip, not infrequently, that he dreams of being made a Commander of the Order of the British Empire by **Queen Elizabeth II**, although he can sometimes be heard—barely heard in his diffident, feathery whisper—claiming (à la **Lyndon LaRouche**) that the **Queen of England** is a degenerate, androgenized thug with a five-o'clock shadow and a hypertrophied clitoris who controls the international drug trade and seeks to liquidate the sovereignty of every nation-state in the Americas.

But how is the "epic" **Ike** portrayed in *The Sugar Frosted Nutsack?*

5.

Poor, polytheistically devout, sex-obsessed **Ike**, cosseted and buffeted by his Gods, their marionette. With the exception of his own family, and possibly his daughter's louche, drug-peddling boyfriend, **Vance** (who finds **Ike** endlessly entertaining and secretly reveres him), no one else in **Ike**'s neighborhood of modest two-story brick homes or perhaps the world (though, for **Ike**, his neighborhood *is* The World) seems to believe in the Gods. So, from a certain psychiatric perspective, one could say that the **Karton** family is clearly and deliberately portrayed as suffering from a form of *folie à famille*—a clinical syndrome in which a psychotic disorder is shared by an entire family, its essential feature being the transmission of delusions from the "inducer" to other family members ("the induced"). Typical characteristics of families with *folie à famille* include social isolation, codependent and ambivalent family relationships, repetitive crises (especially due to economic causes), and the presence of violent behaviors. The "inducer," the original source and agent of the delusions, is usually the dominant family member (almost invariably the father and the symbol of authority, and almost always a Taurus). The other family members, who constitute the "induced," frequently display passive, suggestible, and histrionic personality traits. The suggestion that the **Kartons** suffer from a *folie à famille* raises an interesting question about *The Sugar Frosted Nutsack*. Are the Gods real or is **Ike Karton** just crazy? And the answer is: Yes. There are four explanations for the ambiguous portrayal of the Gods' empirical existence especially as it relates to **Ike**'s (and his family's) mental health. First, obviously the Gods themselves have determined that **Ike**—their mortal champion, their chosen one, their "elect of the elect"—should be anathematized as "a nutbag" by his neighbors, perhaps as a test of **Ike**'s devotion and fortitude, or perhaps to give him the most masochistic bang for his buck, because it doesn't take a psych major to glean from *The Sugar Frosted Nutsack* that **Ike** is a hardcore masochist who has a very florid martyr's complex and chronic, almost continuous fantasies of being flogged by unkempt, overweight, world-weary women. Secondly, perhaps **Ike** (whose cellphone ringtone is **2 Live Crew**'s "Me So Horny") encourages people in his neighborhood to think of him as "crazy" because he is planning to commit "suicide-by-cop" and the determination of an individual's mental capacity, or "soundness of mind," to form an intent to commit suicide may be of consequence in claims for recovery of death benefits under life insurance policies—in other words, if **Ike** seems crazy, his family will get the insurance money after he provokes the ATF or Mossad into killing him (as is his fate). The third explanation is that this is the God **XOXO** fucking with the book, trying to ruin it by making it too confusing, by creating insoluble contradictions and conundrums, by essentially tying the shoelaces of the book together. It's obvious, after all, that **XOXO** has hacked into *The Sugar Frosted Nutsack,* that **XOXO** has contaminated *The Sugar Frosted Nutsack* with a malicious software program or a botnet that's able to compromise the integrity of the book's operating system and/or **Ike Karton**'s mind and/or the entirety of **Ike Karton**'s genome, including, most significantly, his expiration date (i.e., the date upon which, driven by his daemon, his destiny will be fulfilled). Or—and this is the fourth possible explanation—perhaps, in a kind of "false flag operation," it's the Goddess **Shanice** who, upon becoming so indignant at not being named by **Ike** as one of the "Ten Gods I'd Fuck (T.G.I.F.)" in the Second Season, infects **XOXO**'s sharp periodontal curette (the one he uses to ineradicably engrave *The Sugar Frosted Nutsack* into **Ike**'s brain) with a botnet. Most experts now agree that there's overwhelming validity to all four explanations. Though at times it may seem as if the Gods are portrayed as only existing in **Ike**'s mind, *The Sugar Frosted Nutsack* unequivocally represents the Gods as having, in fact, created the world ("During the Belle Époque—that period of time, about fourteen billion years ago, after the Gods were delivered by bus from some sort of 'Spring Break' during which they are said to have 'gone wild'—the Gods put things in order, made them comprehensible, provided context, imposed coherence and meaning, i.e., they created the world as we know it today"). Also, there are frequent instances in which one or several Gods clearly intervene on behalf of or in opposition to **Ike**. For instance, in the Third Season (sometime around 1100 A.D., "sessions" became known as "seasons"), **Doc Hickory**, the God of Money, who was also known as *El Mas Gordo* ("The Fattest One")—the God whose static-charged back hair became the template for the drift of continental landmasses on earth—tries to finagle **Ike** a free rice pudding at the Miss America Diner on West Side Avenue in Jersey City. In the Fourth Season, the Gods **Los Vatos Locos** (also known as **The Pince-Nez 44s**) prevent someone from coming to the aid of **Ike**'s daughter's math teacher when **Ike** threatens to sodomize him. (They're watching this all take place from their perch at the 160-story Burj Khalifa in Dubai, and they're totally cracking up.) In the Fifth Season, **Koji Mizokami**, the God who fashioned the composer **Béla Bartók** out of his own testicular teratoma, helps **Ike** shoplift an Akai MPC drum machine from a Sam Ash on Route 4 in Paramus, New Jersey. And, in the Sixth Season, **Bosco Hifikepunye**, the God of Miscellany (including Fibromyalgia, Chicken Tenders, Sports Memorabilia, SteamVac Carpet Cleaners, etc.) begins supplying **Vance** with the hallucinogenic drug Gravy to sell on the street and also impregnates **Ike**'s daughter. And, as **Colter Dale** (the offspring of that union) postulates—in a postscript that would become the Final Season—"That the Gods only occur in **Ike**'s mind is not a refutation of their actuality. It is, on the contrary, irrefutable proof of their empirical existence. The Gods choose to only exist in **Ike**'s mind. They are real by virtue of this, their prerogative."

6.

Putting aside what might be construed as a cynical attempt to pathologize an authentic oracular hero in order to sell him drugs (e.g., Clozaril, Zyprexa, Risperdal, etc.), in other words, for the financial benefit of the pharmaceutical industry (once we assume an organic basis for *deviant theologies*, we legitimize a market for diagnostic assays and treatment modalities), and putting aside the even more fundamental issue of the pharmacological colonization of the Western psyche, is there any validity to the diagnosis of *folie à famille* for the **Kartons** (the family, not the band)? **Ike Karton** doesn't seem to fit the textbook profile of "the inducer." He can't really be described as domineering, for instance. Of course, in his unassuming way, he casually offers up incidental remarks and observations about the world—that people like **Anna Wintour**, **Gisele Bündchen**, **Ronald Perelman**, and **Jon Bon Jovi** should be dragged from their offices or homes and guillotined on the street, or how it would be much more entertaining in the Winter Olympics biathlon if, instead of shooting at targets, the biathletes shot ski jumpers at the apex of their flights like human skeet, or his admiration for the ferocious Renaissance politician **Cesare Borgia** and Chechen strongman **Ramzan Kadyrov** and the ruthless one-eyed Prime Minister of Cambodia, **Hun Sen**. But he has never tried to "proselytize" or "indoctrinate" his family. He has never sat his wife and daughter down and formally told them the entire saga (i.e., the entirety of *The Sugar Frosted Nutsack*) in the classic style—that is, high on ecstasy, swigging orange soda from a gourd, tapping his aluminum wedding ring on the tabletop to maintain that mesmerizing cadence—from beginning to end. In fact, he won't formally tell the whole saga in the classic style from beginning to end until—in the Penultimate Season, and shortly before being gunned down by ATF and Mossad sharpshooters— he sits down with his half-divine infant grandson, **Colter Dale**, pours out a sacred libation of Sunkist, and, tapping his ring on the tabletop, begins chanting to the rapt, wide-eyed infant from the very beginning: "There was never *nothing*. But before the debut of the Gods, about fourteen billion years ago, things happened without any discernable context. There were no recognizable patterns. It was all incoherent. Isolated, disjointed events would take place, only to be engulfed by an opaque black void, their relative meaning, their *significance,* annulled by the eons of entropic silence that estranged one from the next. A terrarium containing three tiny teenage girls mouthing a lot of high-pitched gibberish (like **Mothra**'s fairies, except for their wasted pallors, acne, big tits, and T-shirts that read 'I Don't Do White Guys') would inexplicably materialize, and then, just as inexplicably, disappear..." And with that unprecedented gesture, **Ike** incorporates (and consecrates) what had heretofore been simply an academic prologue into the very body, the very heart of *The Sugar Frosted Nutsack* (and it has been considered its First Season ever since). But prior to the Penultimate Season, over the years, **Ike** has, every now and then, sat down with his wife and his daughter and his daughter's disreputable boyfriend, **Vance**, and, in his soft, confidential, hoarse whisper, informally shared with them several vivid but isolated and disjointed little fragments. And despite the fact (or maybe due to the fact) that these disjointed little fragments seem to lack any discernable context, **Ike**'s wife, his daughter, and **Vance** are sufficiently enthralled so that they appear (to some experts) to suffer from a form of *folie à famille.* Such is **Ike**'s galvanic (albeit diffident) charisma, his *magnificence.* Such is the inky dye of his faith that, over time, drop by drop by drop, it slowly seeps into and stains the porous minds of his loyal, loving family. (There are some experts, although they constitute a persecuted minority within the expert community, who believe that there has actually been only one bard—that one being **Ike Karton**. And within this group, there is a dissident faction who also believes that there has actually been only one expert, that one also being **Ike Karton**. Although this is an extremely controversial and virtually indefensible position, it does have one vehement and disproportionately influential proponent: **Ike Karton**.)

7.

The key narrative event in (what is now considered) the *Seventh Season* is **Ike** sitting down at the Miss America Diner and writing the lyrics to the narcocorrido "That's Me (**Ike**'s Song)" that his family's band (**The Kartons**) will sing at the "Last Concert"—the front-lawn performance **Ike** intends to give for the benefit of his neighbors earlier on the night he's destined to be gunned down by ATF and Mossad sharp-shooters. His expiration date (his "fate") is pre-encoded into his genome. In fact, **Ike**'s whole genome has been decoded. He has the East Asian version of a gene known as EDAR, which endows people with armpit hair that is thicker and more lustrous than that of most Europeans and Africans. Another gene suggests that he has dry earwax, as do Asians and Native Americans, not the wet earwax of other ethnic groups.

The *Seventh Season* begins with that heavily cadenced and folkloric cadenza subtitled *Ike Always Keeps It Simple and Sexy:*

Ike Always Keeps It Simple and Sexy

What subculture is evinced by **Ike**'s clothes and his shtick, by the non-Semitic contours of his nose and his dick, by the feral fatalism of all his loony tics—like the petit-mal fluttering of his long-lashed lids and the **Mussolini** torticollis of his Schick-nicked neck, and the staring and the glaring and the daring and the hectoring, and the tapping on the table with his aluminum wedding ring, as he hums those tunes from his childhood albums and, after a spasm of **Keith Moon** air-drums, returns to his lewd mandala of Italian breadcrumbs?

Ike always keeps it simple and sexy. He's wearing a hot little white wifebeater. It works for his body and he goes for it! It exaggerates his ripped torso—those monster pecs and sick, big-ass pipes. He's bodaciously buff, and (unlike **Charlie Sheen**) he's never been arrested for beating his wife! And *look*, when he reaches up to point at those birds ("They're house sparrows. And they're gonna eat my fuckin' Italian breadcrumb mandala!" he screams with mock consternation, then cracks up. "But seriously—that's the whole point. It's a sacrificial mandala for the God **Fast-Cooking Ali**. The basic symbolism is that the birds come and carry the crumbs to him up at the Burj Khalifa in Dubai"), *look* how beautiful **Ike**'s abundant chestnut-color armpit hair is, how lustrous and soft and fluffy. (It almost looks as if he blow-dries it for extra volume!) And his baggy gray terry sweatpants look as if they're falling off, which amps up the sex appeal!

Then, in a section subtitled **Ike Shares a Laugh with a God,** **Ike** considers what to have for breakfast, an issue that will eventually lead him to the Miss America Diner. "I can't decide what to have for breakfast today. I don't want something *breakfasty*—that's the problem. You know what I'd really like? A shawarma and a malt. But you can't find good shawarma in this fuckin' town now that it's full of Jews and Freemasons. . . . I'm *serious!*" he cracks up laughing. He muses out loud about several alternatives to shawarma, including pastrami and sliced beef tongue with cole slaw and Russian dressing on rye and a Sunkist orange soda, or maybe just a big bowl of Beefaroni and some chocolate milk. Suddenly, like some hapless **Beckettian** tramp in a white wifebeater and saggy terry sweats, he inadvertently airs his ass-crack as he jauntily genuflects in the general direction of the rocket-shaped Burj Khalifa. "If there's a God who has a minute for an unemployed neo-pagan butcher with a bodaciously buff body who's been out here all morning in his fuckin' guido dishabille making a breadcrumb man-dala, I'd appreciate a quick breakfast suggestion. Please— something relatively inexpensive. I'm unemployed." Then, almost immediately, Ike's cellphone rings. (His ringtone, as we know, is **2 Live Crew**'s "Me So Horny.") He sees from the caller ID that it's **Doc Hickory**, the God of Money, who was also known as *El Mas Gordo* ("The Fattest One")— the God whose static-charged back hair became the tem-plate for the drift of continental landmasses on earth. It's **Doc Hickory** who suggests that **Ike** go to the Miss America Diner. "It's like three blocks from your house, it's cheap, and they have a million things on the menu, including a gyro, which is pretty close to a fuckin' shawarma, big guy." **Doc Hickory** cracks up laughing. His laugh, which is more of a snicker, sounds like that rhythmic, shrill, squeaky-hinge sound that women make in Japanese porn. **Ike** finds **Doc Hickory**'s laugh mocking and malevolent. But, hey, **Doc Hickory**'s a God, and he's supermercurial, and you always have to put up with his cryptic moods and his petulant fatwas. He can be mocking and malevolent one moment and inexplicably generous the next. "Oh, I almost forgot," says **Doc Hickory**. "The rice pudding's on me. Just remind your server or the cashier that **Doc Hickory**—the God whose static-charged back hair became the template for the drift of continental landmasses on earth—is treating you to a rice pudding, and they won't charge you. But you have to use those exact words, that exact epithet. *Buon appetito,* **Mighty Mouse-olini**." The God's snide parting interjection is followed by another dose of that squeaky *ee-ee-ee-ee-ee* laugh of his.

Although the *Seventh Season* wildly exaggerates his extroversion and loquacity, it does accurately represent that, at the end of the day, there's one irrefutable, fundamental fact about **Ike** (who hit the big *forty-eight* last winter, on the same day he got laid off from his butcher job at the A&P Meat Department): he's all about Family and Home (*Blut und Boden*). Priding himself, above all else, on being an exemplary husband and father, he's fanatically devoted to providing for his wife and daughter, and maintaining their modest two-story brick house on Towers Street in Jersey City (his "little hermitage," as he calls it). **Ike**'s a Taurus and, like the typical Taurus man, he's very quiet, practical, composed, and humble. Taurus men are very protective of their loved ones and will always be very gentle toward them. They possess a calm strength and are always prepared for the worst of circumstances. Taurus guys dislike synthetic or "man-made" things, have a tendency to become paranoid and anti-Semitic, and exhibit a higher incidence of thyroid nodules than non-Taurus guys. The Taurus man is stubborn and, if sufficiently provoked, can lash out with genocidal fury. But otherwise you'll have yourself a real man, who'll wrap his big, muscular arms around you and give you money and make you cum. (Famous Tauruses include **Adolf Hitler**, **Pol Pot**, **Jessica Alba**, and **Megan Fox**.) FYI: **Ike** blames losing his butcher job at the A&P on a whispering campaign conducted against him by several Gods, including **Mogul Magoo**, **Shanice**, and **Bosco Hifikepunye**.

Ike's Horoscope

"The stars show that your long-term finances are precarious. Don't try to solve everything all at once, though. Events are fast and furious, but take things one step at a time. Have a conversation with your daughter about why she's· failing math, and also try to ascertain whether her boyfriend, **Vance**, is a drug dealer. Also, this is not a good time to try to persuade the zoning board to grant you permission to build a huge statue of a naked, dildo-impaled **La**

Felina on your front lawn. Think positive—try not to obsess about being killed by the ATF or Mossad. Remember, at the end of the day, you're a bodaciously buff unemployed butcher and the Gods (especially **La Felina**, champion of the unkempt, the plain-spoken, the *Frontschweine*, the *Lumpenproletariat,* etc.) love you very much."

But It's Not the End of the Day. It's Morning.

Ike's wife (she's trendy and gorgeous and believes in the Gods too—it's a *folie à famille!*) comes out to talk to him on their tiny front yard where **Ike**'s just putting the finishing touches to his Italian breadcrumb mandala for the God **Fast-Cooking Ali**. (She makes all her own clothes. She's an anarcho-primitivist too, but she's super-sexy! Her décolletage and sheer prairie dress don't leave much to the imagination!!)

One Good Grab Deserves Another: they both grab each other's asses. Hey, it looks like his wife is sticking her middle finger up **Ike**'s ass! Like she's checking his prostate! False alarm—she's just tickling him. But the marriage is obviously still *muy caliente*. The Jersey City Fire Department might have to come and hose these kids down!!

Ike's wife ("Her name is **Ruthie**!") has an incredible figure. But her secret isn't counting calories. "I eat what I like, but I try to keep it clean and healthy—fruit, vegetables, lean protein—lots of sushi. I don't eat like **Ike**. He likes tonkatsu, shawarma, Beefaroni, Double Whoppers with

Cheese, jalapeño poppers, Dairy Queen shakes, and shit like that. But look at him! Where does it all go?! If I ate like he does, I'd look like **Gabourey Sidibe**!" (Here's the "skinny" from **Ruthie**: "Try swapping out the mayonnaise for mustard.")

8.

Ike Karton: Super-Sexy Neo-Pagan Martyr or Demented Loser?

Cast Your Vote Right This Second! You don't have to go online or call in or anything. Just cast your vote in *your own mind!* And the Goddess **Shanice** (she's telepathically omniscient!) will tally it all up.

He's paranoid and maladaptively hostile. (Paranoia and maladaptive hostility can be super-sexy, right?) He oscillates between chip-on-the-shoulder belligerence and Talmudic introversion. (Isn't the extremely high amplitude of this vibration, in fact, what produces **Ike**'s radioactive charisma?) He operates under what skeptics (his dreary neighbors among them) might call the *erotomaniacal* belief that Goddesses, high on Gravy, are obsessively watching him, that they are forever peering out the windows of the Burj Khalifa in Dubai, across

the Gulf, across the desert, and gazing at him and masturbating. (Compare the visual acuity of the Goddesses here
with the blindness of the bards.) He states it in no uncertain
terms: "The Goddesses watch me like pornography." *That's*
the reason he's such a total gym-rat—he always wants to
look SUPER-SEXY in case **La Felina**, high on Gravy, is
watching him from the 160th floor of the rocket-shaped Burj
Khalifa! His neck and head intermittently jerk toward the
Burj whenever he feels he's being ogled by masturbating
Goddesses. (As would yours.) He's an anti-Semite, although
many experts interpret his anti-Semitism as a form of play-
acting intended primarily to torment his father. (FYI: **Ike**
went to Hebrew school until he was thirteen!) He has a
catarrhal rasp and a criminal record. (Super-sexy!) Whenever he goes to a restaurant, he *always* flirts with the waitress
by asking for a tongue sandwich—same line, every single
time. (That might be a little *demented loserish*.) But check out
how he looks at night—a little looped, a little bleary-eyed
from all the beer and whiskey, standing there in "the soft
pink glow of the sodium-vapor street lights." (It's unanimous—*that's* SUPER-SEXY!!) He likes to sit in the dark at
home, wearing night-vision goggles, watching the Military
Channel, drinking Scotch. By day, he warns men on his
block that their wives are probably Mossad agents. He firmly
believes that most women are Mossad agents. (If you're a
married man and you're reading this, *your* wife is probably a
Mossad agent!) But obscured by all his whispery trash talk,
and embedded deep within his algorithmic solipsism which
transfigures every single thing in the world into a reitera-

tion of *his own mind*, is his extraordinarily tender devotion to *his* wife. Even **Ike**'s philandering is uxorious. His infidelities do not, certainly in *his own mind*, seem incompatible with what he considers his incorruptible rectitude as a husband. They are either seen as the most practical expediencies— before he leaves the house, **Ike** routinely announces to his wife and daughter, "I might have to kill someone or maybe fuck somebody today, but remember, it's for you guys"—or as consistent with the cultivation and honing of his virility, the very virility that **Ike** so solemnly bestows upon his wife as his tribute to her. Would **Ruthie** (or any self-respecting woman, for that matter) want to be married to a man whose appetite for life was so meager and whose libido was so governable that one woman would suffice? What manner of husband would *that* be? (Surely not a super-sexy one!) And what would his love signify, if not a groveling insult?

Sixty-one percent of women say that a scrupulously faithful husband is a TOTAL TURN-OFF!

Of course, some experts say that **Ike**—Implacable Warlord of His Stoop—would kill a human being as casually as a normal person would pop a pimple. But then you see him brushing his wife's hair or coloring her roots, nuzzling her neck, even popping one of her pimples, softly singing "The Shadow of Your Smile" to her....And, of course, we know how—in so many secret, unacknowledged, uxorious moments—he dotes on her, how if he's getting Fig Newtons for them and there are only two left and one's normal and the other one's all mangled and misshapen, he'll take the mangled, misshapen one for himself, or if there are only two

Frozefruits left, one normal, one with freezer burn, he'll invariably take the one with the freezer burn for himself, or—great example—when he and **Ruthie** were completely obsessed with these crab cake sandwiches with lettuce, tomato, and lemon aioli on ciabatta bread and **Ike** would go to the little deli and then realize he only had enough money in his wallet for one crab cake sandwich, he'd get the sandwich for **Ruthie** and he'd just eat a Slim Jim or make himself a peanut butter and jelly sandwich when he got back home. And no one knows he's doing *any* of this, there's no showy, self-aggrandizing display of being a good husband, no "He went to Jared!" moment. It's just part of the texture of uxorious doting that **Ike** is weaving every single moment of every single day. (There is the obvious irony here of characterizing these gestures as "secret" and "unacknowledged" or saying "no one knows he's doing this" since bards—blind, vagrant, and drug-addled—have been chanting these very words for thousands of years, tapping their chachkas against jerrycans of orange soda to maintain that insistent trance-inducing beat.) The portrayal of the **Kartons** in the *Seventh Season*—cavorting on their front lawn in the early AM—is exaggerated to the point of being almost defamatory and flaunts the hyperrealism and saturated colors of a Claritin commercial. In real life, the **Kartons** are, yes, exceedingly loving with each other, but they are also unusually protective of each other's privacy. (It would be considered a monstrous offense even to ask **Ike** if his wife was in good health!) They are utterly inscrutable figures who, paradoxically, understand each other perfectly well. One morning, **Ruthie** came downstairs and found **Ike** sitting at the kitchen table, writing. And she said to him, "You look like you're writing letters to all the officers in your army." There's such profound sympathy and insight and tender irony to that statement, because **Ike** is so alone, so utterly alone in the world of men, so much an army of one. (When **Ike** sits at the kitchen table in the early morning, he's not writing letters or composing narcocorridos, he's typically making lists—lists of which celebrities he thinks should be guillotined, which should go to the gulag, which should be rehabilitated, etc.) In his heart of hearts, **Ike** knows that he's going to die soon at the hands of the ATF and/or Mossad—his "suicide-by-cop"—but he believes that a golden age will come—what he calls "the time when all fettered monsters will break loose"—when he and his wife and his daughter will be reunited for eternity. The bonds uniting this family have been exceptionally strong from the very beginning.

Ike's "10 Things That I Know for Sure About Women" List

Soon after **Ike** and **Ruthie** first met (at the A&P where, at that time, **Ike** was employed as a butcher in the meat department), they had a conversation one spring day in the park about each other's past relationships and about love and about what one could realistically hope for in a marriage, etc. **Ruthie** asked **Ike** if he thought he understood women well. **Ike** got very quiet and thought about this for a while, as he tossed handful after handful of croutons to the swans and mice that had gathered at their feet. Finally, he told **Ruthie** that he was going to make a list. "Not a list of which celebrities you think should be guillotined," she said, coyly averting her eyes and smiling flirtatiously at him. "No," he said, "a list of ten things that I know for sure about women." About a week later—to show **Ruthie** a more delicately registered sensibility than he, a gym-rat and butcher, suspected **Ruthie** gave him credit for—**Ike** presented the list (entitled "10 Things That I Know for Sure About Women" but including an 11th) to **Ruthie** as they sat on the very same bench in Lincoln Park:

1. Even little girls, in all their blithe, unharrowed innocence, have a presentiment of sorrow, hardship, and adversity...of loss. Women, throughout their lives, have an intrinsic and profound understanding of **Keats**'s sentiments about "Joy, whose hand is ever at his lips / Bidding adieu."
2. This sage knowledge of, and ability to abide, the inherently fugitive nature of happiness somehow accounts for the extraordinary beauty of women as they age.
3. Women have an astonishing capacity to maintain their equilibrium in the face of life's mutability, its unceasing and unforeseeable vicissitudes. And this agility is always in stark and frequently comical contradistinction to men's naively bullish and brittle delusions that things can forever remain exactly the same.
4. Women are forgiving, but implacably cognizant.

5. Women are almost never gullible, but sometimes relax their vigilance out of loneliness. (And I believe most women abhor loneliness.)

6. In their most casual, off-hand, sisterly moments, women are capable of discussing sex in such uninhibited detail that it would cause a horde of carousing Cossacks to cringe.

7. Women are, for all intents and purposes, indomitable. It really requires an almost unimaginable confluence of crushing, cataclysmic forces to vanquish a woman.

8. Women's instincts for self-preservation and survival can seem to men to be inscrutably unsentimental and sometimes cruel.

9. Women have a very specific kind of courage that enables them to fling themselves into the open sea, into some uncharted terra incognita—whether it's a new life for themselves, another person's life, or even what might appear to be a kind of madness.

10. Women never—no matter how old they are—completely relinquish their aristocratic assumption of seductiveness.

11. And here is one last thing I know—and I know this with a certitude that exceeds anything I've said before: that men's final thoughts in their waking days and in their lives are of women…ardent, wistful thoughts of wives and lovers and daughters and mothers.

Ruthie found this so beautiful and so moving that she wept as she read it. In the coming weeks, though, she'd discover that **Ike** had plagiarized it, from beginning to end, word for word, from something that had appeared in the November 2008 issue of *O, The Oprah Magazine*. But by then she'd already fallen deeply in love with him, and not at all *in spite of* what he'd done, but, in large part, *because* of it— here was a man willing to steal for her, a man with a big enough nutsack that he was willing to brazenly steal another man's *words,* another man's *ideas* (his most precious intellectual property)...for *her.*

Ninety-seven percent of people think that it was SUPER-SEXY of **Ike** to totally plagiarize that from *O, The Oprah Magazine*!!

The Club Kids Vs. The Hasids

Ike has suffered from irregular clonic jerks of the head and neck ever since he was hit by a *Mister Softee* truck on Spring Break when he was eighteen years old. High on ketamine, wearing silver lederhosen and a hat made out of an Oreo box at the time, he initially claimed he'd been hit by a Hasidic ambulance in an effort to foment an apocalyptic Helter Skelter–type war between club kids and Hasids. Many experts, including **Zsófia Csontváry-Horvath** of the Institute of Linguistics and Classical Philology in Budapest (who's slick with sweat and has a spectacular big-ass ass), maintain that those passages in *The Sugar Frosted Nutsack* about **Ike** making confusing and patently erroneous claims about a Hasidic ambulance are "noncanonical interpolations" and should be deemed "spurious" and deleted. **Csontváry-Horvath** contends that these passages were deliberately inserted by experts who, themselves, were trying to foment an apocalyptic Helter Skelter–type war between club kids and Hasids. Of course, not only is **Ike**'s erroneous contention that he was hit by a Hasidic ambulance considered today a totally canonical and authentic part of *The Sugar Frosted Nutsack,* but **Zsófia Csontváry-Horvath**'s assertion that it's a noncanonical interpolation is considered a canonical and integral part of the saga which audiences expect the chachka-jangling, sightless bards to feature prominently in their recitations. It's also entirely possible that *all* this could just be another example of **XOXO** vandalizing *The Sugar Frosted Nutsack* and trying to confuse people and just fuck everything up. But let's be absolutely clear: **Ike**, when he was eighteen years old, on Spring Break, and high on Special K, staggered into the street and was struck by a *Mister Softee* truck. And ever since the accident, the *Mister Softee* song loops endlessly in his head. This is *not* an auditory hallucination. The song is actually in there—i.e., if you put a stethoscope to **Ike**'s forehead, you can hear the *Mister Softee* song.

But **Ike**'s rage and his lust are strong. He's nursed by the Gods. His honor comes from **El Brazo** and **La Felina** and **Fast-Cooking Ali** and **XOXO**. He's dear to them, these Gods who rule the world.

Throughout *The Sugar Frosted Nutsack,* **Ike** is portrayed as the most soft-spoken, self-deprecating man you could possibly imagine—someone, in fact, almost ostentatious in his soft-spoken self-deprecation—and even on those rare occasions when he might come across as vain or a little smug—he is, after all, a super-sexy neo-pagan hero and a transformative human being—he'll reveal something so disarmingly personal about himself (like his tinea versicolor or his genital psoriasis or his dermatitis herpetiformis, which sometimes requires him to soak for long hours in the bathtub with a vinegar-drenched bandana wrapped around his head) that any hint of hubris is immediately dispelled.

Ike is preoccupied with hidden motives, and nothing makes him happier than when, presented with something fairly straightforward—a bus driver's request for exact change, for instance—he can burrow into deeper and deeper netherworlds of subtext and sub-subtext, disclosing for himself ever-murkier layers of bewildering intrigue and subterfuge, because he believes that it's only when confronted with something that completely befuddles us that we experience the sense of "speechless wonder" (*thaumazein*) that opens us up to a fleeting intimation of the sacred. To **Ike**, the Gods' designs are revealed not in incandescent flashes of lucidity, but in the din of the incomprehensible, in a cacophony of high-pitched voices and discordant jingles. (Hey, maybe this is why he concocted that whole story about being hit by a Hasidic ambulance years ago when he'd so irrefutably been hit by a *Mister Softee* truck—to obfuscate the obvious and thus anoint it with a residue of divinity!) So it shouldn't come as any surprise that the guy would eschew books in his native English and opt instead to pore over texts in languages he can't remotely understand (particularly German). Nor should it come as any great shock that, if he's not at the gym or making a lewd breadcrumb mandala or feeding his wife a Fig Newton, you'll probably find **Ike** ("seething and petulant butcher, coiled with energy") on his stoop or in the park or at the Miss America Diner "reading" his German books, even though he can't understand a single word of German (in the strict sense of the word "understand"), because they are, for him, *in his own mind,* like magical incantations, and he's able to distill the most essential, the most profound, esoteric, and mystical significance, not from their semantic content, but purely from the *sounds* of the words, from their *music.* And so he'll sit there on the hot subway, hunched over his unintelligible text and swaying with concentration (and missing his stop), mouthing a passage—like the following one—out loud, over and over to himself, like some zealous foreign understudy learning his lines phonetically, or—better analogy—like some supersexy (and totally shredded!) priest who's been sent off to a hopelessly remote mission in the jungle, and, sitting on a sweltering train as it steams into the dark interior of the country, is zealously trying to learn the dying language of the head-hunting heathens he's been sent to proselytize, even though he suspects, and perhaps half desires, that instead of gratefully receiving the sacrament, they might very well flog, flay, boil, and consume him:

Mein Kahn ist ohne Steuer, er fährt mit dem Wind, der in den untersten Regionen des Todes bläst.

Comments (Newest First)

SugarFrosted XOXO is introducing junk DNA into the genome of the story. Don't panic. Just keep chanting *Ike, Ike, Ike, Ike, Ike!* And keep in mind that even this junk DNA (cunningly disguised as SMS abbreviations) that XOXO has inserted into these comments is now considered an integral part of the epic, and if the vagrant, drug-addled bards were to recite or perform *Season Nine* without this junk DNA, the audience would feel—and justifiably so—cheated, and probably demand a full refund.

Posted 11:26 AM

Beachgirl What is that? What does that mean?

Posted 11:20 AM

KidComa DYHAB DUM DUWBHTPHFIYAWYC GYPO IWFU DYSL GNOC SMB EWI ATG CTA TCA TTG ACC TTG AGT TAT TAA ATG CTA TCA TTG CAC TTG AGT TGT TAA ATG CTA TCA TTG ACC GTG AGT TAT TAA ATG CTA TCA TTG ACC TCG AGT TAT ATA ATG CTA TCA TTG ACC TTG AGT TAT AGA GTG TGA TTA TAA ATG CTA TCA TTG CCA TCG TGA TAT ATA ATG CTA TCA TTG ACC TTG AGT TAT AGA

Posted 11:17 AM

Beachgirl Ike, Ike, Ike, Ike, Ike!

Posted 11:13 AM

KidComa FMUTA!!!!!

Posted 11:11 AM

Beachgirl XOXO!! That's you, right?! You're vandalizing *The Sugar Frosted Nutsack* again!!!

Posted 11:08 AM

KidComa ROTFLMAO!

Posted 11:06 AM

Beachgirl You're a complete asshole!

Posted 11:01 AM

KidComa LMFAO!

Posted 10:55 AM

Beachgirl I hate people who just laugh at everything. Do you think spina bifida is funny or the Holocaust?

Posted 10:53 AM

KidComa Get your pants off!

Posted 10:50 AM

Beachgirl It is not stupid OR pretentious. You have a great deal of LEARNING to do. You're just too shallow to delve deep into questioning yourself and your life. READ MORE!!!

Posted 10:45 AM

KidComa It's stupid *and* pretentious.

Posted 10:42 AM

Beachgirl What's funny about that? I think it's so profound. And it's so beautifully emblematic of **Ike**.

Posted 10:35 AM

KidComa LOL!

Posted 10:32 AM

Beachgirl It's from Kafka's "Der Jäger Gracchus" (The Hunter Gracchus), dickwad. It means: "My ship has no rudder, and it is driven by the wind that blows in the undermost regions of death."

Posted 10:30 AM

KidComa What the fuck does that mean?

Posted 10:24 AM

Showing 17 of 9,709 comments

Instead of a Monocle and a Walking Stick

It's usually at this point in almost every authenticated version of *The Sugar Frosted Nutsack*—following "Comments (Newest First)"—that **Ike** strolls to the Miss America Diner (on West Side Avenue, at the corner of Culver), where he engages in an extended adagio with **The Waitress**, ordering a tongue sandwich, discussing the erotics of second-person POV during endodontic procedures, and writing the lyrics to the narcocorrido "That's Me (**Ike**'s Song)" that **The Kartons** will sing at the "Last Concert." (In traditional public recitations, the bards—vagrant, drug-addled, and almost always blind, but sometimes just severely dyslexic—are expected to chant all 9,709 of the "Comments," and not just the seventeen included here, especially if the performance is taking place in a remote, rural area "where the pace of life is unhurried, where the air is fragrant with the aromas of shearing sheds and cattle yards, honeysuckle or corn dogs from some fair, and where the appetite for orally transmitted, maddeningly repetitive epic entertainment remains unsated.")

The image of "**Ike** the Flâneur" strolling to the Miss America Diner has become one of the most familiar and iconic representations of the sinewy and reticent hero who, in addition to being convinced that Goddesses are almost continuously leering at him from the top floor of the Burj Khalifa and masturbating, believes that Western materialism—most perfectly embodied by privileged celebrities—is polluting the soul of every living creature in the world (in addition to the souls of human beings, **Ike** believes that

Western materialism is also polluting the souls of animals, especially house sparrows, swans, and mice).

Instead of a monocle and a walking stick, this flâneur sports a tight guinea-T and a baseball bat. But don't worry—he's loaded with gem-like aperçus and aphorisms! For example:

—*If you give people too many things to remember you by, they'll forget them. Pick one.*

9.

For anyone attending a performance of *The Sugar Frosted Nutsack* today, there's likely to be little if any suspense about what actually happens. The story, with its escalating crises, divine interventions, and hyperviolent denouement, is so well known by now that an audience at a public recitation would not only be able to anticipate every single plot point, but would probably know many of the lines by heart and almost be able to lip-sync along with the bards. And they'd know the history of the making of *The Sugar Frosted Nutsack*. They'd know how each "section" became known as a "Session" and then as a "Season." They'd know how these Seasons were produced—over the course of hundreds, even thousands, of years—by nameless, typically blind men, high on ecstasy or ketamine, seated in a circle, and chanting for hours and hours on end as they sipped orange soda from a jerrycan; and how every new improvisational flourish, every exegetical commentary and meta-commentary, every cough, sniffle, and hiccough on the part of the bard is incorporated into the story, and is then required in each subsequent performance; and how numerous unrelated episodes have, over the centuries, fallen into the epic's orbit and gradually become incorporated into the epic itself; and how vernacular variants are incessantly generated in its mutagenic algorithms; how it's been "produced" through layering and augmentation, repetition and redundancy, more closely resembling the loop-based step sequencing we associate with Detroit techno music than with traditional "writing."

Adults and children alike would be familiar enough with the plot to already know (before the bards even opened their mouths to deliver the first words "There was never *nothing*") that the saga of **Ike** begins with him making a lewd mandala of Italian breadcrumbs for the Goddess **La Felina** and then engaging in an extended adagio with the waitress at the Miss America Diner and writing his narcocorrido "That's Me (**Ike**'s Song)"; they'd already know that **Ike** gets high with his daughter's boyfriend, **Vance**, and makes a list for him called "Ten Gods I'd Fuck (T.G.I.F)" and neglects to include the Goddess **Shanice**, which incurs her eternal wrath (FYI: **La Felina** was #1 on his list); and that **Koji Mizokami**, the God who fashioned the composer **Béla Bartók** out of his own testicular teratoma, helps **Ike** shoplift an Akai MPC drum machine from a Sam Ash on Route 4 in Paramus, New Jersey; and that **Bosco Hifikepunye** begins supplying **Vance** with the hallucinogenic drug Gravy to sell on the street; and that **Ike** goes to Port Newark for a tryst with **La Felina**, who's transformed herself into a container ship; and that she promises **Ike** that before he martyrs himself, she'll appear to him in human form and fuck him; and that she says she'll get in touch with him on his cellphone and let him know exactly when and where; and they know that he's photographed there by the ATF; and they'd already know that while **Ike** is interviewing for a butcher's job at Costco, a God impregnates his daughter; and that **Ike** accidentally kills his father as they wrestle for Ike's cellphone because **Ike**'s father is trying to change **Ike**'s ringtone from "Me So Horny" to **John Cage**'s *4'33"*—the composer's notorious "silent composition" consisting of four minutes and thirty-three seconds in which the performer plays nothing (e.g., a pianist going to the keyboard and not hitting any keys for four minutes and thirty-three seconds)—and **Ike** immediately realizes, to his horror, that having **Cage**'s *4'33"* as a ringtone would essentially mean that he'd have *no* ringtone, and that he'd almost inevitably miss **La Felina**'s call, which, for **Ike**, is literally the booty-call of a lifetime; and they'd already know that on the morning of his father's funeral, **Ike** wakes up with a incredibly gross ("grotesquely purulent") case of conjunctivitis and, after delivering the eulogy (a phantasmagorically anti-Semitic diatribe, akin to **Céline**'s *Bagatelles pour un Massacre*), he tries to pull the pillars of the synagogue down and crush the congregation; and that his daughter gives birth to a half-divine, half-mortal infant named "**Colter Dale**"; and that soon after **The Kartons** begin their "Last Concert" (which happens to be their *first* concert), the ATF/Mossad raid on the compound begins; and that after retreating into his two-story brick "hermitage" and reciting *The Sugar Frosted Nutsack* in its entirety to the infant **Colter Dale**, **Ike** is killed.

(And they know that, in a coda, **Colter Dale**—who mythologically functions as **Ike**'s successor—explains how **Ike**'s so-called "delusions" are actually irrefutable proof of the Gods' existence.)

So audiences do not necessarily have to concentrate on each word, gesture, or nuance of meaning that comes from the bards. If your neighbor talks, you don't try to quiet him. The overall impression at most recitations is chaos, as food vendors, children, and adults ceaselessly move up and down the aisles. No one can be expected to sit through an eight- or nine-hour performance without talking, eating, or getting up. Young children romp in the aisles, and when the action gets exciting they mass by the footlights like moths drawn to a flame. The predominantly female audience will continue to talk long after a recitation has begun. Many people doze during less interesting scenes and, in fact, bring their own straw mats on which they sit and sleep.

But when the bards' recitations get particularly lurid (e.g., the scene in the *Tenth Season* in which **Ike** goes to his daughter's school to have a meeting with her math teacher, loses his temper, and threatens to sodomize the teacher if he doesn't agree to give her a passing grade), spectators leap to their feet and the children howl with uproarious laughter, clap, whistle, and yell out encouragement. It may shock some people unfamiliar with orally transmitted epics that audiences would find men threatening each other with anal rape so entertaining. Perhaps it's not hard to understand why uneducated, working-class, middle-aged women might find homoerotic sadism wildly diverting—but children? It could very possibly be that the children don't even under-stand the content of what's being chanted here at all (the language in this Season is almost impenetrably thick with **de Sadean** bombast) and are being whipped into paroxysms of excitement by nothing more than the hysterical cacoph-ony of the bards. Also, the scene has an undeniable slapstick quality, with all its tumultuous, pants-at-the-knees, chase-me-around-the-office antics. And usually bards portray the math teacher as such a stock commedia dell'arte villain—i.e. the sanctimonious martinet moonlighting as JV basket-ball coach and driver's ed instructor, etc.—that it's easy to cheer on **Ike**, even if you disapprove of his cell-block bluster.

There was one prominent and controversial expert who actually believed that the traditional style of the bards (i.e., slurred, mumbling, etc.) so garbles the content of what they are chanting that almost no literal meaning is actually ever transmitted. **Jake S. Emig**, in an erudite and exquisitely reasoned treatise, only slightly marred by vitriolic ad hominem attacks on several female colleagues (who'd report-edly objected to explicit photographs of himself that he'd texted them), contended that since audiences can't under-stand anything that the bards are chanting, they are creating each time, almost out of whole cloth, *The Sugar Frosted Nut-sack* for themselves, out of what they think they hear. After subjecting thousands of hours of taped recitations to so-phisticated audiological analysis, he wrote, "It is more than likely that there is no originative, coherent epic, that there is merely a succession of misinterpretations of the bards' muffled cacophony, of their static, their white noise." **Emig,** an enigmatic figure, started his career as a semiprofessional hockey player. For several years he was a forward for Thetford Mines Isothermic, a team in the Ligue Nord-Américaine de Hockey (LNAH), which is generally considered the most violent hockey league in the world. **Emig**'s teammates on Thetford Mines Isothermic included veteran NHL defenseman **Yves Racine** and right winger **Gaetan Royer**, who played games with the Tampa Bay Lightning in the 2001–02 season and also played for the Bartercard Gold Coast Blue Tongues in the Australian Ice Hockey League (AIHL) in 2008. **Emig** was forced to retire from professional hockey as a result of post-concussion syndrome (PCS) and a succession of DUI arrests. It was then that he became interested in the field of forensic audiology, received his Masters of Applied Science degree several years later, and soon thereafter became an Adjunct Assistant Professor of Forensic Audiology at Lake-Sumter Community College in Leesburg, Florida. Almost immediately upon publication of **Emig**'s study, "Castles of Hardened Bullshit," his work was completely discredited by discoveries that he'd crudely altered much of his audiological research to suit his thesis. Less than a week after these revelations surfaced, **Emig** was found dead at his gym, Bodies-N-Motion, on East Main Street in Leesburg. At first it was naturally assumed that **Emig**, distraught over the self-inflicted damage to his academic reputation, had committed suicide. But forensic allergists were able to determine that the scholar had succumbed to food-associated, exercise-induced anaphylaxis. **Emig**, who was allergic to shellfish, was also receiving weekly immunotherapeutic injections of dust-mite extract to treat his chronic allergic rhinoconjunctivitis. On the afternoon of his death, he'd ordered a bowl of *num pachok chon* (a Cambodian freshwater-snail noodle soup) from a food truck parked near campus. He'd been intrigued by a photograph of the dish taped to the truck, but was completely unaware of its ingredients. After consuming the soup, **Emig** went to the gym and began a vigorous session of aerobic exercise. Within a half hour, he reportedly broke out in giant hives, began to wheeze, vomited, collapsed across the elliptical, and died. There's a significant cross-reactivity between house dust mites and snails, and the combination of dust-mite extract in the immunotherapy injections with the shellfish in the noodle soup and the strenuous exercise proved to be too much for **Jake Emig**'s system to withstand. Soon after his death, a law was enacted—known today as "Jake's Law"— that makes it a federal crime to knowingly sell any noodle soup containing freshwater snails to anyone receiving immunotherapy injections of dust-mite extract.

Intriguingly, when volunteers at Manatee Community College in Bradenton, Florida, who'd been locked in sweltering Porta-Johns and subjected to bards chanting the words "sugar frosted nutsack" nonstop for twelve hours, were asked what visual images occurred to them most frequently, the majority reported envisioning a white planet with a kind of scrotal topography (i.e., "ridged," "wrinkled," "corrugated," etc.). Some simply saw the planet spinning in empty space. Others saw themselves actually on the planet, in a car on an empty highway traversing a desolate, bluish-white, furrowed landscape which radiated out infinitely to the horizon. One of the students (**Heidi**, a junior majoring in Public Safety Administration / Homeland Security who "loves Godiva chocolates and champagne") visualized herself standing on the planet, disproportionately large, "like **The Little Prince**."

The phrase "sugar frosted nutsack" occurs 3,385 times in *The Sugar Frosted Nutsack* (including this sentence). Scholars suspect that this number corresponds to Section 3385, Title 8, of the *California Code of Regulations:* "Appropriate foot protection shall be required for employees who are exposed to foot injuries from electrical hazards, hot, corrosive, poisonous substances, falling objects, crushing or penetrating actions, which may cause injuries, or who are required to work in abnormally wet locations." It's thought that this mystical numerological correspondence might derive from the concern that bards have traditionally had about maintaining the health of their feet, since they are peripatetic and spend the preponderance of their lives walking from village to village. (There are many other eerie mystical numerological correspondences. The flight distance between San Diego, California, and Bogotá, Colombia, is 3,385 miles. The date 3/3/85 is the birthday of Lithuanian supermodel **Dovile Virsilaite**. The sum of the digits — 3+3+8+5 — equals 19. The smallest number of neutrons for which there is no stable isotope is 19. The composer **Béla Bartók** finished his Opus 19 in 1919 when he was 38 (twice 19). The product of the digits — 3x3x8x5 — equals 360. The U.S. Citizenship and Immigration Services Petition for Amerasian,

Widow(er), or Special Immigrant is I-360. The area code for most of western Washington State, including the city of Bremerton, is 360. **Ben Gibbard**, the lead singer for **Death Cab for Cutie**, was born in, believe it or not, Bremerton! There are actually so many mystical numerological correspondences that you're like, this is *so* fucking weird.)

The men who do attend public recitations of *The Sugar Frosted Nutsack* tend to be academic experts, connoisseurs by avocation, or individuals who aspire to be bards. Audiences, though, are composed predominantly of working-class, middle-aged women with little education, who are seeking to establish romantic relationships with the bards. These women chatter, eat, drink, smoke, spit betel juice and pumpkin seeds on the earthen floor, call raucously across the auditorium to each other, and, in imperious voices, order vendors to bring them fried chicken, beer, tampons, whatever they need at the moment. They frequently demonstrate the warmth of their feelings by giving small gifts to bards during the course of a performance. A "donor" will toss them gifts of cigarettes, candy, cologne, or a small amount of money. A gift is often wrapped in a note, requesting a favor of the bard in return. A bard may be asked, for instance, to perform a private recitation. In some cases, bards receive quite large sums of money or valuable gifts ranging from expensive toilet articles and wristwatches to flat-screen TVs, Mercedes-Benz cars, and luxury apartments—anything to pamper them. Often there is a sexual attachment between the donor and the bard. Liaisons between lusty middle-aged women and handsome young bards are especially common.

Some of these women are widows, some are still married. They love to make a show of themselves at the public recitations and squander their husbands' money on bards with whom they've become infatuated.

Most of the blind bards were, at one time, sighted audience members whose wives left them for the bards they met at public recitations. These distraught men, suddenly bereft of their spouses, then blinded themselves and, in turn, became itinerant bards, traveling from town to town, chanting what they remember hearing or think they heard at recitations, although they, too, mumble in such an incomprehensible manner (the traditional style) that it's truly remarkable they convey anything at all to their audiences, one member of which will invariably include the sweaty, lusty middle-aged woman with the spectacular big-ass ass who will become the bard's new wife, leaving yet another jilted man to gouge out his eyes. This is the endless reproductive cycle of the bard.

An *Inside The Sugar Frosted Nutsack* reunion season finale features an exclusive interview with a real husband and real wife who've just emerged from a public recitation of *The Sugar Frosted Nutsack* (an interview which is, of course, immediately incorporated into *The Sugar Frosted Nutsack,* and which experts today consider an integral component of the epic itself, and which audiences naturally expect the bards to ritually chant in its entirety). The real husband and real wife spontaneously perform a power ballad (with its shades of **George Jones** and **Tammy Wynette**) and a **Wagnerian** duet. This combination of declaimed passages (in which the blind, vagrant, drug-addled bards attempt to realistically imitate the voices of characters) and sung passages of greater (or lesser) lyrical beauty provide an enjoyable variety, keeping the recitation—even of long, mind-numbing exegetical monologues—from becoming tedious. Keep in mind that almost immediately after this interview is conducted, the woman leaves her husband for a blind, vagrant, drug-addled bard she met at the very performance she just attended, and that her husband promptly enucleates both of his eyeballs and becomes—what else?—a blind, vagrant, drug-addled bard.

T.S.F.N. If we were to ask you to pick the one thing you liked most about the performance of *The Sugar Frosted Nutsack* you just listened to, what would it be?

REAL HUSBAND The sheer mind-numbing repetitiveness of it. And the almost unendurable length. At first I wanted to just walk out—the bards seemed drunk or fucked-up on something, and I figured, OK, here we go, this is gonna be like **Britney Spears** at the MTV VMAs or Japan's Minister of Finance **Shoichi Nakagawa** at the 2009 G7 meeting in Rome. But then once it got started, I really got into the way the bards kept up that mesmerizing beat by banging their rings on those metal jerrycans of orange soda. And I really like the way that they wander around from place to place...their vagrancy. And I love how they're actually blind—I mean in *real life*. Although, it seemed like a couple of them could see but were...what's the word?...Shit, I'm completely blanking out here....Sweetie, what's that thing where you see words backward or reverse some of the letters?

REAL WIFE *Dyslexic.*

REAL HUSBAND Dyslexic, right. And there was something about their completely mumbled, uninflected delivery that made it...even more sort of mind-numbing. It felt like it was just going around and around in circles and it felt like, at some point, I don't know how to put it...maybe you should talk to my wife, because she's so much better at articulating things like this—she was an arts major (and she has a spectacular big-ass ass, thanks to **Fast-Cooking Ali**).

T.S.F.N. OK, how would *you* describe the effect?

REAL WIFE Well, I don't know how much better I am at articulating any of this, but, to me, that sense of it just going around in circles, in these sort of endlessly spiraling recapitulations—it felt like, at some point, it was just going to drive me crazy. And then I thought, like, duh, this is what it feels like to have **XOXO** inscribing your brain with a sharp periodontal instrument. *This* is what it feels like to be **Ike**. That was one of those epiphany moments, for me at least.

T.S.F.N. An epiphany about what exactly?

REAL WIFE About how—and I think you could say that this is what *The Sugar Frosted Nutsack* is fundamentally about, I mean, this is my interpretation anyway—about how we each have this ridiculously finite number of things inscribed in our minds, and that what we do, moment by moment, is continuously postulate an extrinsic "world" for ourselves by reshuffling and recapitulating these ridiculously finite number of things. But it's a completely closed system—there's no "world" actually extrinsic to it. What makes **Ike** so magnificent is that he's pared down his deck to a single card, *The Hero*—a man standing on his stoop, on the prow of his hermitage, striking that "contrapposto pose, in his white wifebeater, his torso totally ripped, his lustrous chestnut armpit hair wafting in the breeze, his head turned and inclined up toward the top floors of the Burj Khalifa in Dubai, from which the gaze of masturbating Goddesses casts him in a sugar frosted nimbus."

T.S.F.N. Your husband wasn't kidding. That's some straight-up hyperarticulate, high-pitched shit!

REAL HUSBAND (gushing) I told you! She's *pissah smaht!* She's phenomenological!!

T.S.F.N. What else did you especially like?

REAL WIFE There were these two tiny, busty bards with

the T-shirts that said "I Don't Do White Guys." I *loved* them. They reminded me of **Snooki**. . . . Like weird little twin **Snookies**.

T.S.F.N. What else?

REAL WIFE The "10 Things That I Know for Sure About Women" list made me cry. It's so beautiful.

T.S.F.N. It doesn't bother you that it was plagiarized from **Oprah**'s magazine?

REAL WIFE No, are you kidding?! I think that for a man to steal something from **Oprah**'s magazine and say he wrote it—to do that for a woman you're falling in love with—that is just the most romantic thing in the world. Seriously. I think **Ike** is super-sexy. Every time the bards describe his body and talk about his guinea-T and how he's completely shredded and his vascularity and how you can see his butt-crack when he genuflects toward the Burj Khalifa, that kind of thing, it's a *huge* turn-on for me. It makes me sweaty. I have to start fanning myself with my program.

T.S.F.N. That's funny. Wouldn't you rather see a reenactment of *The Sugar Frosted Nutsack* than just hear people reciting the story? Wouldn't that be even more powerful?

REAL WIFE I'd rather listen to something than see it.

It says in *The Sugar Frosted Nutsack,* in *Season Eight:* "The Gods' designs are revealed not in incandescent flashes of lucidity, but in the din of the incomprehensible, in a cacophony of high-pitched voices and discordant jingles." And I believe that. And I'd certainly rather hear a story told by spaced-out blind bards than see it acted out by celebrities.

T.S.F.N. You mean like in a movie?

REAL WIFE Right.

T.S.F.N. You don't like movies?

REAL WIFE I don't particularly want to see two hours of **George Clooney** *playing* a human resource specialist or **Gwyneth Paltrow** *pretending* to die of the plague or **Ben Stiller** *portraying* some disaffected slacker, no. When we come to hear a recitation of *The Sugar Frosted Nutsack,* we're not coming to hear fucking rich celebrities pretending to be bards. These are *real* bards. They are *really* blind. They are *really* itinerant. They are *really* high on ecstasy or psilocybin mushrooms or hallucinogenic borscht. They are not *playing* fucked-up bards. They *are* fucked-up.

REAL HUSBAND Also, we love the whole ambience here, the whole scene—the way people bring their families, and their straw mats and folding chairs, and sit out here for hours, and bring food. And the way they chant along. It's a little like mass karaoke.

T.S.F.N. What did you guys bring?

REAL HUSBAND We packed a lunch. We brought, let's see...we brought shawarma, tongue sandwiches, Fig Newtons, orange soda, of course.

T.S.F.N. How did you and your wife meet?

REAL HUSBAND Well, the funny thing is—we're both from Jersey City, but we met in Manhattan. I was working as a waiter at this place on Seventh Avenue and Nineteenth Street. And my wife was going to Parsons at the time. We met at the Limelight, actually.

T.S.F.N. So you were waiting tables and...anything else? Trying to become an actor? Musician? Putting yourself through school?

REAL HUSBAND I'd actually enrolled in a songwriting workshop at The New School. But I got terminal, fucking insurmountable writer's block immediately. Like the first day of the class. And it was crushing because I'd really made up my mind that I wanted to be a songwriter, even though I'd never written a song before. I'd never really written *anything* except lists, actually. I was a great list maker. So, anyway, I decided—and

this is going to sound crazy, but it's the Gods' truth—
I decided that I'd try to become gay, because so many
of my favorite songwriters were gay, like **Cole Porter**
and **Elton John** and the **Pet Shop Boys**, and I was
thinking that might sort of jump-start me creatively. So
I went to one of those Christian therapists who "cure"
gay people, and I asked him if he'd take whatever he
says to them, y'know, whatever secret incantation he
uses, and say it to me *backward,* so I'd actually become
converted to being gay.

T.S.F.N. That's *so* funny.

REAL HUSBAND Yeah. Well, it didn't work anyway.
And then the two of us met at the Limelight and started
dating, so the whole gay conversion thing became moot.
And it's probably a good thing I never became a lyricist
or a jingle-writer, because she has to help me finish my
sentences all the time!

T.S.F.N. How about you? What were you doing at Parsons?

REAL WIFE It's an interesting question because, during
the recitation, my husband and I were talking about how
people sort of "abuse" **XOXO**, and it made me think
about something that had happened to me at Parsons.

T.S.F.N. Tell us about that.

REAL WIFE Well, I'd been there a couple of years, study-ing painting, and I'd been doing all this, y'know, com-pletely derivative work—**Kenneth Noland** rip-offs, imitation **Agnes Martins**, second-rate **Peter Halleys**, all this shit. And then I came up with this idea, which was to use photographs of very grim, morbid sorts of things and make these kind of unfocused, blurry paint-ings out of them. Really cool idea, and I'd never seen anything like it. So, I'm thinking, y'know, finally, *here I go.* So I did this huge, unfocused, blurry painting of **Joseph Goebbels**'s family, based on a famous photo-graph of **Joseph** and **Magda Goebbels**'s dead chil-dren's pajama-clad bodies (**Helga Susanne**, **Hilde-gard**, **Helmut Christian**, **Hedwig**, **Holdine**, and **Heidrun**) after they'd been put to sleep with morphine and poisoned with cyanide by their parents. And I showed the painting to one of my instructors at Parsons, and he was like, that's amazing, that's brilliant, that's a completely new, unprecedented idea. And I was just totally euphoric. And then, a couple of days later, the same instructor comes up to me and says, you better go check out the new **Gerhard Richter** exhibit at MoMA. And I was like, why? And he said, just go. So I went to MoMA and there's this fifteen-painting cycle of unfo-cused, blurry paintings that **Richter** had done based on photographs of **Andreas Baader** and **Ulrike Mein-hof** and their deaths.... It occurred to me at the time that maybe **XOXO** had taken the idea from my head and given it to **Gerhard Richter**. It crossed my mind.

I'll be honest. And I pretty much gave up on painting after that.

T.S.F.N. What did you mean about people *abusing* **XOXO**?

REAL WIFE I think it's too easy for people to always blame things on **XOXO**. Everyone's always, like, oh, sorry for what I said last night, **XOXO** must have kidnapped my soul and plied it with drugged sherbet, y'know? I think sometimes people just use that as a way of avoiding responsibility for what they say—it's like the equivalent of—oh, I was drunk or I was so tired...

T.S.F.N. Was it a huge disappointment to you that you didn't eventually become an artist?

REAL WIFE No. Look at the so-called "art world." Fucking **David Geffen** sells a **de Kooning** to this hedge fund billionaire **Steven A. Cohen** for 137.5 million dollars. Such "art lovers"! Right? It says in *The Sugar Frosted Nutsack* that a time will come when all fettered monsters will break loose and the plutocrats will be dragged out of office buildings and guillotined on the street. That includes the "art lovers."

T.S.F.N. Some people think that that whole business about **Ike** getting hit by a *Mister Softee* truck on Spring Break when he was eighteen but initially telling people he was hit by a Hasidic ambulance to foment some apocalyptic Helter Skelter–type global war is *really* confusing. Do you agree with that?

REAL WIFE When I went to my first recitation and I heard the bards chant that part, I thought to myself, I don't see how a dispute between club kids and Hasids could set off any kind of apocalyptic global war.

REAL HUSBAND What about World War One? Who was that guy...the Bosnian Serb...the nationalist? Uh...oh fuck!...What was his name, sweetie?

REAL WIFE Gavrilo Princip?

REAL HUSBAND Yeah, **Gavrilo Princip**. **Gavrilo Princip** assassinates the **Archduke Franz Ferdinand** in Sarajevo, right? And it sets off the whole fuckin' First World War. I mean, that's a pretty apocalyptic war. If the conditions are right, you never know what can set it off. Club kids and Hasids could conceivably do it.

REAL WIFE I'm not sure that's the best analogy.

REAL HUSBAND You don't think World War One was an apocalyptic global war?

REAL WIFE That's not what I mean.

REAL HUSBAND You don't think World War One was an apocalyptic fucking global war?

REAL WIFE I never said it wasn't.

REAL HUSBAND Trench warfare. Poison gas. Fifteen million deaths.

REAL WIFE The **Archduke Franz Ferdinand** was heir to the Austro-Hungarian throne. There was an extremely complicated situation...

REAL HUSBAND I'm just sayin'.

REAL WIFE ...with all sorts of interlocking alliances.

REAL HUSBAND I'm just sayin'. If the conditions are right, you never know what can set it off. Club kids and Hasids could conceivably do it.

T.S.F.N. You seem to really identify with **Ike**.

REAL HUSBAND People tell me I sound like him— y'know, the raspy, whispery voice and everything. And I have the same kinds of fantasies he does about big, sweaty, uneducated, working-class women, and about being ogled by masturbating Goddesses...

T.S.F.N. Do you think your wife is a Mossad agent?

REAL HUSBAND (looking askance at his wife with mock suspicion) Hmmm…

T.S.F.N. Possible?

REAL HUSBAND (laughing) Seriously, I tend to interpret that whole "everyone's wife is a Mossad agent" thing in a more sort of metaphorical way—that people you're intimate with might be, like, "double agents," y'know? It's a weird kind of paranoia you get about people you love—that they might turn out to be completely different from who you think they are, that it's all been some sort of diabolically patient plot against you. I think that's a pretty normal fear you have in any serious relationship. And that's why it's such a popular part of the epic, because so many people can relate to that fear. But personally I don't really worry about it too much.

T.S.F.N. Why's that?

REAL HUSBAND Have you ever heard of Cupid's Stigmata?

T.S.F.N. No, what is that?

REAL HUSBAND It's a term they use in online dating. It's when two people share some uncommon anatomical feature with each other, which usually means that they're sort of predestined to be together. And my wife and I both have double ureters draining one of our kidneys (which is an anomaly occurring in, like, 1 in 150 people), and we both have port-wine stains in the shape of Nike swooshes on the smalls of our backs (which is, like, 1 in 10 million people), so...

T.S.F.N. Is that true? That's amazing!

REAL HUSBAND (totally cracking up) No, I'm kidding. I'm busting your chops, man. But seriously—we're really close. Really *really* close. And I think that what they say about **Ike** and **Ruthie** is sort of true about us too—that we're utterly inscrutable figures who, paradoxically, understand each other perfectly well. And we're both lifelong connoisseurs of *The Sugar Frosted Nutsack.*

T.S.F.N. You've been going to recitations your whole life?

REAL HUSBAND Absolutely. And I was in one when I was a kid! In, like, fourth grade. It was a school recitation. I played a fuckin' bard! I probably still know the lines...

T.S.F.N. Do it. Do a little for us.

REAL HUSBAND I don't have a jerrycan of Sunkist to tap my ring on, but...

T.S.F.N. C'mon, do some.

REAL HUSBAND OK.... This is, like, totally from memory...and it isn't verbatim, it's sort of paraphrasing...

T.S.F.N. Go for it.

REAL HUSBAND OK...**Ike** is strolling down to the Miss America Diner. Instead of a monocle and a walking stick, this flâneur sports a tight guinea-T and a baseball bat. Uh...he's loaded with gem-like apercus and aphorisms....He enters the diner and...no, wait a minute...

REAL WIFE Doomed, elusive **Ike**, Warlord of His Stoop...

REAL HUSBAND Doomed, elusive **Ike**, Warlord of His Stoop...never ostentatious, self-righteous, or flamboyantly narcissistic, enters the diner...as if in a trance...a trance abetted by the obbligato of miscellaneous conversations, which is akin to the drone of the bards. "It's his favorite restaurant!" a friend of the hero tells *The Sugar Frosted Nutsack* in an exclusive interview. No, wait— that's not right..." There are two opposed facets to **Ike**'s character, a friend of the hero tells *The Sugar Frosted Nutsack* in an exclusive interview. "He abhors celebrity and yet covets immortality." **Ike** himself is said to be troubled by the ambivalence in his character. "I dwell in anonymity. How is it, then, that I am enchanted by eternal renown?" One of the things about **Ike** that makes him so indisputably a hero is that he doesn't leave his own contradictions to the effete disputations of armchair scholars. He grapples with them himself, in his own lifetime.... Uh—

REAL WIFE Three crazy things to report...

REAL HUSBAND Three crazy things to report: *The Sugar Frosted Nutsack* has received a letter demanding that **Ike** be replaced by actor **Chace Crawford**...six bards were hacked to death by jilted, machete-wielding husbands whose wives had been seduced at a public recitation...we are now learning that the bards have been decapitated, and that the severed heads of the bards continue to cacophonously chant *The Sugar Frosted Nutsack*...hold on...we have just received confirmation that only one head is still chanting—let me repeat that: only *one* head is still chanting...we are now learning that drunken Ukrainian Cossacks, Mexican banditos wearing sombreros and crisscrossed cartridge bandoliers, khat-chewing Somali pirates, Indian Maoists (i.e., Naxalites), and Punjabi Taliban are playing *Buzkashi* with the headless carcasses of the slain bards. OK, we have just received word that all hell has broken loose. Children all over the world are now strangling their fathers with the intestines of their mothers. A single Chinook helicopter has been sent in to evacuate the loyalists, but its blades have been immobilized with what experts are calling "military-grade ass-cheese." Ladies and gentlemen—we have just received an important clarification: all of this is apparently just part of a *Cirque du Soleil* show. Let me repeat that, for the benefit of those of you who are just tuning in: all of this is apparently just part of a *Cirque du Soleil* show. No one could really disregard it or completely purge it from their minds—

REAL WIFE Even though this all turned out to be just part of a *Cirque du Soleil* show, this notion of severed bard-heads was like a remark stricken from the record in a courtroom—no one could really disregard it or completely purge it from their minds...

REAL HUSBAND Right, right.... Even though this all turned out to be just part of a *Cirque du Soleil* show, this notion of severed bard-heads was like a remark stricken from the record in a courtroom—no one could really disregard it or completely purge it from their minds. In fact, in the *Twelfth Season,* some experts begin referring to the vagrant, drug-addled blind bards simply as "Severed Bard-Heads." And a strange idea began to take root in the public imagination—that these severed bard-heads are gathered by itinerant children toting surplus NBA ball bags and sold to "processors" for only several rupees a head. Then the severed bard-heads are crushed in a kind of wine press, resulting in a "juicy pulp," to which is added the spit of the horniest, hairiest, chubbiest, and most uneducated subproletarian women in that particular town or village (aka "**La Felina**'s Angels"). Enzymes in their saliva catalyze various chemical processes that culminate in what we today call "hallucinogenic Gravy."

Some experts devote entire careers to the study of a single scene. For example, the unusually lachrymose (albeit highly ritualized) scene between **Ike** and his father at a restaurant, when **Ike**'s father says to him something to the effect of "I hate to speak ill of the dead, but your mother was a fat, sweaty, uneducated, subproletarian woman who didn't have clue *one*." And **Ike** indicates that he is weeping by slowly touching his sleeve to his forehead. And the father, noting this, says, "You know, I just realized something....My father said almost the exact same thing to me at a restaurant when I was your age." And then the father slowly touches *his* sleeve to *his* forehead. Or **Ike**'s lengthy and disjointed conversation with **La Felina** at Port Newark about whether **Rachel Lee**, the Korean-American mastermind of the "Bling Ring" (the gang of well-off Valley kids who burglarized the homes of **Paris Hilton**, **Lindsay Lohan**, **Orlando Bloom**, and **Audrina Patridge**, a regular on the reality show *The Hills* who famously complained after the burglary that "They took...jeans made to fit my body to my perfect shape"), constitutes a new kind of anarchist insurrectionary, a "Neo-Bandito" representing perhaps the new "lumpen celebutante," or whether she's just someone slavishly in thrall to the celebrities she admired, etc. (This colloquy all by itself is considered by some to be a stand-alone mini-epic.) And there are some experts who devote entire careers to the study of a brief vignette or a single passage: the God **Rikidozen** absently tapping a Sharpie on the lip of a coffee mug, and the unvarying cadence of that tap-tap-tap becoming the basis for the standard 124 beats-per-minute in house music; or the Dwarf Goddess **La Muñeca** turning her mortal girlfriend, Chief Warrant Officer **Francesca DiPasquale**, into a macadamia nut, a jai alai ball, and then 100,000 shares of Schering-Plough stock; or when **Bosco Hifikepunye** makes **Mi-Hyun** fifty feet tall and turns **Lenin**'s corpse and **Ted Williams**'s cryonically preserved head into anal sex toys for her; or when **Ike** says to the God of Money, **Doc Hickory**, "Can I ask you a stupid question? You don't find me *dour*, do you?" and **Doc Hickory**'s like, "Dour?" and **Ike** goes, "Yeah, y'know, humorless," and **Doc Hickory**'s like, "I know what *dour* means. I'm just wondering why you're asking me," and **Ike** goes, "Because I heard that **Mogul Magoo** told **Bosco Hifikepunye** that he thinks I'm all, like, dour and shit"; or when **Shanice** gets **Lady Rukia** to get **XOXO** to sabotage **Ike**'s daughter when she's taking her tenth-grade math final and answering the question "If each of 'Octomom' **Nadya Suleman**'s octuplets also have eight children and then each of their children have eight children and each of their children have eight children, etc., how many offspring would there be in eight generations?"; or **Candace Hilligoss** getting out of the bathtub in *Carnival of Souls* (to creepy organ music); or **Ike** inviting a gob of phlegm to a concert. And then there are those experts who devote entire careers to the study and minute exegesis of a single line. And among these particular experts who were entranced with the phrase "severed bard-heads," there were several who became fixated upon the significance of the line "We have just received confirmation that only one head is still chanting—let me repeat that: only *one* head is still chanting." Contrary to their colleagues, who'd confected a theory of myriad free-floating severed bard-heads—that is, swarms of airborne anthropomorphic "scrubbing bubbles" or "nano-drones" whose punishingly repetitive high-pitched chants comprise what we think of today as *The Sugar Frosted Nutsack*—these experts contend that there is, in fact, only *one* severed bard-head. These experts—who collectively have become known as the "Jersey City School" because most of them actually reside in Jersey City and are, in fact, all people who babysat or taught or coached **Ike** when he was a child (including his driver's ed instructor and the chubby babysitter with the big-ass titties who "mildly molested" Ike while they watched *F-Troop* together)—believe that "the one severed bard-head" is inhabited by all the Gods, which accounts for the polyvocal buzzing or droning quality of the head. They have determined, allegedly through the use of spy satellites, electronic eavesdropping, and information provided clandestinely by the Pakistani intelligence agency, the ISI, that "the one severed bard-head" containing the Gods is kept in a minibar on the top floor of the Burj Khalifa in Dubai. All of which leads inevitably to the question: Is "the one severed bard-head" **Ike** himself?

The identification of "the one severed bard-head" with **Ike** himself is persistent and completely understandable. Of course, one can hear in the cacophonous buzz that emanates from **Ike**'s head an echo—an analogue—of **Claude Lévi-Strauss**'s enigmatic dictum "the myths think themselves in me." Also, the bards' recitations are garbled, fragmentary, repetitive, and almost inaudible. **Ike**'s continuous self-narration is garbled, fragmentary, repetitive, and almost inaudible. They are analogous. But are they one and the same? Isn't **Ike**'s self-narration (and, of course, this very speculation, these very sentences) instantly and retroactively incorporated into the epic *The Sugar Frosted Nutsack* and dutifully transmitted from generation to generation of chanting, drug-addled, blind "severed bard-heads" who maintain their trance-inducing beat by banging their chunky chachkas against metal jerrycans of orange soda? An infinitely recursive epic that subtends and engulfs everything *about* it (i.e., everything extrinsic to it), and that has, for tens of thousands of years, at any given moment, been subject to the impish and sometimes spiteful corruptions and interpolations (or the out-and-out sabotage) of **XOXO**, presents a phenomenon that's difficult to get your mind around.

The Ballad of the Severed Bard-Head

REAL HUSBAND

He abhors celebrity
And yet covets immortality.
What is the meaning of the paradox?
What are its latent properties?

REAL WIFE

These portions can seem hopelessly corrupt.
XOXO is winning the battle to ruin the book,
But he hasn't won the war.

REAL HUSBAND & REAL WIFE

I'm a severed bard-head!
I can't stop reciting what I started!
This shit ain't for the fainthearted!
We ain't toasted, we Pop-Tarted!
So dump me in the toilet bowl and flush me!
Throw me in a garbage truck and crush me!
A trash compactor or a wine press works OK,
It's like all that stupid shit in the *Cirque du Soleil!*
Suicide-by-cop sounds fun,
But you can never find a motherfuckin' cop
When you need one!

REAL HUSBAND

Some scholars have recently compared
The Sugar Frosted Nutsack to Abacus 2007-AC1,
The mortgage investment vehicle which
Goldman Sachs VP **Fabrice Tourre** created.

REAL WIFE

And which he described,
In an e-mail to his girlfriend,
As a "Frankenstein" creation,

"A product of pure intellectual masturbation,
The type of thing which you invent telling yourself:
'Well, what if we created a "thing,"
Which has no purpose,
Which is absolutely conceptual and highly theoretical
and which nobody knows how to price?'"

REAL HUSBAND & REAL WIFE

I'm a severed bard-head!
I can't stop reciting what I started!
This shit ain't for the fainthearted!
We ain't toasted, we Pop-Tarted!
So dump me in the toilet bowl and flush me!
Throw me in a garbage truck and crush me!
A trash compactor or a wine press works OK,
It's like all that stupid shit in the *Cirque du Soleil!*
Suicide-by-cop sounds fun,
But you can never find a motherfuckin' cop
When you need one!

REAL HUSBAND

"Going into the forest to gather wild garlic"
Is a euphemism for those times
When **Ike** stares off into space,
Listening to the voice of a particular
God who's speaking to him.

REAL WIFE

Or when he thinks

The writhing Goddesses are
Ogling him and masturbating,
Or when he thinks he hears
The distant whine of a
Drone aircraft circling overhead.

REAL HUSBAND & REAL WIFE

I'm a severed bard-head!
I can't stop reciting what I started!
This shit ain't for the fainthearted!
We ain't toasted, we Pop-Tarted!
So dump me in the toilet bowl and flush me!
Throw me in a garbage truck and crush me!
A trash compactor or a wine press works OK,
It's like all that stupid shit in the *Cirque du Soleil!*
Suicide-by-cop sounds fun,
But you can never find a motherfuckin' cop
When you need one!

REAL HUSBAND

Ike had a dream about **La Felina**.
There was something dangling from her snatch.
At first **Ike** thought it was a tampon string,
But as he came closer
He could see that it was a fortune.

REAL WIFE

He pulled it out and read it.
It said, "To propitiate **XOXO**,

So he allows your story to be told
In a quasi-coherent way,
You must kill your father, etc.

REAL HUSBAND & REAL WIFE

I'm a severed bard-head!
I can't stop reciting what I started!
This shit ain't for the fainthearted!
We ain't toasted, we Pop-Tarted!
So dump me in the toilet bowl and flush me!
Throw me in a garbage truck and crush me!
A trash compactor or a wine press works OK,
It's like all that stupid shit in the *Cirque du Soleil!*
Suicide-by-cop sounds fun,
But you can never find a motherfuckin' cop
When you need one!

The **REAL HUSBAND** and **REAL WIFE** stop tapping their wedding rings on their cans of Sunkist orange soda, and the tempo slows.

The sky darkens.

REAL WIFE I just want to tell you something. We both knew exactly what we were getting into when we signed on to this whole *Sugar Frosted Nutsack* thing...

REAL HUSBAND I realize that.

REAL WIFE I'm fated to leave you for a blind, drug-addled bard, and then you have to enucleate your own eyeballs. It's all foretold in the epic. You have to really do it—I mean, the eye thing.

REAL HUSBAND I know.

REAL WIFE No regrets?

REAL HUSBAND In the *Thirteenth Season*, when **Ike** tells **The Waitress** at the Miss America diner about his intention (and destiny) to commit suicide-by-cop and thus enable his family to collect on his life insurance policy, **The Waitress** says that "fate is the ultimate preexisting condition." And I believe that.

(The following is sung to the melody of "O Sink Hernieder, Nacht Der Liebe" from **Richard Wagner**'s *Tristan und Isolde*.)

REAL WIFE

At the risk of hoisting myself
On my own petard,
I'm leaving you
For a blind, drug-addled bard.

REAL HUSBAND

What about Cupid's Stigmata?

REAL WIFE

My heart's started an Intifada!

As she departs, he calls out to her—

REAL HUSBAND

Instead of humiliating myself
By begging you to come back,
I'll devote the rest of my life
To chanting *The Sugar Frosted Nutsack*!

He takes a melon baller from the picnic basket...

REAL HUSBAND

'Scuse me while I kiss the sky!

...and blinds himself.

We hear the opening bars of the *Mister Softee* jingle softly repeating over and over again, as if from a vast distance...over and over and over again...for hours, for days...months...years...as if for an eternity...
Until—

114

REAL HUSBAND We've got a caller.

Apparently the *Mister Softee* jingle is the ringtone for the **Husband**'s cellphone, which he retrieves from his jacket pocket.

REAL HUSBAND Hello, you're on *The Sugar Frosted Nutsack*.

CALLER Hello?

REAL HUSBAND You're on *The Sugar Frosted Nutsack*.

CALLER I have a question for **Ike**.

REAL HUSBAND **Ike**'s not here. He's at the Miss America Diner. I can give you his cellphone number or the number for the diner.

CALLER Maybe you could help me.

REAL HUSBAND I'll try.

CALLER OK. I have a couple of questions, but let me start with this one: why is **Ike**'s daughter's name never revealed?

REAL HUSBAND Out of respect for her privacy.

CALLER OK. I know this question will probably make me seem hopelessly provincial, but...why is there *so* much sex in *The Sugar Frosted Nutsack*? You can't listen to even thirty seconds of a public recitation without hearing these drug-addled, vagrant bards chanting about cocks and pussies and clits and tits and balls and asses and shiksa asses and spectacular big-ass asses and hot Jew jizz and fucking and masturbating....Why?

REAL HUSBAND Because it's *sex-drenched* and *death-drenched*.

CALLER But *why* is it sex-drenched and death-drenched?

REAL HUSBAND Because **Ike** is obsessed with sex and death. The seventeenth-century samurai **Yamamoto Tsunetomo**, describing the proper attitude of a warrior, wrote, "Every day without fail one should consider himself as dead. There is a saying of the elders that goes, 'Step from under the eaves and you're a dead man. Leave the gate and the enemy is waiting.' This is not a matter of being careful. It is to consider oneself as dead beforehand." The **Marquis de Sade** wrote, "There is no better way to know death than to link it with some licentious image." Combine the two and you have **Ike Karton**. (FYI, **Vincent van Gogh**'s last words before he shot himself in a wheat field in Auvers-sur-Oise were "Fuck **Kirk Douglas**.")

CALLER There are just these punishingly repetitive references to anal sex toys and bedraggled, sweaty, chubby, mature, subproletarian women and hairy, Asian, midget, hypoglycemic, type-O-negative plumpers who squirt, etc.

REAL HUSBAND There is also—and I don't know if you're aware of this—a punishingly repetitive use of the phrase "punishingly repetitive." In fact, the phrase "punishingly repetitive" is used 251 times (including this sentence) in *The Sugar Frosted Nutsack*.

CALLER Is there any mystical significance to the number 251?

REAL HUSBAND Not to my knowledge. But did you know that it's impossible for a horse to vomit and that Turkish Taffy was **Harry Houdini**'s favorite candy?

CALLER It says, "**Ike** suffers from irregular clonic jerks of the head and neck ever since he was hit by a *Mister Softee* truck on Spring Break when he was eighteen years old." What college was he attending at the time?

REAL HUSBAND Ike was going to F.I.T., but after one semester he dropped out and worked part-time in the meat department at a Gristedes on the Upper West Side.

CALLER You don't happen to have the exact address, do you?

REAL HUSBAND Why?

CALLER Because I'm planning a weekend where I go and visit all the key sites in **Ike**'s life, like the barbershop where he went as a kid and experienced "the thwack of a straight-edge razor on a leather strop, combs refracted in blue liquid, **Jerry Vale** ('Innamorata'), hot lather on the nape of your neck mysteriously eliciting the incipient desire to be whipped by chain-smoking middle-aged women (and/or sweaty Eastern-bloc athletes) in bras & panties," and the park bench in Lincoln Park where he read "10 Things That I Know for Sure About Women" to **Ruthie** when they were dating, and the two-story brick "hermitage" where he and **Ruthie** and their daughter live, etc. So I'd definitely want to go to the Gristedes where he had his first butcher job.

REAL HUSBAND All right, let me put you on hold for a moment and I'll check on that for you.

The **REAL HUSBAND's** MOH (Music on Hold) is **Richard Wagner**'s "O Sink Hernieder, Nacht Der Liebe" from *Tristan und Isolde*. Several moments pass, and then —

REAL HUSBAND You still there?

CALLER Yes, I'm here.

REAL HUSBAND Sorry that took so long. I'm newly sightless. The address of the Gristedes is 251 West 86th Street at Broadway.

CALLER 251? You're kidding.

REAL HUSBAND No, why?

CALLER That is *so* fucking weird.

REAL HUSBAND Why?

CALLER Because 251 is the number of times the phrase "punishingly repetitive" is used in *The Sugar Frosted Nutsack*. And it's the address of the first place where **Ike** had a butcher job. You don't think there's any mystical significance in that?

REAL HUSBAND Honestly, I think it's a complete coincidence.

CALLER You seriously think the fact that the phrase "punishingly repetitive" is used 251 times in *The Sugar Frosted Nutsack* and the fact that the address of the Gristedes where **Ike Karton** had his first butcher job is 251 West 86th Street is a complete coincidence?

REAL HUSBAND I really do.

CALLER You're being serious?

REAL HUSBAND Yeah.

There's a long pause...then—

CALLER It says in the *Fourteenth Season*, "Even within his small, haimish Jersey City neighborhood of attached two-story brick homes, **Ike** conducts himself with the guarded reserve and fateful solemnity of an exile. Doomed hero, dear to the Gods, unwavering, set apart by his fealty and his inexorable fate, but never evincing the hauteur of a freak, he calls his bowel movements his 'little brother.'" I don't completely understand what that means.

REAL HUSBAND You know how some women call their period their "friend"? It's sort of like that. **Ike** is very courtly. He'd never say, "I have to go take a crap" or "a dump" or anything like that. He'd say, "My little brother is visiting." Or "Excuse me, I think my little brother is here." Or "Could you pull into that rest stop over there, I didn't expect my little brother to get here so suddenly. He must have taken an earlier flight." Or "He must have decided to take the Acela, instead of the regular Amtrak."

CALLER Oh...I get it.

REAL HUSBAND And the closer **Ike** gets to the violent death which is his inexorable fate, the more intensely kindred he feels with things that are considered by most people to be base or odious, which is one of the things that makes him such a hero, I think. So there's also a symbolic component to his calling a bowel movement his brother. It's the same sort of thing as in the *Fifteenth Season,* in that scene where he and **Vance** are going to meet the God who's supposedly selling hallucinogenic Gravy to **Vance**, and some guy on the street hawks up a big gob of phlegm and spits it on the sidewalk, and **Ike** stops, and he kneels down, and he says to the gob of phlegm, "Fräulein, my band, **The Kartons**, is giving a Final Concert later this week, and I'd be very much honored if you would attend." This is **Ike**, with his sort of plainspoken eloquence, expressing the paradoxical nature of his character—destined for the glory of a martyr's immortality but, at the same time, fervently wedded to those things most despised, most anathematized, to the lowest of the low.

CALLER You're the one who's actually reciting what I'm saying, right?

REAL HUSBAND Yes. You're like a Japanese *bunraku* puppet and I'm like the chanter (the *tayu*) who performs all the characters' voices.

CALLER So does it have to say "**CALLER**" like that? I

don't feel like being some sort of boldface signifier. Can't I just be part of your recitation?

"Sure."

"That's better. Thank you. It was like being on speakerphone before. I want to ask you a question about these itinerant children who are toting the surplus NBA ball bags around and gathering severed bard-heads and selling them to "processors" for only several rupees a head. Doesn't this drive home the whole issue of how detrimental cheap foreign labor is to American workers? If you have an unlimited supply of these vagrant kids outside the country who are willing to sell severed bard-heads for several rupees a head, it doesn't matter to an American severed-bard-head scavenger how quickly our economy recovers or how fast it grows— the market value of a severed bard-head is going to be several rupees."

"So what do you suggest?"

"A tariff. A tariff on foreign-scavenged severed bard-heads."

"I don't believe in tariffs or quotas or any form of protectionism. I think that protectionism leads to reduced consumer choice, higher prices, lower-quality goods, and, in the long run, economic stagnation and coercive monopolies."

There's a long pause...then—

"What does 'military-grade ass-cheese' mean?"

"I've always thought that military-grade ass-cheese is just basically the shit that gums up the works in your life. Do you know what I mean? This is just my interpretation, but I think it's basically the shit that just fucks everything up."

"OK. Is it true that **Ike** buys a grenade launcher from an undercover FBI agent at the Miss America Diner?"

"No, that's not true. This whole business of **Ike** buying a grenade launcher from an undercover FBI agent at the Miss America Diner is what experts call a 'noncanonical blooper.'"

"But is it in *The Sugar Frosted Nutsack* or not?"

"It is now. Thanks to you. Thanks to you bringing it up."

"OK. I guess this is my last question: There's a vignette involving a pet groomer named **Rebecca Nesbit** and a Beverly Hills plastic surgeon by the name of **Dr. Giancarlo Capella**. And I'm not sure why it's even included in the epic—if, in fact, it is—because it doesn't appear to involve **Ike** or any of the Gods. And I was just wondering if it's also considered a noncanonical blooper. And I'm also curious as to whether you think that noncanonical bloopers are the work of **XOXO**."

"First of all, yes, this is an out-and-out noncanonical blooper that was not part of the original epic, although, again—as of right now—it's considered totally authentic. **Rebecca Nesbit** was a pet groomer (actually, I think she advertised herself a 'pet stylist') who, following her divorce in Jersey City, New Jersey, moved out to Southern California with her kids and had a laser vaginal rejuvenation performed by **Dr. Giancarlo Capella** in Beverly Hills. As a result of the procedure, **Nesbit**'s vaginal muscle strength was increased so excessively that it resulted in traumatic penile injuries to two of her boyfriends—**Donald De Vries**, who, during intercourse with **Nesbit**, suffered a tear of the tunica albuginea (an injury sometimes referred to as a penile 'fracture'), and **Sonny Ghazarian**, who, under similar circumstances, suffered a crushed penile shaft with extra-albugineal and bilateral cavernosal hematomas. **De Vries** and **Ghazarian** filed a joint medical-malpractice lawsuit against **Capella** (who was uniformly portrayed in the press as a combination **Richard Simmons / Josef Mengele**, or luridly compared to the **Mantle** brothers, the twin gynecologists in **David Cronenberg**'s film *Dead Ringers,* or to **Dr. Heiter**, the demented surgeon in **Tom Six**'s *The Human Centipede*). In a dramatic courtroom demonstration before a rapt gallery, a pneumatic squeeze-bulb dynamometer was used to show that **Nesbit** now had a vaginal grip-strength of well over 4,500 pounds per square inch (PSI). (Keep in mind that a commercial trash compactor typically has a maximum operating pressure of only about 3,000 PSI.)"

"This is *exactly* why we need comprehensive tort reform in this country. There's an epidemic of these frivolous lawsuits and it's bankrupting our health care system. I have a very good friend who's a pet stylist in Jersey City, and he's been doing 2,500-PSI vaginal rejuvenations on some of his dogs, but he told me that because of all the publicity generated by the case in Beverly Hills, he's had to stop. He can't afford the insurance anymore or risk the litigation."

"There are a number of experts who actually think that **Nesbit** and **Capella** were impersonated by **Fast-Cooking Ali** and **La Felina**."

"Why?"

"You gotta look at the injured parties here, the plaintiffs, these guys **Donnie De Vries** and **Sonny Ghazarian**. They're exactly the kind of rich, privileged, good-looking scumbags that **Fast-Cooking Ali** and **La Felina** loathe with a passion, tooling down the PCH in their little Porsche 911 Cabriolets, in their fuckin' **Moss Lipow** sunglasses."

There's a long pause...

"You there?"

Another long, long pause...then—

"Are you still on?...I can barely hear you....I'm going to put you back up in boldface."

CALLER I was just saying that I was listening to **Tony Bennett** singing "The Shadow of Your Smile" on YouTube. And I read this comment that someone had posted about how "The Shadow of Your Smile" had been her late father's favorite song. And how he always used to sing it walking down the street, and how, when this person was a little girl, she would be so embarrassed and beg him to stop singing. And she ends the post by saying, "Oh, what I would give to hear him sing one more time!" And that made me so sad that I just started crying. And it's so weird because my own father died recently, and I don't really think of him that much and when I do it's not with much emotion. My first conscious memory of my dad—he's wearing one of those, y'know, those belligerent T-shirts that say, like, "Stop Reading

My Shirt, Asshole!" and these polyester Hawaiian swim trunks, and Velcro sandals he got at Dollar Tree, and socks, and he's drinking fuckin' Keystone Light from a go-cup, and I was like, "Ewwwww, that's my dad?" So, y'know, I don't really miss him in that painful way you miss someone when you're really grieving. But that comment on YouTube made me feel so much intense grief on behalf of this person I don't even know. It's so weird...

REAL HUSBAND I don't think that's so weird at all. I completely get that. Everyone typically thinks that when you're intimately close to someone, like your husband or your wife or your mom or your dad, that it opens you up so much to all these powerful feelings of connectedness and enables you to understand the other person with such incredible empathy. But I really think that when you become habituated to someone, it can actually do completely the opposite—totally anesthetize you, totally numb you out and blind you to the other person. But then you'll be somewhere completely random or you'll just be reading, and you'll come upon something so *abstract*, like, I don't know, an equation in a math book or some mask in a museum or a comment by a complete stranger on YouTube, and suddenly you're just flooded with all this raw emotion. I really think that the *idea* of grieving for a father, I mean *in theory*—the abstract notion of children grieving for fathers—can actually cause us to experience so much more anguish than our *own* personal grief for our *own* fathers.... Do you know what I mean? Does that make any sense?

CALLER I love you. If your wife ever leaves you for a vagrant, drug-addled bard, I'll be waiting.

REAL HUSBAND (cuing **Foreigner**'s "Waiting for a Girl Like You") She's already left me for a vagrant drug-addled bard.

There's a long pause...like an eternity...and then...nothing.

It's sometimes said that, here, for a moment, the world disappears, that there's a fade to pure white...like a T-shirt bleached of sentiment...like an empty page...like the tabula rasa of an erased mind...and then—
a flourish of calligraphy:

Eleventh-Century Poem by **Su Tung-p'o** *Entitled*
"Re: ***Ike Karton***"

> ***Ike*** *is known to sometimes walk backward*
> *To leave misleading footprints.*
> *Or to wade through puddles,*
> *Leaving no tracks at all...*

P.S. **Ike** also walks backward to hide his face from security cameras.

Backward, **Ike** enters the Miss America Diner. With the exception of a **Chloë Sevigny** doppelgänger who frets over cold pancakes in the corner, all the other patrons are the ostentatiously generic people whose photos are already in the picture frames you buy at the store. They are the world's most famous nobodies: **Joe Shmoe** and **John Q. Public** sit at the counter drinking coffee and eating buttered rolls; **Every Tom, Dick, and Harry** are squeezed into a banquette across from **Mr. and Mrs. Consumer**, tucking into large breakfasts of eggs, sausage, and toast; **Jane Doe** and **Your Average American Sports Fan** clasp hands across unopened menus on a table. They all fall silent as **Ike**, dear to the Gods, Warlord of His Stoop, the world's most anonymous somebody ("illustrious and unknown"), enters, backward.

How Can *T.S.F.N.* Defeat XOXO?

The *Fifteenth Season* is rough going. Many people find sitting through a public recitation of the *Fifteenth Season* almost unbearably harrowing. It features some of **XOXO**'s most vicious and cunning assaults on *The Sugar Frosted Nutsack,* and includes attacks on the itinerant bards themselves, attacks that leave hundreds massacred, maimed, and mutilated. It is also the first time that **XOXO** resorts to such "asymmetric tactics" as deploying what's referred to as "military-grade ass-cheese" and momentarily effacing the world and scrawling across its white emptiness in his elegantly insouciant calligraphy. (In a recent poll, 59 percent said **XOXO** was winning, only 21 percent thought *T.S.F.N.* was making progress.) Also, in a ruthless effort to humiliate **Ike**, at the behest of the Goddess **Shanice** who remains (and will forever remain) implacably hostile to **Ike** for omitting her from his list, "Ten Gods I'd Fuck (T.G.I.F.)," **XOXO** steals ideas from the minds of exceptionally brilliant scientists, cultural theorists, and scholars and transplants them into the minds of dim-witted celebrities, enabling them to write erudite and abstruse books, which are released by prestigious publishing houses to tumultuous critical acclaim. Within the same three-month period, reality-TV star **Heidi Montag** comes out with *Capitalism and the Florentine Renaissance* (Hill & Wang), **Kate Gosselin** quickly follows with *Mirror Neurons: The Bio-Epistemology of Countertransference* (W. W. Norton & Company), and Abercrombie & Fitch model and *90210* star **Trevor Donovan** weighs in with two prodigious tomes, *The Jade(d) G(l)aze: Twelfth-Century Goryeo Celadon Pottery and Ceramics* (Abrams) and *Proust, Mallarmé, Racine: The Intersexuality of the Text / The Intertextuality of Sex* (Yale University Press).

Ike—unfailingly self-abnegating, a hero cast into the maelstrom of life—of course, violently abhors the exaltation of rich, privileged celebrities, for whom he prefers the gulag and the guillotine. (This is the central reason he's so beloved by **La Felina** and **Fast-Cooking Ali**.) **Shanice**'s vindictive utilization of **XOXO** against **Ike** is tacitly abetted by **Mogul Magoo**, because it avails the plutocratic God of Bubbles yet another way of vexing, by proxy, his eternal nemesis **La Felina**, who champions the lumpen, the subproletarian, the unsung, the village idiot with his half-witted smile and tear-filled eyes, the anomic, the disaffected and misshapen, the disinherited, the lame and crippled, the unheralded; who loves everything that's defiled and damned; who loves everyone who's pockmarked and putrid; who exalts the physically deformed and the mentally unbalanced and the sans-culottes and the scum of the earth; and who wet her pants during the September Massacres of 1792.

XOXO attacks *The Sugar Frosted Nutsack* where it's most vulnerable, when it's most "keyed up," most "hyperesthetic." In the face of mounting criticism for his indiscriminant use of military-grade ass-cheese, **XOXO** simply shrugs. "I'm a legitimate businessman," he'll say, slyly assuming the role of one whose motives are eternally misinterpreted.

In the spring of 2013, a group of experts, including former Federal Reserve chairman **Alan Greenspan**, **Dog the Bounty Hunter**, and controversial Beverly Hills plastic surgeon **Dr. Giancarlo Capella**, make a startling assertion. After conducting what they describe as "an insane amount of research," based on new information made available through "totally unprecedented access to the Myanmar military junta's secret archives," they reach the conclusion that the actual title of the epic is not—nor has it *ever* been—*The Sugar Frosted Nutsack,* but is instead—and has *always* been—*What to Expect When You're Expecting.* Although, that summer, **Dr. Capella** and **Dog the Bounty Hunter** (who are both in Lithuania to promote a chain of vaginal rejuvenation clinics) recant their assertion, claiming that **XOXO** had plied their souls with drugged sherbet, **Greenspan** continues to defend his findings. **Greenspan** admits that, yes, his soul was plied with drugged sherbet, kidnapped, and taken to **XOXO**'s garish hyperborean hermitage miles beneath the earth's surface in Antarctica, where it was kept captive for five and a half God-years, and, yes, there was a suffocatingly sweet smell at the hermitage, as if Eggnog Febreze was being continuously pumped in through the ventilation system, and, yes, every so often **XOXO** would chastely kiss his soul on the mouth, and that, at some point, **XOXO** shampooed and cornrowed his soul's hair, and that, using a sharp periodontal curette, he carved secret wisdom into **Greenspan**'s soul's mind. This wisdom includes, according to **Greenspan**, the curious notion that *The Sugar Frosted Nutsack* isn't—and never was—really about **Ike Karton** at all, but is—and always has been—about the war between **XOXO** and *the epic itself,* i.e., the war between the boldfaced and the italicized.

Why Is It SO FUCKING EASY for XOXO to Hack into *T.S.F.N.?*

A. By clicking on a link and connecting to a "poisoned" website, a *T.S.F.N.* employee inadvertently permitted **XOXO** to gain access to *T.S.F.N.*

B. Having access to the original programmer's instructions—or source code—provided **XOXO** with knowledge about subtle security vulnerabilities in *T.S.F.N.*

C. Understanding the algorithms on which *T.S.F.N.* is based enables **XOXO** to identify and locate weak points in the system.

Then **Greenspan** admitted—not realizing that his microphone was still on—that **XOXO** might be a cluster of multivariate, random variables, or possibly entropic vectors...

Thanks to the contradictory conclusions of **Greenspan**, **Dog the Bounty Hunter**, and **Dr. Capella**, there was a great deal of confusion about what the real name of the epic actually was. Some experts, deliberately or inadvertently, began corrupting or blithely mixing-and-matching the titles, e.g., *The Sugar Frosted Bard-Head* or *The Severed Nutsack*, etc. So this bunch of guys in Arizona decided to conduct an experiment in which they called the epic using various names in order to determine which of those names the epic would respond to most readily: "Heeere, *The Sugar Frosted Nutsack* [or *The Ballad of the Severed Bard-Head* or *The Sugar Frosted Bard-Head* or *What to Expect When You're Expecting* or *The Severed Nutsack* or *T.S.F.N.*], [kissing or clicking sounds], come!"

It turns out that the epic most obediently and enthusiastically responded to the name *T.S.F.N.* And so "This Bunch O' Guys" (as they came to be known) announced with great fanfare, at a hastily convened press conference held in a huge open-air outdoor mall called the *Promenade at Casa Grande*, that *T.S.F.N.* is the epic's authentic name (a finding many experts around the world admittedly endorsed for no other reason than it's the easiest title to type).

Keep in mind that even though *T.S.F.N.* is an epic whose origins date back thousands, if not tens of thousands, of years, an epic which has accrued and been transmitted via public recitations by drug-addled, vagrant bards (still referred to as "severed bard-heads" in some parts of the world, e.g., Phlegmish-speaking regions of the Upper Peninsula), it still responds more readily to the "come" command when it's delivered in a friendly, welcoming, and soothing voice. (You could even wave a tasty treat around to lure your epic over if necessary.) Your "come" command should be something your epic looks forward to hearing, something with which it has a positive association. Remember, there are many things an epic could be doing at any given moment—it could be subjecting itself to recitation by severed bard-heads, of course, it could be yielding to scholarly exegesis, it could be undergoing adaptation by **Peter Brook** for performance at the Bouffes du Nord theater in Paris or by **Robert Wilson** or **Gisli Örn Gardarsson** for the Brooklyn Academy of Music. Your goal is to make coming to you a more attractive option to your epic than any other alternative action.

You're Gonna Love This

In the *Sixteenth Season*, **Dog the Bounty Hunter** captures a fugitive **Lloyd Blankfein** (ex–Chief Executive Officer and Chairman of Goldman Sachs). As part of **Blankfein**'s community service, he's ordered to play the role of the poet **Sebastian Venable** in a *Cirque du Soleil* production of the **Tennessee Williams** play *Suddenly, Last Summer*. (It would be more accurate to say that **Blankfein** is, winkingly, playing himself playing **Sebastian Venable**.) In the **Williams** play, **Venable** is cannibalized by the street urchins / male prostitutes he's been paying for sex. (In the play, we only *hear* the story as narrated by **Sebastian**'s insane cousin, **Catharine Holly**. In the movie version, we actually *see* fragments in flashback, as **Catharine** (played by **Elizabeth Taylor**), under the influence of Sodium Pentothal, relates the grisly story to the lobotomy specialist, **Dr. John Cukrowicz** (played by **Montgomery Clift**), of how, while vacationing in the Galápagos Islands, her cousin was beaten by street urchins / male prostitutes, who then tore him apart and ate his flesh.) At the end of the *Cirque du Soleil* production, **Blankfein** is actually cannibalized by street urchins / male prostitutes. No one in the audience even lifts a finger to try and help **Blankfein**. Even though it's horrifically grisly — **Blankfein** is hacked and torn apart by flesh-eating, subproletarian *ragazzi di vita* (hustlers) — his agonized cries for help go unheeded. Everyone in the audience thinks it's just part of the *Cirque du Soleil* show. But it actually happens. In *real life*. These are not actors (i.e., rich fucking celebrities) pretending to be flesh-eating, subproletarian *ragazzi di vita*. These are real flesh-eating, subproletarian *ragazzi di vita*.

XOXO's fingerprints are all over these mutations and deformities (i.e., the mind-fucking God's "trashing" of the epic) — the power ballads; the operatic self-enucleation of the **REAL HUSBAND**'s eyeballs; the talk-radio drivel about cheap foreign labor and tort reform; the suborning of experts with the expedient of an abbreviated, user-friendly title; the suggestion that an epic that's been declaimed by chanting, drug-addled bards for tens of thousands of years is actually some sort of compliant, domesticated pet that can be beckoned merely with the tantalizing display of a bacon-flavored treat; etc. The frat-boy prank of changing the word "Flemish" to "Phlegmish" is classic **XOXO**, as are the screeching gossip-magazine headlines that plunge **Ike** into the cauldron of his own contradictory abhorrence of celebrity and yearning for immortal renown, his introversion and diffidence and how shamelessly he revels in the masturbatory gaze of moaning Goddesses. And although the ritual dismemberment and cannibalization of Wall Street titan **Lloyd Blankfein** by feral male hustlers (or *ragazzi di vita*) "reeking of **Thierry Mugler**" bears the unmistakable imprint of **La Felina**, the abrupt and arbitrary switch from German to Italian as *T.S.F.N.*'s pet foreign language (e.g., *ragazzi di vita*) seems right out of **XOXO**'s bag of tricks.

An expert once observed that **XOXO** "totally gets off on injecting military-grade ass-cheese into the synapses of the epic." But is the "**XOXO** effect" always harmful? It undoubtedly maximizes the mutability of the epic, which is a good thing, right? And although the *Sixteenth Season* is rough going and many people find sitting through a public recitation of it almost unbearably harrowing, it is also one of the most beloved Seasons. Grafting the culturally prestigious melody of "O Sink Hernieder, Nacht Der Liebe" from **Richard Wagner**'s *Tristan und Isolde* into "The Ballad of the Severed Bard-Head," especially to cue the **REAL HUSBAND**'s self-enucleation by melon baller, couldn't really be called "bad," right?

But last September, the highly regarded but reclusive Caltech biochemistry professor **Pot Pi**, or someone writing under his name, issued a controversial statement declaring that **XOXO** was, in fact, a form of delusional parasitosis, akin to Morgellons disease. (Not much is known publicly about **Pot Pi**. There are no official photos of him. And the authenticity of existing images is debated. Apart from the fact that he is missing one eye, accounts of his physical appearance are wildly contradictory. Some people who have met him describe him as having the voluptuous curves of a **Beyoncé** or a **Serena Williams**, while others describe him as more closely resembling **Representative Henry Waxman**. And while he has been characterized by some as shy and untalkative with foreigners, others contend that if you get a few Mike's Hard Lemonades into him, he becomes a screeching cockjockey.) **Pot Pi**'s hypothesis that **XOXO** is a form of delusional parasitosis is one with which **Ike Karton** *violently* disagrees. **Ike** unequivocally rejects any suggestion that the Gods are symbolic or allegorical. And just as he would dismiss any pantheistic or structuralist or semiotic interpretation of the Gods, he categorically repudiates a psychopathological one. **Ike** communes with the Gods themselves, he is their beloved, he is their sexual fantasy, he is their chosen one, even though they occasionally array themselves against him when they've taken umbrage at something, e.g., **Shanice**'s pique at having been left off the "Ten Gods I'd Fuck (T.G.I.F.)" list. But the bottom line is: the Gods are real and they intervene in human affairs. Period. And this is why **Ike** sent one of his elegant little **Joseph Cornell / Unabomber** boxes to **Pot Pi** at Caltech—a box containing a butcher cleaver stuck to **Pot Pi**'s photograph and splashed with blood and cold vomit, and a note that read, "You must not forget that traitors (i.e., thorns in the eyes of the Gods) have ALWAYS been slaughtered by cleavers."

It's Almost Impossible to Get One's Mind Around XOXO

What shape does one's mind need to assume in order to *get around* (i.e., "apprehend"—with both its meanings of "capture" and "understand") **XOXO**?

1. It's impossible to know where **XOXO** ends and you begin.
2. **XOXO** calls into question the provenance and chain of custody of every single thought in your head.
3. **XOXO** is the inside and the outside.

Sometimes it actually appears as if *T.S.F.N.* is holding its own against **XOXO**. Maybe, with an invulnerability conferred by its morbid ingestion of everything extrinsic to it, *T.S.F.N.* simply cannot be killed, like **Jason Voorhees** or **Freddy Krueger** or **Michael Myers**. So powerful is the human tropism toward boldface signifiers that whenever the severed bard-heads manage, even momentarily, to wrest control of the epic from **XOXO** and return to the basic story of **Ike** and **Ruthie** and **Vance**, the audience (which has glazed over, staring torpidly at their feet during the interminable and frequently incoherent exegetical Seasons) perks up, looking alive and avidly interested. But these moments are far and few between, and given the overwhelming perception that **XOXO** has carte blanche access to the bards' brains and to your brain (via public recitation, book, Kindle, Nook, iPad, iTunes, etc.), it's reasonable to ask: Why hasn't **XOXO** just killed *T.S.F.N.* by now? And the answer is, according to the experts, because **XOXO** is content to simply toy with the epic, to just keep fucking with it forever.

XOXO, who sometimes likes to pose as "an innocent Canadian tourist," once boasted—not realizing that his microphone was still on—that when he kidnaps someone's soul and brings it to his hyperborean hermitage, he likes to fillip the soul's mind with his index finger so that it oscillates back and forth trillions of times a second between, what he called, "its regular state and its antimatter state." This hyperoscillation, **XOXO** explained, is that state of mind called "going into the forest to gather wild garlic."

Of course, one could reasonably say (along with the **CALLER**) that there's "too much" sex in *The Sugar Frosted Nutsack*, that it's punishingly repetitive. But whether that's a function of **Ike Karton**'s fixations and fetishes and his compulsion to be punished or whether it's the result of the impish perversity and malice of **XOXO**, we can't possibly know. Nor can we know ultimately—because of **XOXO**— whether what you're hearing or reading is what was originally intended. We can't know—thanks to the legerdemain of the God **XOXO**—whether what you're reading is what was written.

Mogul Magoo V$ El Brazo

.In *Season Seventeen,* a protracted battle begins between **El Brazo** and **Mogul Magoo** over who owns the rights to *T.S.F.N.* **Mogul Magoo** (who was originally the God of Bubbles) had asserted himself as God of the Nutsack. He'd dutifully submitted his boilerplate rationale: Anything Enveloping Something Else. Just as a bubble is a globule of water that contains air, the scrotum is a pouch of skin and muscle that contains the testicles. Ergo, it's perfectly logical and reasonable to conclude it falls within his purview. Thus, he reasoned, he owns exclusive worldwide rights (including all derivative works) to *T.S.F.N.* This completely infuriated **El Brazo**, also known as *Das Unheimlichste des Unheimlichen* ("The Strangest of the Strange"), who, as the God of Urology and the God of Pornography, considered the nutsack his inviolable domain and thus claimed ownership of exclusive worldwide rights (including all derivative works) to *T.S.F.N.* The antipathy that developed between these two Gods (and, subsequently, between **Magoo** and the Goddess **La Felina**) would have significant consequences. **El Brazo** threatened **Magoo** and his cohorts with liquidation in a "Night of the Long Knives." In response, **Magoo** beefed up his posse of "**Pistoleras**"—the divine, ax-wielding mercenary vixens who are total fitness freaks with rock-hard bodies, each of whom has a venomous black mamba snake growing out of the back of her head, which she pulls through the size-adjustment cutout on the back of her baseball cap. Neither of them could care less about the literal or the allegorical and mystical implications of the epic, or

139

that many fashion critics are saying "Finally, a drug-induced epic that celebrates real women's contours and silhouettes." This is just a heavyweight dick-swinging contest between two Gods. Even though most legal experts conclude that **Mogul Magoo** can make the more compelling case for ownership of *T.S.F.N.*—its tail-chasing, vortical form is clearly consistent with his proprietary concept of "enveloping," and there's no question that severed bard-heads (aka "scrubbing bubbles") fall within his realm—he is, characteristically, playing several moves ahead of everyone else. After tense marathon negotiations conducted at the 160-story, rocket-shaped Burj Khalifa in Dubai, this shrewd, uncannily prescient, and relentlessly enterprising businessman—who already owns the entire **Rodgers and Hammerstein** music catalogue, as well as the rights to such all-time favorites as "The *Mister Softee* Jingle," "Under My Thumb," "Tears of a Clown," "White Wedding," "What Have I Done to Deserve This," "Party in the U.S.A.," **Billy Joel**'s "Movin' Out (Anthony's Song)," "The Shadow of Your Smile," **Foreigner**'s "Waiting for a Girl Like You," **Richard Wagner**'s "O Sink Hernieder, Nacht Der Liebe," and "The Ballad of the Severed Bard-Head"—shocks everyone by suddenly conceding ownership of *T.S.F.N.* to **El Brazo** in return for acquisition of the ringtone rights to the narcocorrido "That's Me (**Ike**'s Song)" ("Do you hear that mosquito, / that toilet flushing upstairs, / that glockenspiel out in the briar patch? / That's me, Unwanted One, Filthy One, Despised / Whore, Lonely Nut Job...").

Whether **Magoo**'s wager that he can make more money from the ringtone rights to a single neo-pagan narcocorrido

than from the public performance royalties that would accrue to him from thousands of years of spaced-out blind
bards chanting a mind-numbingly repetitive fugue-like epic
while swilling from jerrycans of orange soda remains to be
seen. But financial history has shown that it doesn't pay to
bet against the chubby, pockmarked God of Bubbles.

Ike's New Horoscope (SPOILER ALERT)

The A&P will start carrying that Kozy Shack butterscotch
pudding you like so much. Your anal fissure will start bleeding again (so don't wear the tight white jeans, in case you
start spotting). Your daughter will get pregnant. You're going
to have dinner with your father to try to persuade him to
change his will, and you're going to get into a really nasty
fight with him, and you're going to say, "You know how they
say the apple doesn't fall far from the tree? Well, I'm like an
apple that **Vladimir Guerrero** picked up and threw as far
as he could. That's how far from your fucking tree I fell."

What Is the Mystical Significance of Bold v. Italics?

This is the innermost secret of the epic.

Before the arrival of the Gods, *everything* was wildly italicized. This was the time of the so-called "Spring Break."
There were only phenomena and vaguely defined person-

ages, and there was really no discernable distinction between phenomena and personages. There were no "Gods" per se, no dramatis personae, there was only an undifferentiated, unidimensional *T.S.F.N.*—only the infinitely recursive story and its infinitely droning loops, varying infinitesimally with each iteration. But once the Gods arrived and got off the bus, they insisted on being **boldfaced signifiers**.

This whole epic is about the war on the part of *T.S.F.N.* to vanquish the **boldfaced signifiers** and reestablish the "golden age" when things happened without any discernable context; when there were no recognizable patterns; when it was all incoherent; when isolated, disjointed events would take place only to be engulfed by an opaque black void, their relative meaning, their *significance,* annulled by the eons of entropic silence that estranged one from the next; when a terrarium containing three tiny teenage girls mouthing a lot of high-pitched gibberish (like **Mothra**'s fairies, except for their wasted pallors, acne, big tits, and T-shirts that read "I Don't Do White Guys") would inexplicably materialize, and then, just as inexplicably, disappear.

One possible conclusion that could be drawn from this, of course—and it happens to be precisely the conclusion reached by the apocryphal "Justices of the Eighteenth Season" (these Justices who seem almost bard-like in their black hoodies, their scrotums dusted with confectionary sugar)— is that **XOXO**, whose ongoing and indefatigable campaign to undermine context and disrupt cohesiveness (i.e., his vandalism and vajazzlement of the epic) is, by now, familiar to anyone who's not totally brain-dead, is actually working in collusion with *T.S.F.N.* And, in fact, the majority of the Justices—the vote was 8–1—question whether the so-called "war between **XOXO** and *T.S.F.N.*" might not have always been a front or a pretext for this collusion between **XOXO** and *T.S.F.N.*

But this whole notion of "Justices in black hoodies, whose scrotums are dusted with confectionary sugar" seems suspect. Who are these "Justices"? Are we meant to infer that they are the habitués from the Miss America Diner—**Joe Shmoe**, **John Q. Public**, **Every Tom, Dick, and Harry**, **Your Average American Sports Fan**, etc.—those men who so shamelessly and ostentatiously flaunt their vaunted anonymity? And what of this so-called "8–1 decision" suggesting that **XOXO** and *T.S.F.N.* are now working in cahoots, that they are, one or the other or both of them, double agents of some kind? Isn't this all beginning to sound suspiciously familiar? Isn't it more than plausible that *all of this* is part of the incredibly sophisticated disinformation campaign being waged by **XOXO**? This vexing suspicion is the very basis for the lone, dissenting vote—that lone, dissenting vote belonging, of course, to **Ike Karton**.

The hero **Ike**—unwavering, irreproachably self-abnegating, aloof, Warlord of His Stoop—offers neither oral nor written opinion. His dissent is mute. He strikes a pose of implacable mute dissent. He just stands there on his stoop, on the prow of his hermitage, and he strikes that contrapposto pose in his white wifebeater, his torso totally ripped, his lustrous chestnut armpit hair wafting in the breeze, his head turned and inclined up toward the top floors of the

Burj Khalifa in Dubai, from which the gaze of masturbating Goddesses casts him in a sugar frosted nimbus. (This is the "glaze of the gaze"—the onanistic scrutiny that sugar frosts **Ike**'s every move—which Abercrombie & Fitch model and *90210* star **Trevor Donovan** analyzes in his book *The Jade(d) G(l)aze: Twelfth-Century Goryeo Celadon Pottery and Ceramics.*)

Many of the epic's most perceptive commentators have underestimated or missed altogether or dismissed as so much incoherent, dilettante bullshit (or as the product of the Brownian motion of **Ike**'s paranoid ideation) the complexities of the **Boldface** v. *Italics* case and this whole notion of "Justices in black hoodies, whose scrotums are dusted with confectionary sugar" (with its choral judgment of the dissenting voice—that judgment and that doomed voice staking out the dialectical polarities of martyrdom). One expert said, "With most of *T.S.F.N.*, we can sing along by 'following the bouncing ball,' as **Mitch Miller** (whom many experts consider to be the 'inventor' of karaoke) used to instruct viewers of his 1960s television show, *Sing Along with Mitch.* But in this Season, we're being asked to follow the red rubber tip of a paranoid flâneur's walking stick as he jabs it at your head."

After the massacre of drug-addled, blind bards by jilted husbands (a bloodbath purportedly masterminded by **XOXO**), a shadowy splinter group was formed, calling itself *T.S.F.N.—General Command.* This group, which was fanatically anti-**XOXO**, began recruiting members in the fetid, overcrowded refugee camps to which the surviving bards fled after the massacre. After establishing links with **La Felina**, they forged an unlikely alliance of convenience with the nihilistic, glue-sniffing street punks who'd hacked to death and cannibalized **Lloyd Blankfein**. On an oppressively hot summer night, marked by a bizarre outbreak of ball lightning which left all of Jersey City reeking of sulfur, an assassination commando unit comprised of blind *T.S.F.N.*— *General Command* bards and glue-sniffing street punks— who'd recently taken to calling themselves *giovanetti martirizzati* ("martyred youth") from the *zozzo mondo* ("slob world")—supposedly descended on the Miss America Diner and slaughtered the eight "Justices in black hoodies, whose scrotums are dusted with confectionary sugar," in retaliation for their having promulgated the idea that *T.S.F.N.* is working in collusion with **XOXO**.

What Makes Ike a Hero?

A. His implacable hatred of the rich is, among other things, what makes **Ike** a hero. An anarcho-primitivist, he strives to restore the world to an antediluvian arcadia (what he calls "Spring Break") where no one man or woman seeks more wealth or notoriety than the next, and where the Gods are content to be indistinguishable from phenomena. And he dreams of a new Jacobinical Terror, of deploying guillotines outside *Soho House* (in West Hollywood and New York), of harvesting the severed heads of Hollywood A-listers and dropping one down the chimney of each and every child who's been good that year (i.e., each child who's militantly resisted celebrity worship in his or her school and who's been modest, reticent, and almost naively kind to others, especially the misshapen and the misbegotten).

B. Basically, at every moment, **Ike** is trying to figure out how to constitute himself and how to situate himself in history. And this, among other things, is what makes **Ike** a hero.

C. Like all epic heroes, **Ike** hears the narration of the epic in his head and frequently mouths the words (sometimes audibly) to himself as he ritually reenacts the epic. This, of course, is what is meant by the term "epic karaoke" or "recursive karaoke" or "karaoke *mise en abyme*." The ritual reenactment and murmured karaoke recitation of the epic of which he is the hero constitutes **Ike**'s life. This is the life to which **Ike** is doomed. This is why he is so frequently described as "death-drenched."

D. This is **Ike the Chimera**—the hybrid beast with the severed head of a bard and the sugar frosted nutsack of a hero.

E. That statement, "This is **Ike the Chimera**—the hybrid beast with the severed head of a bard and the sugar frosted nutsack of a hero," is considered to contain the innermost embedded secret within the many embedded innermost secrets of the epic, i.e., this is the very moment when the epic most suggests a Russian Matryoshka doll or a Chinese nested box.

F. How can **Ike** be ritually reenacting something that he

appears to be doing extemporaneously and for the very first time? It is because this takes place in the "realm or the zone of the heroic," on a "heroic plane"—it is fated, choreographed by the Gods.

G. **Ike** is the hero of the epic about the bard who simultaneously recites and reenacts the epic of which he is the extemporaneous, albeit inexorably doomed, hero. This is why scholars frequently refer to **Ike** as the "Möbius Stripper," i.e., the man whose lascivious dance (i.e., "his life") is performed for the delectation of masturbating Goddesses.

H. **Ike**'s ongoing self-narration (which is an echolalic karaoke recitation of what he hears streaming in his head) is extremely similar to—and thought by many experts to actually derive from—the flowing auto-narrative of the basketball-dribbling nine-year-old who, at dusk, alone on the family driveway half-court, weaves back and forth, half-hearing and half-murmuring his own play-by-play: "…he's got a lot going on that could potentially distract him…algebra midterm…his mom's calling him to come inside…his asthma inhaler just fell out of his pocket…but somehow he totally shuts all that out of his mind…crowd's going *ca-razy!*…but the kid's in his own private Idaho…clock's ticking down…badass craves the drama…*lives* for this shit…*Gunslingaaah*…he can hear the automatic garage-door opener…that means his dad's gonna be pulling into the driveway in, like, fifteen seconds…*un-fucking-believable* that he's about to take *this* shot under *this* kind of pressure, with the survival of the species on the line...and look at him out there—dude's *ice*...is this guy human or what?...his foot's hurting from when he stepped on his retainer in his room last night...but he can play with pain...we've seen that time and time again...he's stoic...a cold-blooded professional...*Special Ops*...*Hitman with the Wristband*...hand-eye coordination like a *Cyborg Assassin*...his mom's calling him to come in and feed the dog and help set the table for dinner...the woman is doing everything she can possibly do to rattle him...but this guy's not like the rest of us...he is *un-fucking-flappable*...he dribbles between his legs...OK, hold on...he dribbles between his legs...hold on...he dribbles...hold on...he dribbles between his legs (yes!)...fakes right, fakes left, double pump-fakes...there's one second left on the clock...and he launches...an impossibly...long...fadeaway...*jumpaaah*...it's off the rim...but he fights for the offensive rebound like some kind of rabid samurai...throwing vicious elbows like lethally honed swords...the severed heads of his opponents litter the court...spinal cords are sticking out of the neck stumps...but there's no ticky-tacky foul called, the referees are just letting them play...there's somehow still .00137 seconds left on the clock...now there's a horn honking...might that be the War Conch of the Undead?...etc., etc."

I. **Ike** is constantly testing his own self-narration against "empirical reality" (which is itself actually an illusory construct inscribed by **XOXO** in **Ike**'s mind, which **Ike** realized after being hit by the *Mister Softee* truck).

So, **Ike**'s tactical response to **XOXO** (everyone's, for that matter) is not far from a kind of delirium. **Ike**'s methodology is to echo the epic: "**Ike**'s doing this, **Ike**'s doing that," and to compare what he's saying he's doing with what he's actually doing, and see if there's any "wobble." This, among other things, is what makes **Ike** a hero.

J. **Ike Karton**, unemployed butcher, inveterate mumbler, Warlord of His Stoop, believes—and justifiably so—that he's fated to die very soon at the hands of Mossad sharpshooters. And he will stand in front of the Miss America Diner (sometimes in close proximity to this other solitary psycho who angrily paces the perimeter of the parking lot bellowing at passersby, "Are you staring at my girlfriend's tits?!") and murmur to himself, "He is fated to die very soon at the hands of Mossad sharpshooters," to which he will almost immediately append, "He is also fated to stand in front of the Miss America Diner (sometimes in close proximity to this other solitary psycho who angrily paces the perimeter of the parking lot bellowing at passersby, 'Are you staring at my girlfriend's tits?!') and murmur to himself, 'He is fated to die very soon at the hands of Mossad sharpshooters.'" These bracketing redundancies, the compulsive conjuring up of these Matryoshka dolls or Chinese nested boxes, can occupy **Ike**'s thoughts for hours upon hours. This is one of the reasons (in addition to the whispering campaign conducted against him by **Mogul Magoo, Shanice**, and **Bosco Hifikepunye**) that **Ike** was fired from his job in the A&P Meat Department, and it is one of the things, among many, that makes **Ike** a hero.

K. For doomed **Ike**, everything—every concept and every percept—is a totem of death. Everything bespeaks evanescence. Even a brand new *Quiznos* on the corner of West Side Avenue and Stegman Parkway (a *Quiznos* that hasn't even opened yet!) reeks of *mono no aware* ("the pathos of things") and *lacrimae rerum* ("tears of things").

L. Of course, we know that **Ike**'s soul has been repeatedly kidnapped by **XOXO** and taken to **XOXO**'s hyperborean hermitage. And we know that **Ike** has developed (or is perhaps feigning, as a tactical ploy) Stockholm syndrome.

M. **Ike**'s heroic maneuvering to situate himself in an appositional space vis-à-vis **XOXO**—that is, to juxtapose himself somehow in relation to **XOXO**, to find a place interior to him or outside of him—may account for **Ike**'s fractured motion, for the sort of cubistic way he has of moving through space ("the feral fatalism of all his loony tics").

N. **Ike** was asked at the zoning board hearing if his soul had ever had a homosexual relationship with **XOXO**, and **Ike**—ever the discreet, gallant, old-world gentleman— said that they'd merely had "tickle fights." (And this, among other things, is also what makes **Ike** a hero.)

O. None of the above.

P. All of the above.

ANSWER: ~~P~~. All of the above.

Note to self: *P. All of the above* includes *O. None of the above.* Consider mystical significance.

10.

Ike's Agony:
Why His Own Family Fears for His Life
How his obsession with polytheism and martyrdom (and on-line porn) is tearing his family apart. **Ruthie** lashes out! She leaks X-rated pics of **Ike**, and gossips about **La Felina**'s "sham marriage" to **Fast-Cooking Ali**.

T.S.F.N. Shocker:
99% of All Unmanned Drone Attacks & Robotic Prostatectomies Are Being Conducted by the Same Nine-Year-Old Kid in a Mumbai Call-Center Cubicle!

Miss America Diner Waitress:
"I'm fired!"
- Furious owner axes humiliated St. Peters sophomore for giving **Ike Karton** free tongue sandwich
- Inside her legal battle to regain her part-time job

REAL HUSBAND on **CALLER**:
"She's using me to get to **Ike**."

Vance: "**Ike**'s bonkers."

Drug-Addled, Blind Bard Steps Out to Flaunt New Super-Sexy Sumo Body:
"I gained 165 pounds from drinking 40 cans of Sunkist orange soda a day!"

75 Sex Tips from Gods:
Sizzling, Sinful, Surprising Things They're Craving Now

- Act like a skanky slut with a train-wreck personality who's all about appealing to *my* needs while expressing none of your own. That's a total turn-on to a God! With your tongue, trace the head of my penis in a circular motion, and then look up at me with your slutty trout-pout and say, "Determine my destiny capriciously, like you don't even give a fuck. Give me a fate befitting the dirty little whore that I am! Use me and then fling me into the abyss where I belong." I'll have a huge orgasm.

  —*El Brazo*

- Just at the moment I enter you from behind, sharply contrast my divine omnipotence with your human inadequacies. Say something like, "You're immortal, I'm not. You remain eternally young and beautiful, whereas I'm going to get wrinkles, age spots, spider veins, osteoporosis, or diabetes, or have a stroke or something." Or, if you're riding me on top, reach back, grab my balls, and say, "You're omniscient—I, on the other hand, can barely follow an episode of *Dora the Explorer* without becoming hopelessly befuddled and breaking into tears!" I'll climax so convulsively and with such a magnitude of semen that hundreds of thousands of people in low-lying regions will drown!

—*Bosco Hifikepunye*

- This might sound stupid (but women don't do it and we love it *so* much and it's *so* easy)—refer to me occasionally as a "God." Say things like "Oh, my God...oh, my God!"

—*Mogul Magoo*

- My favorite thing is spontaneity. So, say we've got courtside seats for the Lakers game. When we know the TV camera is right on us, and there we are up on the giant HDTV screen hanging over the arena, kiss me and put two of my fingers inside your underwear, so I can feel how excited you are. Then we'll immediately head out to Death Valley, where you'll slather my genitals with chopped meat or chicken giblets so that buzzards will swoop down and tear at my nutsack with their razor-sharp talons. (It won't hurt me—I'm a God!) Then we'll have punishing (i.e., super-hot) sex under the merciless desert sun for eternity (literally). The fact that you'd leave a Lakers game with a God, go to the desert and let him fuck you forever with his mangled, giblet-covered dick will show me that you're into completely spontaneous, raw, gotta-have-you-now sex—which is a total turn-on!

—*Doc Hickory*

• Plus 71 more!!

T.S.F.N. Announces New Fall Lineup

Monday: 8 PM Eastern
"**Ike**'s Narcocorrido"

In the Season Premiere, **Ike** sits down in a booth at the Miss America Diner (West Side Avenue at the corner of Culver Avenue), with a pad of unlined white paper and a blue-ink pen, perhaps to make a list of celebrities to be gassed, but with no conscious intention to write a narcocorrido. "I might totally flirt with you," he tells **The Waitress**. "I don't mind," she says coyly, with a slight Mississippi drawl. **Ike**'s rage and his lust are strong. He's nursed by the Gods. His honor comes from **El Brazo** and **La Felina** and **Fast-Cooking Ali**. He's dear to them, these Gods who rule the world. In his soft voice, he orders a tongue sandwich (this is apparently what he meant by "flirting"). She can't hear him and leans way over so he can whisper directly into her ear. She's like some hapless **Beckettian** tramp in a white waitress uniform so short that it barely covers her spectacular big-ass ass. She's got big-ass titties as well. As she leans over, her face in and out of oblongs of sunlight, she gently nuzzles his head, almost accidentally.

"What is that?" she asks, hearing something.

"Oh, it's just this song I can't get out of my head," he says.

She puts her ear, now deliberately, to his temple and listens. "That's the *Mister Softee* jingle," she says.

He smiles.

"You know a lot about tongue," she says.

"I'm a butcher."

"Are you related to **Bilinda Butcher**, the guitarist in **My Bloody Valentine**?"

"No. My name is **Ike Karton**. I play Akai MPC drum machine in **The Kartons**."

"Did you know that the **Baal Shem Tov** was a *shohet* (a ritual butcher) in Kshilowice, near Iashlowice?" (She's totally flirting with him right now.)

Meanwhile, the **Chloë Sevigny** doppelgänger, who's fretting over cold pancakes in the corner, is ritually reciting everything that **Ike** and **The Waitress** are saying as they say it, as if she were mouthing the lyrics to a favorite song or the dialogue from a scene she'd assiduously memorized by heart.

"When I eat," **Ike** explains, in his shy, measured, Taurus way, "I always propitiate the Gods by offering them a portion of my food. But I don't want to seem obsequious, so I try to be very casual and sort of uninflected. Do you know that expression actors use, where you just 'throw your line away'? I'll just jerk my head toward the Burj Khalifa in Dubai and say something, almost under my breath, like:

'You want some fries? I can't eat them. That tongue sandwich was huge. Did you see the size of that sandwich?'"

"I bet you're too vain to eat fries anyway," **The Waitress**
says, giving his ripped torso a slow, flirtatious once-over.
"And you're married," she adds, noticing the aluminum
wedding ring that **Ike** taps on the table in rhythm to the music in his mind.

Ike explains to her that he and his wife are soul mates,
but that she's too gorgeous, too soft-spoken and articulate,
too sophisticated. Her mind is too agile and nuanced, her
sensibility is too refined and delicate. She's a bit too petite.
Too ethereal. Too patrician. "Sexually," he confides, "I'm
more attracted to coarser women … sweatier, bigger, less hygienic women … women who have trouble understanding
even simple things."

"You love your wife deeply," **The Waitress** responds,
"but you have this completely specific psychosexual / socio-
political fetish, this *nostalgie de la boue.* I totally get that."

"I like the bodies of women who don't like their bodies,"
he says.

Then **Ike** reveals his intention to get himself killed by the
ATF or Mossad in order for his wife and his daughter to
collect his life insurance. **The Waitress** asks, "If you purpo-
sively get yourself killed—isn't that like suicide-by-cop? Insurance companies won't pay out on suicide, will they?" And
Ike explains to her that, yes, he's destined to die by suicide-
by-cop, but that the determination of an individual's mental
capacity, or "soundness of mind," to form an intent to commit suicide is of consequence in claims for recovery of death

benefits under life insurance policies. In other words, if it's determined that a person is of unsound mind when he commits suicide-by-cop, his family is entitled to receive life insurance benefits. And the fact that he's intent upon neo-pagan martyrdom, that he's under twenty-four-hour erotomaniacal surveillance by masturbating Goddesses, and that he's the "inducer" in a family suffering from a form of *folie à famille* would probably constitute more than sufficient evidence, if needed, that he's of "unsound mind." **The Waitress** ponders this for a moment, and then asks rhetorically, "Isn't fate, like, the ultimate preexisting condition?"

Later, as she serves **Ike** his breakfast, **The Waitress** asks him if he's into online porn at all.

"Yes, totally," **Ike** replies.

"Well," she says, "you know how in porn movies the women always narrate what's happening to them in the second person? The 'you're doing this, you're doing that' thing? 'You're licking my hard nipples' or 'You're putting your big cock in my juicy pussy' or 'You're gonna pound that pussy, you're just gonna tear that pussy up, aren't you?'" (She is *so* totally flirting with him right now.)

Ike looks intensely into her eyes for a moment, and then he says, "You're serving me a hot tongue sandwich; you're putting the plate right in front of me; you're setting an ice-cold Sunkist orange soda down right next to my big, crunchy onion rings."

And **The Waitress** smiles. "Second-person present-tense narration makes everything super-fucking-hot. I don't know why exactly. You know how dentists always keep you apprised of everything they're doing as they're doing it, so you don't get all freaked out? 'I'm putting a dental dam in your mouth.... I'm making an opening through the crown of your tooth to gain access to the pulp chamber. I'm using an en-dodontic file to remove the diseased pulp tissue from the root canal.... Now I'm using a plugger to place the gutta-percha points into your empty root canals to replace the pulp tis-sue which I removed.' Wouldn't it be super-fucking-hot in the second-person, if the patient was like, "You're making an opening through the crown of my tooth to gain access to the pulp chamber. You're using an endodontic file to re-move the diseased pulp tissue from the root canal.... Oh, God, now you're using a plugger to place the gutta-percha points into my empty root canals to replace the pulp tissue which you removed'? Except that you probably wouldn't be able to understand anything she's saying with all that stuff in her mouth."

Experts have made much of the links between the garbled speech of the dental patient; the mumbled, almost incoher-ent, shoegazey chanting of the vagrant, drug-addled bards; and the murmured, diffident, barely audible utterances of **Ike Karton** himself. But what implications are latent in these links? (That anagogic significance is not conveyed through discursive meaning, maybe?)

"Second-person present-tense narration somehow de-taches the link between your actions and your own voli-tion," **Ike** says, "as if what you think you're doing spon-taneously has already been predetermined, as if it's been reenacted countless times before. It ritualizes the extemporaneous. It can make every mundane thing you do feel like a dénouement that's been gestating since the beginning of time."

"Totally," **The Waitress** says, cracking her gum.

And it's here, for the first time, that we begin to suspect that we (and **Ike**, for that matter) may have been *had*, that **The Waitress** may be far less disingenuous and far more calculating than she seemed at first blush, i.e., much more of a professional waitress (perhaps the professional waitress *par excellence*) who knows just how to say all the right things and use all that cogent body language and instinctively acclimate herself to all the psychological idioms of her customers, peppering them with risqué innuendos, buttering them up with all sorts of blandishments, and milking them for helplessly exorbitant tips—although, it must be said, that this reading of her as merely **Machiavellian** is mitigated by the indisputable authenticity of her affect (i.e., her "humanity") in this episode's final scene.

Whether it's because he's genuinely inspired by her or simply avails himself of the opportunity once she leaves to tend to her other tables, **Ike** now dashes off his narcocorrido:

That's Me (Ike's Song)

> *Do you hear that mosquito,*
> *that toilet flushing upstairs,*
> *that glockenspiel out in the briar patch?*

That's me, Unwanted One, Filthy One, Despised
   Whore, Lonely Nut Job...
I am looking up at your face
   through the chartreuse froth
   of your female ejaculate.

I am the sexual messiah
   of every bespectacled bipolar girl
   in her library carrel,
   every lesbian lacrosse star,
   every dorm-room slut, degenerate babysitter,
   and fat, euthanizing, anal-sex-freak nurse.
I am the sexual messiah of the three-legged,
   bulimic crypto-nympho rank and file.

The black cleft between your buttocks
   is the primordial vector.
It's the first line
   drawn in the sands of time.

When the waitress returns with another ice-cold can of
Sunkist orange, **Ike** shows her the narcocorrido. (Compare
Ike's anxiety as **The Waitress** reads the lyrics of his song to
XOXO's anxiety as **Shanice** read his poem.)

The Waitress tells **Ike** that the song is totally anthemic
and romantic, and that she feels like he wrote it just for
her because all her life people have called her a fat bipolar
whore. She adds that it's a little self-vaunting (the sexual messiah part), but that she really likes that aspect of it because it

makes it even more super-fucking-hot, but that, to be honest, it did surprise her a little at first because **Ike** seems so modest and reserved. **Ike** explains that it's exaggerated for dramatic effect and that the first-person narrator of the song isn't him; it's a character, it's the persona of a Gravy trafficker (which is what makes the song a narcocorrido, by the way). She says she totally gets that—that **Eminem** isn't **Slim Shady** and **Daniel Dumile** isn't **MF Doom**. "Exactly," Ike says. "Take a song like the **Bee Gees**' 'I've Gotta Get a Message to You.' You've got the narrator of the song who's a guy who's about to be executed in the electric chair for killing his wife's lover, but **Robin Gibb** never killed his wife's lover and he obviously hasn't been executed in the electric chair. It's just a character." **The Waitress** says it's sort of like that **Ass Ponys** song "Hey Swifty," and she recites all the lyrics to the song, which she's assiduously memorized by heart.

Ike then tells her that his narcocorrido definitely expresses, in a poetic way, his beliefs about smashing the cultural and sociosexual hegemony of rich, privileged celebrities, and how fervently he's wedded to those things most despised, most anathematized, to the lowest of the low, to the lumpen, to the misshapen and the misbegotten. Then he says, "I'm sort of surprised you remember an **Ass Ponys** song so well," and she says that she originally just liked the band because of its name, because her father had always called her his "Ass Pony."

And **Ike** pauses for a moment (for dramatic effect) and says, "So did mine."

Some experts contend that showing the narcocorrido to

The Waitress—which seems like an overt act of seduction—is actually a means to simply ingratiate himself with **The Waitress** (and, by extension, the entire waitstaff at the diner) so that **Ike**'s family can get discounted food there after his imminent death. But this reading of **Ike** as merely **Machiavellian** is mitigated not only by the fact that **The Kartons** do indeed perform the narcocorrido at "The Last Concert" but by the indisputable authenticity of his affect (i.e., his "humanity") in this episode's final scene.

When it turns out that the God **Doc Hickory** ("whose snarky, adenoidal laugh is a snide reproach to those of simple purpose and modest means") played a trick on **Ike** by assuring him that he was entitled to free rice pudding at the Miss America Diner, **Ike** gets into a brawl with the manager of the diner and is pepper-sprayed.

As he's leaving, **Ike** turns back and grabs **The Waitress** and turns her around so she's facing him, and he holds her in his arms, tears in his eyes, blinded by the pepper spray, perhaps experiencing a presentiment of his own imminent and hyperviolent demise, knowing he'll never see her again. "Never forget," he says fervently, "how close—in the end—we really turned out to be." **The Waitress** watches **Ike** leave the diner; then, through the window, she watches him recede in epileptic jump-cuts, a marionette of his Gods, a clutter of spasms and ticks, a nude descending a staircase. She can't move for a moment. Her throat is clogged with emotion. She knows she's been traversed by tragedy.

Monday: 10 PM Eastern
"Ten Gods I'd Fuck (T.G.I.F.)"

Ike discovers that his daughter's boyfriend, the glassy-eyed, unscrupulous **Vance**, has been stealing his underpants—two pairs of gray **Tommy Hilfiger** boxer briefs and one pair of smoky blue **Calvin Kleins**. Later, as **Ike** and his daughter sit together on the stoop in the late afternoon, he gives her a pep talk about an upcoming math midterm, and then casually broaches the subject of the stolen underpants. "What does **Vance** want to do, anyway—I mean, as a career?" he asks. "He's really interested in doing something in music," his daughter says. "What aspect of music is he interested in pursuing?" inquires **Ike**. "I think just listening to it," she replies. Meanwhile, **Vance**, who was raised by three hard-drinking lesbian fisherwomen in a squalid shack under the **Pulaski** Skyway, is seen tooling around town on a battered red BMX bike, making various stops, selling drugs. (Some experts interpret the threesome of alcoholic lesbian fisherwomen as a mortal analogue to the motif of the "triadic goddess," i.e., a variant of the three tiny teenage girls in the terrarium who mouth a lot of high-pitched gibberish (like **Mothra**'s fairies, except for their wasted pallors, acne, big tits, and T-shirts that read 'I Don't Do White Guys') and also of the three Gods known variously as **The Pince-Nez 44s** and **Los Vatos Locos** ("The Crazy Guys")). After dinner, **Ike** resumes work on the fifteen-foot lewd statue of **La Felina** ("naked, dildo-impaled") that he's begun constructing on the front lawn, adjacent to a jerry-rigged "stage." Later, just as **The Kartons** begin rehearsing the narcocorrido that **Ike** wrote at the Miss America Diner ("Do you hear that mosquito, / that toilet flushing upstairs, / that glockenspiel out in the briar patch?")—with **Ike** on vocals and Akai MPC drum machine, **Ruthie** on guitar and vocals, and his daughter on bass—a neighbor calls the police to complain about the noise. Three squad cars pull up in front of **Ike**'s hermitage, and, after verbal sparring with the cops escalates into a physical confrontation, **Ike** is pepper-sprayed and Tasered. The next day, when he and **Vance** drink Sunkist orange soda and get high on a smokable form of Gravy as they sit on the curb in front of a convenience store, **Ike** confronts him about the stolen underpants. But **Vance** totally disarms **Ike** with the remark "Did you know that hiccoughs are a form of myoclonic seizure?" (One may recognize here an epic application of a folkloric motif found frequently in the tales of every continent: a hero confronts his son-in-law or his daughter's suitor about stolen underpants, only to be disarmed with a fascinating factoid.) **Ike** confides in **Vance** that he knows his violent death is imminent.

"Damn!" **Vance** says, with emphatic sympathy, shaking his downcast head as he absently spins a wheel of his battered red BMX bike, which lies on its side against the curb, and he lets his empty soda can rattle against the spokes. "How do you know for sure you're gonna die so soon?" he asks.

"**La Felina** came to me in a dream," **Ike** says, "and she pretty much promised me."

And probably because he's getting pretty high, **Ike** tells

Vance about the dream, about how there was something dangling from **La Felina**'s snatch, and how, at first, he thought it was a tampon string, but, as he came closer, he could see that it was a fortune, and he pulled it out and read it, and it said: "You're going to be assassinated by Mossad in a week or so." **Ike** tells **Vance** that when **La Felina** spread her legs, it perfumed the room, that it was like the warm smells from a halal truck, and that it made him so hungry that he woke up from the dream with a ravenous appetite and went straight to the Miss America Diner and ate an enormous tongue sandwich. **Vance** says that if he knew that he was going to die in a week, he'd do every fucked-up thing he could think of. **Ike** gently admonishes **Vance**. "That's the wrong approach," he says. "Here's what you'd do: You'd shave every day. You'd keep your shoelaces nice and snug. You'd work on your posture. You see what I'm saying?" Although **Ike** suspects that beneath **Vance**'s glazed stupor lurks a reptilian cunning, he senses that the semiliterate underpants-jacker is having trouble with the concept of Bushido asceticism, and proceeds to tell him a story illustrating exemplary conduct in the face of imminent hyperviolent death. How, early one morning in fifteenth-century Edo, a loyal retainer inadvertently offended a thin-skinned and legendarily fastidious nobleman. Stricken with remorse and shame at his conduct, the retainer immediately offered to commit *seppuku* at dawn the following day. The nobleman, now ashamed of his petulance, attempted to dissuade the retainer from taking such drastic action, but the retainer was adamant that, having offended his master, he must pay the ultimate price. The nobleman, sensing the unimpeachable rectitude and indomitable valor of this man, had no choice but to accept his decision to commit ritual suicide, but he invited the man to be his honored guest at his castle and, for the twenty-four hours before his death, partake of anything he desired—food, drink, concubines, etc. The retainer, bowing deeply, accepted his master's invitation. Soon after he arrived at the opulent abode of the nobleman, as he wandered the labyrinthine hallways of the castle by himself, the retainer's nose began to itch. A man of irreproachable manners and discretion, he exerted all his willpower in an effort not to scratch his nose and appear uncouth. But the more he tried to ignore the itch, the more maddening it became. Finally, he furtively reached up to his nose (furtively, even though he was completely alone—such was his rectitude) and felt an overgrown hair curling just a bit out of one nostril. He impulsively yanked it out, bringing tears to his eyes. Now he had the tiny hair between his thumb and forefinger. But so scrupulous was this man that he wouldn't even consider the possibility of simply dropping the hair and letting it float harmlessly and unnoticeably to the floor. Knowing that his nose hair had befouled the gleaming tile of his master's palace would have filled him with deep, intolerable shame. So he tried to find a small garbage bin or a pail of some sort or even an ashtray or a chamber pot where he could discreetly discard the nose hair. But the palace of the fastidious nobleman was so exceptionally pristine that there was no such vessel to be found anywhere—all the garbage bins and chamber pots had been tastefully ensconced out of sight. Still, the retainer absolutely refused to litter the floor with this single nose hair. And he spent the next twenty-four hours in their entirety—the very last twenty-four hours of his life—stubbornly, but fruitlessly, wandering the halls of the palace in search of something, anything, into which he could deposit the hair. He ate not a morsel, drank not a drop, and spent not even a single moment with any of the voluptuous concubines who awaited him. And, at dawn, he committed *seppuku,* solemnly disemboweling himself, the nose hair still pressed between the fingers of his hand.

"Damn," **Vance** says, spinning the wheel of his BMX bike, the spokes rhythmically thrumming the empty Sunkist can.

Later, **Ike** tells **Vance** about his special diet for the week preceding his violent death: two meals a day, each meal consisting of 16 oz of cole slaw served in a "sacred" blue Dansk plastic salad bowl and two rounded scoops (44 g each) of BSN Syntha-6 banana-flavored protein powder mixed into 12 oz of Sunkist orange soda. "The cole slaw is for roughage," he explains to **Vance**. "I want to have a clean colon when I die," he tells him, "because when the Mossad kills you, Israeli law requires them to do a colonoscopy on your corpse as part of the autopsy. It's this Yid fixation with the gastrointestinal tract." **Ike** (SO high) totally cracks up at the sheer perversity of his rancid, self-loathing anti-Semitism. And then he tells **Vance** about how he had an appointment with his urologist the other day, and the Discovery Channel was on the TV in the waiting room, and there was a show about the origin of cole slaw, about how it was originally called "Cossack Saddle Cabbage," and about how a Cossack horseman would take a razor-sharp hatchet and shred a couple of raw cabbages and pack it into a rawhide sack and actually use that as a saddle, and how, over long distances, the horse sweat would actually pickle the cabbage, producing a version of what we today call "cole slaw," and how the name "Cole Slaw" is actually the result of a careless transliteration of the phrase "Cossack Saddle Cabbage" by a harried immigration official at Ellis Island. (Note, here, a foreshadowing of **Ike**'s discussion about the significance of *naming*.) **Vance** (high school dropout) is too gullible and too fucked up to know whether **Ike** is putting him on or not. Also, some people (e.g., experts) wonder whether **Ike**, in reality, wasn't in the living room of his two-story hermitage, watching the Discovery Channel on his own TV, in his wifebeater and night-vision goggles, with his bottle of Scotch, and simply *imagined* that he was in the waiting room of a urologist. One never knows with **Ike**, who must perpetually contend with the mischievous and mind-manipulating **XOXO**, who, in turn, persists in booby-trapping the epic with nihilistic apocrypha. Meanwhile, in the course of discussing the change in his diet and needing to be strong for "The Last Concert" and his martyrdom, **Ike** apologizes to **Vance** for not inviting him to be in the band (**The Kartons**).... "You're not a **Karton**, though," he says. And **Vance** goes, "I know, *names have talismanic power; when you're given a name, your defining destinies magnetically accrue to that name; the infinite contingencies that arise at every given moment in your life are magnetically reconfigured by that name; a person is* *just a hash of glands and myelin sheathing and electrochemical im-pulses, but there's no discernable context, no recognizable pattern, it's all incoherent, until it's organized and orchestrated into a story, into a fate, by that name."* (Experts today are in almost unanimous agreement that this scene and the scene that follows it are in the WRONG ORDER! **Vance** is sarcastically parroting, almost verbatim, **Ike**'s ideas about naming that **Ike** hasn't even expressed yet, and won't until the *next* scene. So, un-less the Gravy has endowed **Vance** with uncanny powers of precognition, the two scenes should obviously be reversed. But this remains the canonical sequence, because bards— surprisingly hidebound for drug-addled vagrants—insist on continuing to recite the epic as it's traditionally been recited for thousands, if not tens of thousands, of years.) At any rate, there's something so mocking and provocative about **Vance**'s tone (probably because he's SO high on Gravy) that it makes **Ike** momentarily furious. His great impacted anger flares, his festering **Maoist / Mansonesque** rage. (In his coiled fury, **Ike** is like **Tetsuo, the Iron Man**. He dreams of Red Guard maenads, of flesh-eating **Maoist** zombies tear-ing celebrities apart.) And he almost impulsively smashes **Vance**'s face in with his bat. And he would have done it so quickly and so brutally that **Vance** would never have had a chance to even pull his Glock 17 from the waistband of his jeans. But **La Felina** (who, of course, with a Goddess's telescopic vision, is ogling **Ike** from the penthouse of the Burj Khalifa in Dubai) intervenes by swooping down into Jersey City and impersonating a young nanny from Côte d'Ivoire (with a spectacular big-ass ass and big-ass titties), who sashays past pushing a white baby in a stroller, distracting **Ike** (he imagines that look on the nanny's face, that moment of surrender to her own indigenous pleasure, etc., etc.), and by the time she passes out of sight, **Ike**'s temper has cooled, and, high as he is, he smiles and shakes his head abashedly at his own propensity for explosive violence. His lust and his rage are strong. He never dithers. Thrown into this world, he maneuvers himself with the unfaltering aplomb of a somnambulist, but a somnambulist in blazing daylight, in the "blaze of the gaze." (Whether this scene is intended to augur the hyperviolent demise of **Ike Karton** or this is merely identifiable with the benefit of hindsight remains a question contested by experts, but it is surely tempting to see in the overt symbolism of **Ike**'s bat and **Vance**'s Glock a prefiguration of the epic's death-drenched climax.) As if to atone for his transient wrath, **Ike** offers **Vance** another fascinating factoid: that, in the week before he himself was guillotined, **Maximilien Robespierre** (another one of **La Felina**'s "boy-toys") subsisted on black coffee and marzipan.

"I may not understand life," **Ike** says, paraphrasing **Joseph Goebbels**, "but I know how to die magnificently."

"For real," **Vance** avers, spinning the wheel.

"I love my fate," **Ike** says, channeling **Friedrich Nietzsche**.

"If you love your fate so much, why don't you marry it?" **Vance** (who's *so* high) asks.

"I'm fervently wedded to my fate," answers **Ike**.

And here, of course, as throughout, you feel **Ike**'s fealty to his fate in his smile, not in his solemnity.

"How are things going with you and my daughter?" **Ike** asks, not using his daughter's name out of respect for her privacy.

Vance describes being raised by hard-drinking lesbian fisherwomen as "*The Vagina Monologues* if it were hosted by **Jerry Springer**.... There was a lot of disclosure, a lot of sharing, followed by a lot of violence...so I'm used to all that obstreperous emoting.... But with your daughter, it's impossible to know what's really going on inside her." (That line, "it's impossible to know what's really going on inside her," will become critically important relative to the daughter's impending pregnancy on Thursday night's episode.) Then, **Vance** asks **Ike** how he got his wife, **Ruthie**, to fall in love with him, and **Ike** tells him that the first time he saw **Ruthie** she was thrashing on a patch of grass at Lincoln Park in Jersey City, wearing a see-through prairie dress and no underwear, wildly plucking at a zither. "I was immediately struck by her anarcho-primitivist hypersexuality. Although, she was more petite and hygienic than the women I usually go for, and she seemed educated to me—which I usually don't like. I usually go for women who can barely follow an episode of *Dora the Explorer* without becoming hopelessly befuddled and breaking into tears. I just find them, on the whole, more wonder struck (*thaumazein*)." So he read every book and saw every movie and every play that features a character named **Ruthie** or **Ruth**—every single boldface **Ruth** or **Ruthie**—including **Dr. Ruth Westheimer** in *Dr.*

Ruth's Sex After 50: Revving up the Romance, Passion & Excitement!; **Ruth Bader Ginsburg** in **Jeffrey Toobin**'s *The Nine: Inside the Secret World of the Supreme Court*; **Ruth** ("a woman in her early thirties") in **Harold Pinter**'s play *The Homecoming*; the patio-sealant huffing **Ruth Stoops** in *Citizen Ruth* (the **Alexander Payne** movie starring **Laura Dern**); and, of course, **Ruth** in *The Book of Ruth*, in which **Ruth**'s mother-in-law, **Naomi** (which means "the delightful one"), changes her name to **Mara** (which means "the bitter one"): "And she said unto them, 'Call me not **Naomi**, call me **Mara**: for the Almighty hath dealt very bitterly with me.'"

"A person's name is a fate-conjuring incantation," **Ike** tells **Vance**, and then proceeds to tell him a story illustrating the mystical significance of names: "A guy walks into an agent's office and says, 'I'd appreciate it very much if you'd consider representing me. I hear you're one of the best agents in the business and that you could really give my career a terrific boost.' The agent says, 'OK, what do you do?' And the guy says, 'I do a bit of everything. I sing, I dance, I do impersonations, I act—straight drama, musical theater, comedy, slapstick—the whole megillah.' And the agent says, 'That sounds great. What's your name?' And the guy says, 'My name is **Penis van Lesbian**.' And the agent's taken aback for a moment, and then he says, 'With all respect, son, you're going to have to change that name.' And the guy says, 'Why?' And the agent says, 'That name, **Penis van Lesbian**, just isn't going to work in show business. So if I'm going to represent you, you're simply going to have to change it.' And the guy sighs and says, 'That's a shame, because **van**

Lesbian has been the family name for generations upon generations, and it would be terribly disrespectful of me to change it. And my parents gave a lot of thought to naming me **Penis**, and I wouldn't want to offend them in any way either. So I'm afraid changing my name is out of the question.' And the agent says, 'Well, I completely understand that, and I wish you all the luck in the world.' And the guy leaves. So, about five years later, the agent's sitting in his office and there's a knock on the door. And in walks this same guy, looking a little bit older and considerably more prosperous. And he takes out a check for fifty thousand dollars made out to the agent, and he puts it on his desk. The agent's totally nonplussed. 'What's this for?' he asks. And the guy says, 'Well, about five years ago I came in here and you told me that to make it in showbiz, I needed to change my name, and I said no. And after knocking my head against the wall and getting absolutely nowhere, I finally changed my name, and I've been a fabulous hit. You were *completely* right, and you deserve to share in my success.' The agent shrugs. 'Thank you,' he says. 'What did you change your name to?' '**Dick van Dyke**,' the guy says." As he recounts the parable, **Ike**'s whispery rasp is almost inaudible against the percussive rattle of the soda can thrummed by the slowly spinning spokes of **Vance**'s battered red BMX bike and the buzz of several enormous iridescent-winged horseflies who sip at dazzling rivulets of bright orange soda that trickle from the mouths of the discarded cans. **Vance**, because he's *so* high on Gravy, is momentarily fixated on the flies—a surreal tableau of mutant nomadic nymphs feeding on chromium sludge in some postapocalyptic wasteland...he's thinking. And the horse-fly/nymphs seem to be serenading each other in some sort of high-pitched gibberish.... Tiny, voluptuous nymphs plucked out of a painting by the English Pre-Raphaelite **John William Waterhouse** and cast in some Disney/Pixar 3-D animation...he's thinking. The very words he's thinking—the very language he's thinking in—scrolling across the bottom of his visual frame...like karaoke, he's thinking...he's SO high...

For **Ike**, the Gravy seems to have deepened his understanding of his relation to **XOXO**. **Ike** is "reading" (i.e., thinking) what **XOXO** is writing, what he's inscribing in **Ike**'s mind with his sharp periodontal curette. **Ike**'s *denken* is **XOXO**'s *dichten*. **XOXO** has also has made a series of "drill-drawings," for which he inserts a periodontal curette into a motorized drill to produce circular patterns in **Ike**'s mind, thus divorcing the hand of the artist from the work of art. This is what produces the effect that links **Ike**'s simultaneous enactment of *hero* and *bard* to "the flowing auto-narrative of the basketball-dribbling nine-year-old who, at dusk, alone on the family driveway half-court, weaves back and forth, half-hearing and half-murmuring his own play-by-play." (A periodontal curette inserted into a motorized drill to produce circular patterns would also explain the epic's "tail-chasing, vortical form.")

Some of the nymph/horseflies are attracted to **Ike**'s armpits (which are said to be "redolent of sex and death").

Meanwhile, **Ike** expounds further upon the talismanic power of "the name," about how—whether you're mortal (*sterbliche*) or divine (*göttliche*); **Ike Karton**, **Vance**, or **DJ Doorjamb**; **Mogul Magoo**, **Bosco Hifikepunye**, or **Mister Softee**—when you're given a name, your defining destinies magnetically accrue to that name, and about how the infinite contingencies that arise at every given moment in your life are magnetically reconfigured by that name, and about how a person is just a hash of glands and myelin sheathing and electrochemical impulses, but there's no discernable context, no recognizable pattern, it's all incoherent, until it's organized and orchestrated into a story, into a fate, by that name. "Isn't what you *call* something the crucial question?" he asks **Vance** rhetorically. Certainly, the experts have always maintained that what you call the epic is the crucial question. Is it *The Sugar Frosted Nutsack*? Is it *The Ballad of the Severed Bard-Head*? Is it *T.S.F.N.*? And, at one point, near the finale, swilling Scotch and swinging his bat at flitting nano-drones, **Ike** calls out "**XOXO!**" as if *that* were the title of the epic: *Trotzdem schrie **Ike** noch aus aller kraft den namen, der name donnerte durch die Nacht.* ("Nevertheless, with full force, **Ike** shouted out the name, the name thundered through the night.")

Vance—louche, semiliterate, BMX-borne Gravy dealer—was diagnosed with attention deficit hyperactivity disorder (ADHD) and put on a daily dose of 72 mg of Concerta (Methylphenidate) when he was twelve years old, and was kicked out of high school for "habitual truancy." Because he's so high from the Gravy and/or because the God **XOXO** ("The Ventriloquist") is using his sharp periodontal curette to indelibly engrave these ideas into his mind, **Vance**

now finds himself discoursing upon the "problematics of the name," identifying naming as both a *taxonomy* (a "hegemonic system of classification") and a *taxidermy* (an "attempt to capture, chloroform, and neuter the referent").

He shrugs, befuddled by the stream of high-pitched gibberish that's coming out his own mouth. Then he loses his train of thought, and they both totally crack up.

At first, it seems as if **Vance** is finishing **Ike**'s sentences, as if he's able to anticipate verbatim what **Ike**'s going to say... as if they're performing some ritual they've reenacted countless times before... soon they're actually riffing back and forth, a spirited give-and-take, the teasing interplay between tabla and sitar in some woozy raga they've played countless times before. (Note again here, as throughout, *the tellers* and *the told* folded in on themselves.)

When **Vance** stops spinning the BMX wheel, **Ike**'s whispery rasp is suddenly foregrounded in utter silence, imparting great drama to whatever he's saying. And so too will the blind, drug-addled, vagrant bards when they re-create this scene, and cease rhythmically banging their chunky chachkas against their jerrycans of orange soda, and intone, in the sudden sepulchral hush, the words "At dawn, he commits *seppuku,* solemnly disemboweling himself, the nose hair still pressed between the fingers of his hand," or "'You were absolutely right, and you deserve to share in my success.' The agent shrugs. 'Thank you,' he says. 'What did you change your name to?' '**Dick Van Dyke.**'"

Because he's so high on Gravy, **Ike** mentions to **Vance** that the Goddesses use him as pornography when they masturbate. **Ike** also makes the curious statement that fate enables a Goddess to know exactly when to watch him. "If I'm doing something, say, at 10:38 PM EST on a Monday night, it's because I'm fated to be doing it then—it's precisely scheduled that way so a Goddess can find me easily. These are what they call my *listings*. Long ago the Gods ordained these things." If only **Vance** were his son, perhaps **Ike** could be even more forthcoming and discuss his impending tryst with **La Felina**. Nonetheless, he does disclose to **Vance** that the thought of being shamelessly ogled by writhing autoerotomaniacal Goddesses makes his nutsack tingle as if it were a "sachet of plutonium potpourri." **Vance** is like, "Sometimes I get so horny that one of my nuts starts gnawing on the other one."

And it's here that **Ike** makes the cryptic—and endlessly analyzed—assertion that his scrotum contains two eyeballs.

The Gravy's made them both telepathic, so **Ike** knows that **Vance** is wondering what it's like to fuck a Goddess, and **Ike** tells him—without having to say a word—that the greatest thing about having sex with a Goddess (or a human woman, for that matter) is the expression on her face when she capitulates to her own pleasure. It's a return, a homecoming, riffs **Ike**. It's that sublime moment when she defects to the *old country,* to her ancestral homeland, to her own private *paradise*— "where everything was *italicized,* where things happened without any discernable context, where there were no recognizable patterns, where it was all incoherent; where isolated, disjointed events would take place, only to be engulfed by an opaque black void, their relative meaning, their *significance*, annulled by the eons of entropic silence that estranged one from the next; where a terrarium containing three tiny teenage girls mouthing a lot of high-pitched gibberish (like **Mothra**'s fairies, except for their wasted pallors, acne, big tits, and T-shirts that read 'I Don't Do White Guys') would inexplicably materialize, and then, just as inexplicably, disappear." It's that moment she succumbs to herself, surrenders to her depersonalized, oceanic subjectivity, uncorrupted by the narratives of fathers, husbands, village elders, etc. It's a renunciation of modernity, thinks **Ike**—doomed, compulsively hermeneutic, unemployed, anarcho-primitivist, gym-rat. "What does it look like?" wonders **Vance** wordlessly. "Like the grimace of someone throwing herself on an electrified fence at a border crossing or the imperturbable serenity of someone about to do a reverse three-and-a-half somersault tuck into the abyss," **Ike** replies in his thoughts. And **Vance** wonders whether **Ike**'s entire hermetically enclosed, paranoid, narcissistic *Weltanschauung* isn't simply the fetishization of this single snapshot of female *jouissance*... but then he shrugs, unable to remember (never mind comprehend) a single word of what he just thought.

Ordinarily **Ike** probably wouldn't be so candid with **Vance**, except that he's SO high on Gravy. It's like military-grade Gravy, and **Ike** suspects that **Vance** is being supplied by a God. And sure enough, once **Vance** describes the "guy" he's getting his shit from, **Ike**'s almost certain that it's someone who's being impersonated by the God **Bosco Hifikepunye**. (The incident in which **Ike** actually encounters

this "guy" is the basis for the celebrated and extensively studied episode from the *Fifteenth Season,* during which **Ike** will
kneel down and say to a gob of phlegm, "Fräulein, my band,
The Kartons, is giving a Final Concert later this week, and
I'd be very much honored if you would attend," accentu-
ating the dignity he bestows on the lowest of the low. **Ike**'s
suspicion that **Vance**'s supplier is **Bosco Hifikepunye** is
confirmed when **Ike** discovers fresh loot drops (or "God
guano") in the vicinity.)

They are SO high.

This Gravy is super-potent.

It's military-grade Gravy.

Their eyes are glazed over and orange dribble runs down
their chins...

The mesmerizing metronomic tick
        of the spokes thrumming against
                the empty Sunkist can...

Vance spins the BMX wheel not as if it were a Himalayan
prayer wheel (as some shit-for-brains experts have stupidly
suggested)....He spins it like **Goethe**'s *Gretchen am Spinnrade.*
Gretchen is singing at her spinning wheel, in anguished
erotic contemplation of **Faust**. *"Mein armer Kopf / Ist mir ver-
rückt, / Mein aremer Sinn / Ist mir zerstückt."* ("My poor head /
Is crazy to me, / My poor mind / Is torn apart.")

Like **Gretchen**, **Vance** seems here like someone smitten,
someone besotted. Yes, **Vance** is captivated by **Ike**'s diffident magnificence, his "death-drenched luminosity." But

there's something vaguely homoerotic in the way he absently spins his wheel and stares vacantly at his girlfriend's father, something of the grotto-groping Goddesses' vacuous gazes, that so perfectly reflects the slack drift of the masturbating mind.

"Oh my god, we love the *same* song!" **Vance** says at one point, in such a lilting tone of blithe, unalloyed affection that it's hard not to read at least *some* element of homoeroticism into the remark.

Just as the piano in **Schubert**'s *Lied* stops as **Gretchen** becomes completely distracted by the thought of **Faust**'s kiss and forgets to keeps spinning— *"Mein Busen drängt sich / Nach ihm hin. / Ach dürft ich fassen / Und halten ihn, / Und küssen ihn, / So wie ich wollt, / An seinen Küssen / Vergehen sollt!"* ("My bosom urges / Itself toward him. / Ah, might I grasp / And hold him! / And kiss him, / As I would wish, / At his kisses / I should die!")—**Vance** forgets to keep spinning the BMX wheel...

At this point, there is a break—a missing section—in the epic of nearly four hours. This has come to be known as *The Big Lacuna*. Reconstruction of *The Big Lacuna* can never be more than conjectural, but its contents, at least in outline, are tolerably clear. (Experts consider *The Big Lacuna* to be over when **Vance** snaps out of his reverie and asks **Ike** whom he'd rather fuck, **Jenny Sanford** or **Silda Spitzer**.) Blame for *The Big Lacuna* obviously and immediately falls on **XOXO**. Given the tendency of the embittered poet manqué to brazenly interpolate something gratuitously titillating or abstruse or jarringly incongruous, i.e., to preemptively corrupt the epic beyond redemption, it wouldn't surprise anyone if he'd capriciously paralyzed **Ike** and **Vance** for four hours. But what other means might **XOXO** have at his disposal to cause a *Big Lacuna* in the epic? Well, he could go directly after the bards themselves. He could use a nebulized mixture of military-grade ass-cheese and 3-Methylfentanyl (the aerosolized fentanyl derivative that Russian Spetsnaz forces used against Chechen separatists in the 2002 Moscow theater hostage crisis), and he could have any one of those department store perfume saleswomen simply sashay by a group of bards as they recite the epic and casually spray a small amount of the mixture in their vicinity. This would be enough to cause a *Big Lacuna*. **XOXO**, who says he's retired and lives on his pension, dismisses any such allegations as "absolute nonsense." Speaking by telephone from his hyperborean hermitage, he says, "I have no hand in it." He adds, "*T.S.F.N.—General Command* is pulling the wool over your eyes"—referring to the splinter group allied with a radical faction of exiled bards. But we all know what **XOXO** is capable of doing to the bards. He can make some of their pianissimo phrases breathy. He can cause them to suddenly chant in a laughable falsetto or stutter helplessly. And, of course, he can make them recite high-pitched gibberish. (Because the bards are traditionally blind, drug-addled vagrants, experts tend to underplay what great shape they need to be in, especially to perform some of the more physically demanding and rigorously choreographed reenactments in the epic, e.g., when **Ike** is pepper-sprayed at the Miss America Diner or when he chases his daughter's math

teacher around the room or restrains himself from bludgeoning **Vance** with his baseball bat, etc. A bard's heart rate can
surge from 60 beats a minute to over 240 beats a minute
during a recitation of *The Sugar Frosted Nutsack*. The lateral
G-forces exerted on a bard who's rocking back and forth to
the rhythmic ostinato of spokes against a jerrycan could be
as much as 4.5 G, which means about 25 kg of pressure on
the neck.)

Whatever the cause of *The Big Lacuna*, for the entirety of
its duration, **Ike** remains frozen in one immutable cataleptic posture. This tableau vivant demarcates in physical space
the deep authenticity of **Ike**'s mode of experiencing the passage of time—to strike a single pose under the unflinchingly
prurient gaze of the moaning Goddesses, a gaze which casts
him in a sugar frosted nimbus, the "glaze of the gaze," that
Abercrombie & Fitch model and *90210* star **Trevor Donovan** analyzes in his book *The Jade(d) G(l)aze: Twelfth-Century
Goryeo Celadon Pottery and Ceramics*.

Ike presses himself like a gargoyle or a figurehead on the
prow of a ship against the onrush of his own fate.

This tableau of **Ike** batting flies from his armpits as the
glassy-eyed **Vance** spins his BMX bike wheel is, arguably,
one of the most famous and iconic in the world.

And although the epic reaches a state of absolute stasis
here, this continues to be one of the single most popular
parts of the epic repertoire. Its hieratic solemnity and mag-
isterial, almost inert choreography have given rise to com-
parisons with Noh drama, Khmer royal ballet, and Indian
classical dance forms, including Bharatanatyam, Kathak,

and Kuchipudi. Connoisseurs appreciate the degree to which bards are willing to deform themselves into stunted and crippled shapes as they reenact the interminable tableau, risking grotesque injuries (although probably only the most discerning cognoscenti could distinguish these stoop-shouldered, drooling, cataleptic postures from the stoop-shouldered, drooling, cataleptic postures that the drug-addled vagrants typically assume, even when they're not performing the epic). A bard is expected to have extraordinarily precise control over every single part of his body. For instance, when reenacting the scene in which **Ike** is distracted from bludgeoning **Vance** with his bat by the Goddess **La Felina**, who swoops down into Jersey City and impersonates a young nanny from Côte d'Ivoire (with a spectacular big-ass ass and big-ass titties), who sashays past pushing a white baby in a stroller, the bard, miming **Ike** with his brandished bat frozen in mid-air, must remain perfectly still except for the gentle rising and falling of his erection which choreographically registers the modalities of **Ike**'s emotions, achieving a tumescence and a flaccidity that's precisely synchronized with the narration of the nanny's approach and recession into the distance.

Among the world's most illustrious blind, drug-addled bards, **Meir** and **Aaron Poznak**—feral twins abandoned as infants by their parents at Bergdorf Goodman and raised by a wild pack of Yorkipoos near the pond at the southeast corner of Central Park—are especially celebrated for their performances of the "Bat and Nanny" scene, to which they have added their own inimitable flourish. They can actually swivel their testicles from left to right in tandem to signify **Ike** "watching" the nanny as she sashays by—a sly allusion to, and literalization of, his cryptic assertion that his scrotum contains "two eyeballs." In addition to their ultrasophisticated interpretations of **Ike**'s complex and hieratic poses during *The Big Lacuna,* the **Poznak Twins** are also renowned as unrivaled virtuosos of "high-pitched gibberish." (Recently, **Meir Poznak** has receded from the public eye, purportedly becoming the shadowy leader of *T.S.F.N.— General Command.*)

Meanwhile...

Ike seems to see two suns blazing in the heavens, and new mothers who had left their babies behind at home, their breasts swollen with milk, nestling gazelles and young wolves in their arms, suckling them.

"Is this a private jihad, or can anyone join?" a nymph/horsefly murmurs to **Ike**, flitting from armpit to armpit.

Ike's aura is sugar frosted.

Vance is lost in some hallucinatory K-hole of his own.

The mesmerizing metronomic ostinato of the spokes ticking against the empty Sunkist can...the high-pitched gibberish of the nymph/horseflies (the "**Ikettes**")...the buzz of the unmanned drones that represent **Ike**'s inescapable destiny...

They are SO high. This Gravy is super-potent. It's military-grade Gravy. Their eyes are glazed over and orange dribble runs down their chins.

They're SO high.

They're SO FUCKING high.

* * *

According to a report issued by the organization *Psychophar-macologists Without Boundaries,* the amount of hallucinogenic Gravy which could be contained in the period at the end of this sentence, if ingested on an empty stomach, would be enough to cause a person to mistake a rocket-propelled grenade for a Vietnamese *bánh mi* sandwich. But is it simply Gravy that **Ike** and **Vance** are smoking in this episode? They seem SO high. Well, some experts have concluded that the Gravy **Vance** is buying from the God **Bosco Hifikepunye** has been cut with military-grade ass-cheese, which would make it exponentially more potent and potentially neurotoxic. The amount of military-grade ass-cheese / Gravy blend that you could snort off the hyphen between the words "ass" and "cheese" in this very sentence is said to be enough to induce a full-blown psychotic episode. And, if all the letters in the sentence *This tableau of **Ike** batting flies from his armpits as the glassy-eyed **Vance** spins his BMX bike wheel is, arguably, one of the most famous and iconic in the world* were infused with the military-grade ass-cheese / Gravy blend and a person were to ingest the entire sentence, that person would almost certainly become an incurable paranoid schizophrenic. (Keep in mind, too, that boldface signifiers like "**Ike**" and "**Vance**" contain up to three times the amount of the binary psychotropic drug as words in a regular or italicized font do.)

Although it's not the consensus opinion, many scholars suspect that during *The Big Lacuna,* **XOXO** has kidnapped

Ike's and **Vance**'s souls and spirited them off to his hyperborean hermitage beneath Antarctica. **Vance**'s soul doesn't know where the fuck it is. And it gets a little agitated. And **XOXO** starts telling it some bullshit just to calm it down, like "We have a salon on premises and I promise you our stylists don't push products on the customers. Don't you hate it when you go get your hair cut and the stylist tries to push a product on you, etc."—just some bullshit to calm **Vance**'s soul down. He also tells them that there's a restaurant at the hermitage: "You'll love it," he says. "It's like a weird version of *Hooters*." He takes the two souls out back behind the restaurant where Zaporozhian Cossack cavalrymen are just returning from raiding an Ottoman village with freshly made cole slaw under their saddles. Inside, all the waiters are famous Casanovas who are now impotent, incontinent, doddering old men, traipsing from table to table in diapers, using walkers, enormous hydroceles sagging their scrotums to the floor—**Hugh Hefner**, **Warren Beatty**, **Jack Nicholson**, **Wilt Chamberlain**, **Tommy Lee**, **Julio Iglesias**, etc.

Vance's soul is like, "I thought he said this was like *Hooters*." And **Ike**'s soul says, "I think he just meant that there's, like, a theme going on with the waiters."

The waiters are all suffering from dementia and can't remember your orders (never mind their grandchildren's names or the last movie they saw), so you have to write down what you want directly on their grotesquely exposed cerebrums with a sharp periodontal curette.

The allegorical interpretation of **XOXO**'s hermitage as

hell and **Ike** and **Vance**'s brief sojourn there as some sort of *perilous infernal descent*, which dominated the critical debate about *The Sugar Frosted Nutsack* for, like, five minutes in the late '80s, is now widely discredited. Yes, the hermitage is un-derground—miles beneath the surface of Antarctica. And yes, **Ike** refers to it as *unten*—literally "under" or "below." But, *hello*, it's "hyperborean"—of or relating to the arctic, frigid, very cold. The opposite of infernally hot. Well, what if it's WAY underground down near the inner core of the earth, where it's like 10,000 degrees? Well, what if it's up your ass where it's like *10,000,000* degrees? Well, what if you're a cocksucking dwarf racist retard midget dickwad? Well, what if you're a fucking scatological-bakery urinal-cake-boss motherfucking fist-fucked cow-pie anal-fissureman motherfucker?

...And so this debate, rendered incontrovertibly moot years ago (if not tens of thousands of years ago), curiously rages on.

Ostensibly a sequence intended to reinforce the scope of **XOXO**'s omnipotent mischief (his *mojo*) and/or the super-potency of the hallucinogenic Gravy that the God **Bosco Hifikepunye** is selling **Vance**, the so-called "Playdate at the Hermitage" (whether apocryphal or not) has the perhaps unintended consequence of showcasing, of all things, **XOXO**'s *tenderness* (an anomaly in the epic, with the excep-tion of his ill-fated literary courtship of **Shanice**). The big fuss he makes about the cole slaw behind the restaurant is clearly **XOXO**'s way of winking at **Vance** and sympathet-ically acknowledging that he knows that **Vance** was sort of punk'd by **Ike** re: the Cossack Saddle Cabbage and the harried immigration official at Ellis Island, etc. More significantly, in this scene (and again, experts are divided about whether it's an authentic scene or a noncanonical blooper), **XOXO** clearly conveys a strong ideological solidarity with **Ike** via the abject humiliation of the celebrity Casanovas at his Dantean "*Hooters.*"

Whether this perhaps vindicates some experts' queasy faith in **XOXO** has yet to be determined, but it surely feeds a growing suspicion that **XOXO** may have a more sympathetic if not a distinctly symbiotic relationship with **Ike** (and with the epic itself) than previously thought—something that even **XOXO**'s most indefatigable detractors may have to wearily concede.

Suddenly, the following ("without any discernable context, etc."):

Four girls on the subway, back from a Yankees game...one in a white pinstripe #2 **Derek Jeter** *Yankees jersey, tight, short white skirt, no underwear, drinking a big Burger King shake through a straw...white wristbands...chubby arms...pink fingernail polish, blue toenails, gold sandals...huge face...HUGE...almost like the kid in that movie* Mask *with* **Cher** *...not with craniodiaphyseal dysplasia, just a really, really big face...and hot fleshy freckly chubby thighs.... The other three have knockoff* **Marc Jacobs** *bags...but the chubby one with the Burger King shake and the thighs and no underwear has the real deal: a $45,000 Hermès black crocodile Kelly bag.*

Here, many people (e.g., audience members at public recitations, experts, metaphysicians, etc.) are like:

"Huh? 'The fuck just happened???"

This has gotta be **XOXO** totally fucking with the epic, right? Plying the epic with drugged sherbet. Shooting it up with military-grade ass-cheese, right? **XOXO**—who persists in booby-trapping the epic with nihilistic apocrypha.

Well, not so fast, contend some scholars. In a scrupulously researched monograph coauthored by **V. S. Naipaul** and **C. C. Sabathia**, a cogent case is made for the possibility that there is no *Big Lacuna* (i.e., that this is not **XOXO** vandalizing the epic), that during this mute interstice, **Ike** and **Vance** are simply too fucked up to talk and that **Vance** keeps up the tranced-out empty-can-against-the-spinning-spokes rhythm while **Ike** just stares off into space (a whole desultory lifetime tacitly exchanged between them, as if between two dogs) and that, at some point, **Vance**, emerging from some hallucinatory K-hole of his own, is like, "Four girls on the subway, back from a Yankees game…one in a white pinstripe #2 **Derek Jeter** Yankees jersey, tight, short white skirt, no underwear, drinking a big Burger King shake through a straw…white wristbands…chubby arms…" In other words, that it's simply his spacey elliptical reportage of something he observed recently (probably apropos of something **Ike** had been saying before about how sexy he thinks sweaty plus-size women are) and not just a piece of completely incongruous bullshit that **XOXO** plopped in to gum up the epic (perhaps at the behest of the flagrantly snubbed and pissed-off **Shanice**). Other experts, though, contend that the **V. S. Naipaul** / **C. C. Sabathia** monograph itself is a crude forgery, an obvious noncanonical blooper lobbed in by **XOXO** to gum up the epic. (It bears repeating that all noncanonical bloopers are almost immediately subsumed into the realm of the canonical and are, at the first opportunity, dutifully chanted by vagrant, drug-addled bards.)

As the individual earlier identified as "**REAL WIFE**" said (this is the woman who attended the public recitation of *The Sugar Frosted Nutsack* with her husband but then ditched him for a vagrant, drug-addled bard, the one who gave up painting when she saw **Gerhard Richter**'s paintings of **Andreas Baader** and **Ulrike Meinhof**), "It's too easy for people to always blame things on **XOXO**." Although, clearly, **XOXO** is perfectly capable of turning the epic into a celebrity gossip magazine or TV listings if he feels like it, so why not a *Big Lacuna*? Question, though: Might not the chubby girl in the subway without underwear be **La Felina**? Wouldn't her fabulously expensive Hermès Kelly bag in this context signal a *theophany*—the appearance of a deity? A message to **Ike** re: their tryst, maybe? Or is the meaning of the *Big Lacuna*— this stand-alone mini-epic—ineffable? (Or, perhaps, as one noted metaphysician put it, simply too *stupid* for words?)

It's at this point, during a public recitation, that a bard will stand and hysterically exclaim:

XOXO's got the epic by the nutsack!!!
Ike Ike Ike Ike Ike!
Ike Ike Ike Ike Ike!
Ike Ike Ike Ike Ike!

Ike Ike Ike Ike Ike!
Ike Ike Ike Ike Ike!

This chant, accompanied by the frenzied banging of gaudy rings against jerrycans of orange soda, continues unabated for a stupefying four hours, at which point (in almost every credible version of *The Sugar Frosted Nutsack*), **Ike**, in response to the defibrillating incantation of his name ("**Ike Ike Ike Ike Ike!**"), finally snaps out of his cataleptic reverie and addresses his galvanic "Apostrophe to the Bards"—"apostrophe" because the bards are not literally present (in the *epic dimension* which **Ike** inhabits), although the fact that they respond (echoing **Ike**'s words, but *backward*) suggests that they are *present* (perhaps in some purely metaphysical sense) but not *proximal*. **Salinger/Foyt** will later suggest that the bards here are *hyperproximal*, i.e., present in a purely *intracranial* sense. This is difficult to understand. When experts talk about the bards' "hyperproximity" to **Ike**, about their presence being "intracranial," they are correlating the motif of **Ike**'s head (filling with the perpetually inscribed narration of the epic and the ever murmuring voices of masturbating Goddesses) with the motif of the minibar at the Burj Khalifa (the underlying notion here being that all of the Gods actually compress or collapse themselves within the minibar itself). This is what some highly regarded pseudo-intellectuals mean when they speak of **Ike**'s head *as* minibar. These interlocking motifs represent something that is simultaneously infinitely small and infinitely capacious.

Ike

Let me hear all my fuckin' big-dick drug-addled blind
bards from Jersey City say "HEY!"

Big-Dick Drug-Addled Blind Bards
from Jersey City

YEH!

Ike

Let me hear all my fuckin' big-dick drug-addled blind
bards from Jersey City say "AHH!"

Big-Dick Drug-Addled Blind Bards
from Jersey City

HHA!

Ike

Let me hear all my fuckin' big-dick drug-addled blind
bards from Jersey City say *"Tuer tous les célébrités!"*

Big-Dick Drug-Addled Blind Bards
from Jersey City

Sétirbéléc sel suot reut!

Ike

Cut their motherfuckin' heads off!

Big-Dick Drug-Addled Blind Bards
from Jersey City
Ffo sdaeh 'nikcufrehtom rieht tuc!

Ike
Death to every name on the *Forbes* Celebrity 100 list.

Big-Dick Drug-Addled Blind Bards
from Jersey City
Tsil 001 Ytirbelec *Sebrof* eht no eman yreve ot htaed.

Ike
Guillotine **Jerry Bruckheimer, James Cameron, Bono, Simon Cowell,** and **Elton John.**

Big-Dick Drug-Addled Blind Bards
from Jersey City
Nhoj Notle dna, **Llewoc Nomis, Onob, Noremac Semaj, Remiehkcurb Yrrej** enitolliug.

Ike
Guillotine **Spielberg.** Guillotine **Jennifer Aniston** and **Michael Bay.** Guillotine **Coldplay.**

Big-Dick Drug-Addled Blind Bards
from Jersey City
Yalpdloc enitolliug. **Yab Leahcim** dna **Notsina Refinnej** enitolliug. **Grebleips** enitolliug.

Ike

Guillotine fucking **Jerry Seinfeld**. Guillotine **Tom Hanks** and **Ryan Seacrest** and **Brad** fucking **Pitt** and **Leonardo DiCaprio** and **Dr. Phil** and **Judge Judy** and **Alec Baldwin** and **Bethenny Frankel**!

Big-Dick Drug-Addled Blind Bards
from Jersey City

Leknarf Ynnehteb dna **Niwdlab Cela** dna **Yduj Egduj** dna **Lihp Rd.** dna **OirpaCid Odranoel** dna **Ttip** gnikcuf **Darb** dna **Tsercaes Nayr** dna **Sknah Mot** enitolliug! **Dlefnies Yrrej** gnikcuf enitolliug.

Ike

Long live the flesh-eating, subproletarian *ragazzi di vita!*

Big-Dick Drug-Addled Blind Bards
from Jersey City

Ativ id izzagar nairatelorpbus, gnitae-hself eht evil gnol!

Ike

Let me hear all my fuckin' big-dick drug-addled blind bards from the Upper Peninsula say "HEY!"

Big-Dick Drug-Addled Blind Bards
from the Upper Peninsula

YEH!

Ike

Let me hear all my fuckin' big-dick drug-addled blind bards from the Upper Peninsula say "**XOXO**—we takin' our motherfuckin' epic back!"

Big-Dick Drug-Addled Blind Bards
from the Upper Peninsula

Kcab cipe 'nikcufrehtom ruo 'nikat ew—**OXOX**!

In a provocative (though virtually incomprehensible) essay titled "Memory and Obsolescence," first published in the August 1958 edition of the children's magazine *Highlights,* coauthors **J. D. Salinger** and **A. J. Foyt** analyze this mirrored call-and-response between **Ike** (doomed introvert, implacable neo-pagan, coy Taurus, Saint Laurentian fusion of the tough and the tender) and the bards, which is driven by the mesmerizing beat of empty soda can against BMX spoke. **Salinger** and **Foyt** explain the incongruity of **Ike**'s profane, clamorous exhortations ("a full-bore venting of all his fevered antipathies toward celebrities and, implicitly, an impassioned avowal of his devout affiliation with the humble and abject") by suggesting that they are "whispered, if not wholly tacit"—after all, if you're addressing bards who are "hyperproximal" or who reside "intracranially" (i.e., in your "minibar"), there's really no need to raise your voice. **Salinger** and **Foyt** go on to claim that "the fact that the bards are represented here as repeating what **Ike** says but backward means that, essentially, **Ike** is continuously pulling himself out of his own ass, inside-out."

"**Ike** is continuously pulling himself out of his own ass, inside-out" is another way of depicting the *inside-outness* of **Ike**'s simultaneous narration and enactment of the epic. When you think (and you don't have to actually say it out loud) "I am a hero," you immediately become a *karaoke bard* because you're simply *reading* what **XOXO** is inscribing into your brain. But because the epic subsumes everything extrinsic to it, the karaoke bard is instantly turned back into content, i.e., back into a hero. **Salinger** and **Foyt** call this unending process "enveloping inversion." And they liken the *inside-outness* of **Ike**'s simultaneous narration and enactment to the In-N-Out Burger "secret menu," and specifically the "3x4"—three beef patties, four slices of cheese. Not only do the alternating layers of cheese/beef/cheese/beef/cheese/beef/cheese parallel the alternating inversions of hero/bard/hero/bard/hero/bard/hero, but the 3x4 configuration corresponds to the three letters in the name "**Ike**" and the four letters in the name "**XOXO**" and, most significantly, to the license plate HPG-XOXO, a license plate analyzed in stupefyingly granular detail over the course of an essay that runs some thirty thousand words (every one of which audiences expect the vagrant, drug-addled bards to recite verbatim).

Ike's "Apostrophe to the Bards" could also be "A Cry from the Smallest Box," i.e., a *cri de coeur* from the depths. What **Salinger** and **Foyt** mean here is that **Ike** could be calling out from within **XOXO**'s hyperborean hermitage or, more likely, that in *The Big Lacuna*, **Ike** finds himself in an extreme spiritual state, in the innermost embedded place, in the innermost and smallest of all the epic's ever-diminishing Chinese nested boxes or Russian Matryoshka dolls (or "M-dolls"). The smallest, most deeply embedded version of the "**Ike** M-doll" (which is a purely practical construct—in theory, of course, there is no *terminus* in an infinitely recursive *reductio ad infinitum*) is basically a freeze-frame at the very threshold of existence which is called "The Minibar." This is why the Gods are sometimes said to reside in "The Minibar," which is sometimes likened to an infinitesimal zero-dimensional point called a Severed Bard-Head, and which is sometimes thought to symbolize **Ike**'s head. The amplitude of the vibration of a "terminal" infinitesimally recursive Severed Bard-Head is referred to as "high-pitched" or "HPG" ("High-Pitched Gibberish"). And, of course, HPG-XOXO is the license plate of the *Mister Softee* truck that hit **Ike** during Spring Break and the final license plate that traverses **Ike**'s field of vision as he orgasms at the precise moment of his assassination by the ATF/Mossad.

Most original, though, is **Salinger** and **Foyt**'s theory that has come to be known as "**Rapunzel**'s Braid," in which they contend that the images of wafting armpit hair ("look how beautiful **Ike**'s abundant chestnut-color armpit hair is, how lustrous and soft and fluffy. It almost looks as if he blow-dries it for extra volume!"), the tampon string and Chinese fortune-cookie fortune in **Ike**'s dream of **La Felina**, the pendulous breasts of the ubiquitous "chubby middle-aged women," even the hanging hydroceles of the decrepit waiters in **XOXO**'s Dantean *Hooters*, represent "lifelines," i.e., means of extricating the hero from some underworld (i.e., from death or from some perilous spiritual journey). "**Ike Ike Ike Ike Ike!**"—the incantatory concatenation of the *Name*—is a string of words (analogous to a tampon string or a paper fortune or a loyal retainer's nose hair) upon which the hero can climb back into the world of the living. **Ike** configures himself as an in-and-out alternation of bard/hero, which constitutes a kind of "braided identity." When we chant "**Ike Ike Ike Ike Ike!**" (the first **Ike** in the string a hero, the second a bard, the third a hero, the fourth a bard, the fifth a hero), we are forming a plaited lifeline that **Salinger** and **Foyt** refer to as "**Rapunzel**'s Braid." And isn't **Ike**'s vaunted tongue sandwich, they proceed to ask, the figurative instrument *par excellence* for depicting the inside-outness of chanting the braided name (the bard) and of being consumed (the enveloped hero)? This is the "Swallowed Tongue"—a metonymic symbol for epilepsy. So clearly, according to **Salinger** and **Foyt**, the epic intends to associate **Ike**'s "pulling himself out of his own ass, inside-out"—his perpetual high-pitched oscillation between bard and hero—with a form of seizure (e.g., "the feral fatalism of all his loony tics—like the petit-mal fluttering of his long-lashed lids and the **Mussolini** torticollis of his Schick-nicked neck").

Even those who consider all this total bullshit have to concede that it's upscale, artisanal bullshit of the highest order. It's also worth noting that **Salinger** and **Foyt** were the very first experts to notice a change from **Ike**'s Spartan pre-martyrdom diet of cole slaw and protein shakes to a more epicurean regimen of salami and provolone sandwiches, egg rolls, Frosted Cherry Pop-Tarts, Kozy Shack Butterscotch Pudding, and Absolut Peppar vodka shots.

For deliberately demented gobbledygook, nothing tops a group of experts who call themselves "Chineans" after **Vincent "The Chin" Gigante**, the mob boss who wandered the streets of Greenwich Village in his bathrobe and slippers, mumbling incoherently to himself, in an act to avoid prosecution. The Chineans maintain an evangelical belief in the surpassing significance of **Vance** and swear allegiance to the nose-thumbing, mind-fucking God **XOXO**, for which they have earned the implacable enmity of the reclusive, shadowy paramilitary leader **Meir Poznak**, who has placed a high-price bounty on the head of the equally reclusive and shadowy impresario of the Chineans—a man called **The High-Talking Chief** (and who is also known as "The Craziest of the Crazy," "The Pazzo di Tutti Pazzi," and "The Capo di Tutti Frutti"). **Meir Poznak** has threatened **The High-Talking Chief** of the Chineans with the ritual punishment of eye enucleation by melon baller and guillotining. No one's ever seen **The High-Talking Chief**. There are no official photos of him. And the authenticity of existing images is debated. Apart from the fact that he is already missing one eye, accounts of his physical appearance are wildly contradictory. Some people who have met him describe him as having the voluptuous curves of a **Beyoncé** or a **Serena Williams**, while others describe him as more closely resembling **Representative Henry Waxman**. **The High-Talking Chief** has said, "We did a complete simulation of *The Big Lacuna* and sliced the code to its deepest level. We have studied its protocols and functionality. We're convinced that **XOXO** has nothing to do with it." **The High-Talking Chief** of the Chineans has also said that the most serious attacks on the epic have been mounted not by **XOXO**, but by **Fast-Cooking Ali** (supposedly acting out of jealousy, because his girlfriend **La Felina** has such an obsessive crush on **Ike Karton**). **The High-Talking Chief** of the Chineans has said that what **Fast-Cooking Ali** does is "ramp up the frequency of the epic, so that it spins faster and faster, causing it to hit 1,410 Hertz (or cycles per second)—just enough to send it flying apart." Although this is all self-serving and unsubstantiated bullshit, it is upscale, artisanal self-serving and unsubstantiated bullshit of the highest order, and the Chineans are responsible for certain findings which have broadened our understanding of the epic immeasurably. For instance, it was the Chineans who uncovered identical e-mails sent by **Ike**, on the night before his death, to the three top heavyweight competitors at the Women's Sumo World Championship in Warsaw, Poland—**Anna Zhigalova** of Russia, and **Svitlana Iaromka** and **Olga Davydko**, both of the Ukraine. Although their precise content is unknown, they are said to be lengthy and unusually coherent, alternating between crude sexual bravado and weary resignation. **Ike** purportedly quotes **Thomas Hardy** (without attribution, of course): "Remember that the best and greatest among mankind are those who do themselves no worldly good." It was the Chineans who discovered numerous inscriptions in **Ike**'s Snyder High School yearbook reading "See you at Rutgers!" irrefutably debunking the myth that **Ike** ever attended the Fashion Institute of Technology (F.I.T.). The Chineans were the first experts to grapple with the question of why **Oprah Winfrey**'s name is conspicuously omitted from the roster of those sentenced to the guillotine in **Ike**'s galvanic "Apostrophe to the Bards." She is, after all, #1 on the *Forbes* Celebrity 100 list. The Chineans contend that the answer lies in **Ike**'s habit of plagiarizing from her magazine and his self-professed fondness for the bodies of women who don't like their bodies. And it was the Chineans (who claim to "strip away the accretions of the epic") who determined that the definitive title of the epic is—and always has been—*The Sugar Frosted Nutsack 2: Crème de la Sack.*

The Chineans advocated that the bards actually negotiate with **XOXO**, and went so far as to publicly suggest "positive interventions" he might undertake to expand the epic's audience, e.g., "Hmm, how about deleting all the references to **Ike**'s rancid, self-loathing anti-Semitism?" and "Hey, why not make **Vance** much more prominent? How about posting on YouTube footage of **Vance** tooling around Jersey City on his BMX bike with his Glock tucked into the waistband of his jeans to the **Boys Noize** remix of the **N.E.R.D. / Nelly Furtado** track 'Hot-N-Fun'? Or how about **Vance** with the lesbian fisherwomen, in their squalid shack under the **Pulaski** Skyway, drinking, smoking, playing dominoes, cooking, laughing to the **Four Tet** remix of the **Pantha du Prince** track 'Stick to My Side'? Just a real cool, tranced-out video. That would definitely appeal to a younger, hipper demographic" and "Consider losing **Ike**'s fetish for chubby, sweaty, hairy, unkempt, and uneducated middle-aged women and replace it with a predilection for smokin' hot young chicks. This would make it significantly easier for that whole coveted eighteen-to thirty-four-year-old male demographic to identify with **Ike**." The Chineans offered their consulting services to **XOXO** in return for a 5 percent stake in royalties generated by the narcocorrido **Ike** wrote at the Miss America Diner ("Do you hear that mosquito, / that toilet flushing upstairs, / that glockenspiel out in the briar patch?") which is weird because—unless the Chineans know something we don't know (which they very well might)—the rights to **Ike**'s narcocorrido belong exclusively to **Mogul Magoo**. The Chineans also criticized **Ruthie** for parading around on her front lawn, wearing a transparent "prairie dress" and no underwear (calling the look "Ruby Ridge meets **Tila Tequila**") and offered her a free makeover from celebrity stylist **Andrea Lieberman**. This was such an egregious affront to **Ike**—suggesting to someone who fervently yearns for the massacre of celebrities that his own wife get a makeover from a "celebrity stylist"—that it spawned a stand-alone fantasy episode in the *Twenty-Eighth Season*. In a sort of *The Sugar Frosted Nutsack 2: Crème de la Sack* meets *Zatoichi: The Blind Swordsman*, **Ike**, blinded by a particularly disgusting case of conjunctivitis, bludgeons to death a group of Chineans, clad in their trademark bathrobes and slippers (which are associated not only with **Vincent "The Chin" Gigante** but also with the old, decrepit waiters from **XOXO**'s Dantean *Hooters*), who have encircled him on the corner of West Side Avenue and Culver in Jersey City. Unlike the episode in which **La Felina** distracts **Ike** from his impulsive rage by impersonating a voluptuous au pair from Cote d'Ivoire, this time, **La Felina**, watching from the top floor of the 2,717-foot Burj Khalifa in Dubai, completely gets off on **Ike**'s "helmet-to-helmet" violence and masturbates until she has an outrageous gushing orgasm that lasts for fifty years and fills a 143,200-square-mile endorheic basin between the Caucasus Mountains and the steppe of Central Asia that is today called the "Caspian Sea."

Meir Poznak, whose hard-line faction *T.S.F.N.—General Command* adamantly rejects any suggestion that the epic functions under the aegis of **XOXO**, considers this "the single greatest episode of *The Sugar Frosted Nutsack 2: Crème de la Sack* ever made." (**Poznak** relentlessly excoriates the Chineans. He is their irreconcilable enemy. In a series of blistering communiqués, **Poznak** inveighs against the Chineans' perversely counterintuitive (but increasingly plausible) contention that there's active collusion or some secret pact or modus vivendi between **Ike Karton** and **XOXO**.)

Slaughtering Chineans is straight-up **Poznak** shit. Experts who express even the slightest affinity for Chinean precepts are viciously beaten and crippled by *T.S.F.N.—General Command* thugs acting on orders from **Meir Poznak**. On the other hand, bards are routinely butchered by packs of pipe- and machete-wielding Chinean enforcers at the behest of the **Capo di Tutti Frutti**. True, **Meir Poznak** emerged from within the milieu of the bards and the **Capo di Tutti Frutti** emerged from within the milieu of the experts. But there are highly regarded Poznakian experts and celebrated Chinean bards. (Although, for those who haven't made a close study of the schism, it might be difficult, if not impossible, to distinguish between a Poznakian and a Chinean bard. Either would be a chanting, drug-addled vagrant who maintains his trance-inducing beat by banging chunky chachkas against metal jerrycans of orange soda, either would assume the classical stoop-shouldered, drooling, cataleptic posture during the so-called *Big Lacuna,* etc.)

Some Chineans have floated the idea that **Vance**—the louche, semiliterate, BMX-riding Gravy dealer—may actually be a God. This is based primarily on an interpretation of the line "experts consider *The Big Lacuna* to be over when **Vance** snaps out of his reverie and asks **Ike** whom he'd rather fuck, **Jenny Sanford** or **Silda Spitzer**." These Chineans (a breakaway sect known as the "Some Chineans" or the "These Chineans") suggest that **Vance**'s so-called "snapping out" is a form of extricating himself from or becoming extrinsic to the epic, and that since only a God can extricate himself from or become extrinsic to the epic, **Vance** is, ipso facto, a God. This theory is bolstered by the suspicion that **Vance** is the father of **Ike**'s teenage daughter's infant, **Colter Dale**, who is generally considered to be quasi-divine, and that given the fact that **Ike**'s teenage daughter is mortal (she almost failed math!), **Vance** is, ipso facto, a God, although there is equally compelling evidence that **Bosco Hifikepunye**, the God of Miscellany (Fibromyalgia, Chicken Tenders, Sports Memorabilia, SteamVac Carpet Cleaners, etc.), who used **Ted Williams**'s cryonically preserved head as an anal sex toy with the Korean flower-shop clerk **Mi-Hyun**, and who supplies **Vance** with hallucinogenic Gravy, is the actual father of **Colter Dale**.

Monday: 11:30 PM Eastern
"The Stone Mind"

Most Chineans and Some Chineans contend that **Ike** is a *statue*. This is, of course, the theory with which the Chineans are most notoriously associated. There's always a suspicion about the Chineans that their most wildly preposterous assertions are simply part of their act to "avoid prosecution" (i.e., to evade or confound critical scrutiny). But what had once seemed beyond the pale—**Ike**, a statue? An inanimate object?—has steadily gained credence.

The idea that **Ike Karton**—valiant, brooding neo-pagan, "despot of his stoop (*n'est-ce pas?*)," with his pomaded pompadour, hazy and queasy from the Gravy, whose "rancid, self-loathing anti-Semitism" is "just a way to stick it to his dad," who's beloved by **La Felina** for his loathing of celebrities and plutocrats and for his ardent solidarity with the lowest of the low, who likes the bodies of women who don't like their bodies, who's continuously pulling himself out of his own ass, inside-out—is actually in an advanced state of petrifaction (i.e., that he's a statue, a stone homunculus, a lawn jockey) may have initially been broached for sheer shock value, but it soon developed into a finely calibrated theory which today is widely considered the finest calibratcd theory for which the Most Chineans and the Some Chineans (aka the *These Chineans*) are most notoriously associated.

Could they mean all this figuratively or metaphorically— that **Ike** is simply *statue-like* or *statuesque?* Well, maybe at first. It's easy to see how, given the fact that **Ike**'s been in a sort of dissociative fugue state ever since he was hit by a *Mister Softee* truck on Spring Break when he was eighteen years old ("high on ketamine, wearing silver lederhosen and a hat made out of an Oreo box at the time, he initially claimed he'd been hit by a Hasidic ambulance in an effort to foment an apocalyptic Helter Skelter–type war between club kids and Hasids"), and that the Some Chineans surmise that he's been mute (not just reticent or soft-spoken, but mute!) since the *Mister Softee* accident, and that, for most of the epic, **Ike** stands on his stoop, "on the prow of his hermitage, strik- ing that contrapposto pose, in his white wifebeater, his torso totally ripped, his lustrous chestnut armpit hair wafting in the breeze, his head turned and inclined up toward the top floors of the Burj Khalifa in Dubai, from which the gaze of gasping, masturbating Goddesses casts him in a sugar frosted nimbus," they might conclude that **Ike** is *like* a statue or *like* a lawn jockey.

After all, he *does* seem to largely exist in a state of sus- pended animation, and his "taunting, lascivious dance along the precipice of incoherence" *does* make him "a frozen figure in a tableau vivant," "a taxidermied gym-rat in a habitat diorama," "a paralyzed player," "a cataleptic kike," etc. This is, of course, why **Ike** is so frequently called a "Nude Descending a Staircase"—because he is a static image of movement ("a ruptured contraption," "a clutter of spasms and ticks").

But the Chineans have gone way beyond the mere kinesics of **Ike**'s vaunted inertia. **Ike** literally goes nowhere, they claim. His birth and his death are the only real (i.e., the only *measurable*) events in his life and, thus, constitute the true polarity of the epic. These two events, though antipodal, simultaneously occupy one point in space. **Ike** is born (in the heroic sense) in the arousal of the gasping Goddesses' desire, and he dies (heroically) in the self-satisfaction of that desire. In other words, he is born on his stoop and he dies on his stoop without having traversed any distance, without having moved a muscle—ergo, **Ike** the Statue. Everything in between his heroic birth and death (if anything can be said to be "between" events which coincide) is represented by an ellipsis. In other words, each dot in the ellipsis is made out of a zero-dimensional dollop of military-grade ass-cheese that's been extruded from what the Chineans call "the pastry bag" (i.e., from a God's ass). These are also called "loot drops" and "God guano."

The Chineans don't mean that at some point in recent history a statue of **Ike Karton** was erected in Jersey City to commemorate the hero of *The Sugar Frosted Nutsack 2: Crème de la Sack*. They mean that **Ike Karton**, the hero of the *The*

Sugar Frosted Nutsack 2: Crème de la Sack is, literally, a fucking statue.

Ike the hero—porn addict, Taurus, marionette of his Gods—is sculpted in time, in vectors of time, veering inexorably inward, inexorably toward his fate. Although his martyr's death (at the hands of Mossad sharpshooters perched in trees) is a hyperviolent implosion, a convulsive centripetal rupturing, it is imperceptible to the external observer. Yes, **Ike** subjectively experiences it as "driving a Pagani Zonda into a concrete wall at 300 mph," but his neighbors perceive the hyperviolently imploding **Ike** as basically the same **Ike** they see every day ("on the prow of his hermitage, striking that contrapposto pose, in his white wifebeater, his torso totally ripped, his lustrous chestnut armpit hair wafting in the breeze, his head turned and inclined up toward the top floors of the Burj Khalifa in Dubai, from which the gaze of masturbating Goddesses casts him in a sugar frosted nimbus").

Ike is riddled, infested, consumed,

Devoured from within by Gods.

Only Gods can inhabit a stone mind.

So this whole massively involuted epic, which has variously been called *Ten Gods I'd Fuck (T.G.I.F.)*, *The Ballad of the Severed Bard-Head*, *What to Expect When You're Expecting*, *The Sugar Frosted Nutsack*, and, finally and definitively, *The Sugar Frosted Nutsack 2: Crème de la Sack*, with all its excruciating redundancies, heavy-handed, stilted tropes and wearying clichés, its overwrought angst, all its gnomic non sequiturs, all its off-putting adolescent scatology and cringe-inducing

smuttiness, all the depraved tableaus and orgies of masturbation with all their bulging, spurting shapes, and all the
compulsive repetitions about **Freud**'s repetition compulsion … is essentially, at the end of the day, about a man who
just stands on his stoop, rooted to the spot, making crypto-
grams out of passing license plates, watching a kid tooling
around the block on a BMX bike. (What's interesting is that
you never really know with overwrought angst or heavy-
handed, stilted tropes—they can seem terrible on the page,
but *totally* work at a public recitation. Same's true with
cringe-inducing smuttiness and off-putting adolescent scatology—it can seem lame on paper, but completely come
alive when delivered by vagrant, drug-addled bards banging chunky chachkas against metal jerrycans of orange
soda.)

FYI: The Chineans also believe that **Ruthie** and the
Daughter and **Colter Dale** are "superfluities," i.e., later
additions (noncanonical bloopers) which were inserted to
"mainstream" the figure of **Ike**—to create a more norma-
tive version of **Ike**, i.e., to give *a famille* to his *folie*.

And they believe that if you put a stethoscope to the stone
head of **Ike**, the Lawn Jockey, you can hear, against that endlessly looping sample from the *Mister Softee* jingle …

> *All the rapturous, orotund eroticism of*
> ***Ike**'s erudite, oxymoronic doxologies,*
> *And all the demagogic authority*
> *Of his psychosexual serenades*
> *("Do you hear that mosquito,*

That toilet flushing upstairs,
That glockenspiel out in the briar patch?
That's me, Unwanted One, Filthy One,
Despised Whore, Lonely Nut Job...")

And finally, the Chineans ask: Do the **Kartons** comprise an organized crime family? According to the federal law against organized crime in Mexico, "when three or more people make an agreement to organize or form an organization to engage, in an ongoing or reiterated fashion, in activities that by themselves or together with other activities have as a goal or a result the commission of any or several crimes, they will be legally classified and penalized because of these actions as members of organized crime." Clearly, the Chineans assert, the **Kartons** have engaged in a conspiracy to build a dildo-impaled statue without a permit and a conspiracy to perform a narcocorrido ("Do you hear that mosquito / that toilet flushing upstairs / that glockenspiel out in the briar patch?") in a residential area.

The Chineans are part of **Vance**'s reverie. Since many people believe that **Vance** is a God (significantly, **Vance** himself happens *not* to believe that he's a God), this means that the Chineans are part of a God's reverie, which confers enormous prestige upon them at least for the duration of the reverie, but consigns them to oblivion once **Vance** "snaps out" of his reverie (an event said to be augured by "the mysterious appearance of a mah-jongg tile on the floor of some cabana").

It goes without saying that all of this could simply be another case of **XOXO** slipping something into the epic's drink (i.e., drugging its sherbet). **XOXO** is forever doodling on **Ike**'s mind, and on the minds of bards (doodling on *all* our minds) with his sharp periodontal curette, and forever feeding "the apophenic mania of experts to find hidden and farfetched links and correlations. Is it possible to predict **XOXO**'s behavior toward human beings based on his alliances with other Gods? For example, what is his position vis-à-vis the **La Felina / Mogul Magoo** schism? **Shanice** had, from the beginning, cliqued up with **Mogul Magoo**, so **XOXO** (after **Shanice**'s withering critique of his poem) had naturally cliqued up with **La Felina**. But **XOXO** is too intractable a nihilist to ever be considered aligned with any single faction. And it always bears repeating that the Gods view human beings with a fundamental detachment, almost as if they were characters in a video game. They are *entertained* by humans. Sure, they have their favorites (**Ike** is famously **La Felina**'s *favorite*), but the Gods basically *love* to fuck with people— literally, in the sense of having sex with them (e.g., **Bosco Hifikepunye** with **Mi-Hyun** and **Ike**'s daughter), and in the sense of fucking with their minds (e.g., **XOXO**).

A Chinean comandante decries what he calls "the selfflagellation over our affinity for **XOXO**." The shadowy death-squad leader says that, although experts routinely call **XOXO** "a resentful poet manqué who plies the epic with drugged sherbet and shoots it up with military-grade asscheese," what the God has actually done is taken a single static tableau (that of **Ike Karton** "standing on his stoop, on the prow of his hermitage, striking that contrapposto pose, in his white wifebeater, his torso totally ripped, his lustrous chestnut armpit hair wafting in the breeze, his head turned and inclined up toward the top floors of the Burj Khalifa in Dubai, from which the gaze of masturbating Goddesses casts him in a sugar frosted nimbus") and, thanks to all his filigreed interpolations (i.e., noncanonical bloopers), turned it into a massive, stupor-inducingly redundant epic, and he deserves major kudos for that. (As he's giving this interview, the severed heads of fifteen vagrant, drug-addled bards, strung together with coaxial cable, are found floating in the Passaic River under the **Pulaski** Skyway. These fifteen bards had recently signed a statement which urged aficionados of the epic to rapidly chant "**Ike, Ike, Ike, Ike, Ike**!" ("it should sound like **Popeye** laughing, or like **Billy Joel** in 'Movin' Out (Anthony's Song)'—'But working too hard can give you / A heart attack, ack, ack, ack, ack, ack'" as a way of "fucking with the mind of the mind-fucking God"—an obvious reference to **XOXO**). The notorious Chinean death-squad comandante (whose nomme de guerre is "**lol**") quickly issues the following addendum: "Don't want my previous statement to be misconstrued in any way as a condemnation of self-flagellation. If it's inconvenient to have someone else flagellate you, there's absolutely nothing wrong with flagellating yourself. It's an excellent way to relieve tension, which can increase your risk of stroke or heart attack." "When I was a kid," **lol** reminisces later, over coffee, "most of my friends loved the Macy's Thanksgiving Day Parade, but I preferred the Shia Day of Ashura processions in which young men ceremonially whip their own backs with barbed chains and razors." He says that the first movie scenes that gave him a hard-on were when seaman **John Mills** (played by **Richard Harris**) gets flogged with a cat-o'-nine-tails in *Mutiny on the Bounty* and when **Lucrèce Borgia** (played by **Martine Carol**) is whipped by her brother, **Cesare** (played by **Pedro Armendáriz**), in *Lucrèce Borgia* (aka *Sins of the Borgias*). Favorite poem? The poem **XOXO** wrote for **Shanice** about the businessman who became so terribly aroused when he was flogged in the woods by some of his colleagues ("They gang up on the 'new guy'— someone who'd only recently been transferred to their division—and, in what appears to be a sort of hazing ritual, they tie him to a tree and whip him with his own belt. His pants fall to his ankles, and it's obvious that he's aroused." Reminded that most experts interpret the poem to mean that the protagonist is aroused not by the robust flagellation, but because he sees an ineffably beautiful butterfly flit by, **lol** shakes his head vehemently. "I think he's aroused by the robust flagellation.")

The Goddesses prefer gazing at inert and immutable images ("onanistic ornaments") while they masturbate. This is why, the Chineans insist, the only significant image of **Ike** in the entirety of the epic is the one of him "standing on his stoop, on the prow of his hermitage, striking that contrapposto pose, in his white wifebeater, his torso totally ripped, his lustrous chestnut armpit hair wafting in the breeze, his head turned and inclined up toward the top floors of the Burj Khalifa in Dubai."

In an event at the Celeste Bartos Forum of the New York Public Library billed as **THE CAPO DI TUTTI FRUTTI** *in conversation with* **Lorena Bobbitt** (who was replaced at the last moment by **Malcolm Gladwell**), a man purporting to be

The Capo di Tutti Frutti (his face was covered by a bala-clava) answers the question "What do you think is the sexiest inert and immutable image?" by proposing "A photograph of a chubby, perspiring fifty-year-old woman bending over to pick up a mah-jongg tile from the floor of some cabana, co-quettishly exposing her hairy hole." This creates quite a stir, prompting some in the audience to call out their own sugges-tions: "What about a Hummel figurine of a plus-size Bavarian beer maid getting a dental X-ray, wearing a low-cut dirndl and a lead apron," someone proposes. "Some defaced plinth in a piazza," someone else says. "A magazine layout of models showing the half-chewed-up food in their mouths," says an-other. **The Capo di Tutti Frutti** (or whoever he is) glares at the audience, shaking his head vehemently. "A photograph of a chubby, perspiring fifty-year-old woman bending over to pick up a mah-jongg tile from the floor of some cabana, co-quettishly exposing her hairy hole," he repeats.

That night, thousands of rats descend on an enormous obelisk of baklava that's been erected by bearded, bare-chested intellectuals in cargo shorts to protest a significant uptick in the number of vagrant, drug-addled bards who are being slaughtered.

Tuesday: 8:00 PM Eastern
"Snapping Out"

Here, as anyone with even the faintest familiarity with *The Sugar Frosted Nutsack 2: Crème de la Sack* knows, **Vance** is supposed to snap out of his reverie and ask **Ike** whom he'd rather fuck, **Jenny Sanford** or **Silda Spitzer**. And **Ike the Kike**—"haloed martyr, edged in splendor, the stone homunculus, who never curdles into the comprehensible"—is supposed to impassively ignore the question, his eyes remaining fixed in the direction of the Burj Khalifa in Dubai, and then **Vance** is supposed to ask, "Well, who do you think are the hottest Goddesses?" prompting **Ike** to compile his "Ten Gods I'd Fuck (T.G.I.F.)" list (headed, of course, by his beloved **La Felina** and including **Lady Rukia**, **La Muñeca**, **Las Pistoleras**, and several others, including a hitherto unknown Goddess named **Hmm Uh**, who is now considered a Goddess of surpassing significance, although some experts continue to believe that "Hmm Uh" was simply what's called a "speech disfluency" or "verbal placeholder"—a meaningless interjection that **Ike** unconsciously inserted as he tried to think of other Goddesses he'd fuck). And this is the list in which **Ike** fatefully neglects to include **Shanice**, which sets into motion an inexorable concatenation of events culminating in **Ike**'s death at the hands of Mossad sharpshooters hiding among the leaves of the trees across the street from **Ike**'s hermitage.

But **Ike** doesn't compile his list. And **Vance** spins the wheel of his BMX bike, faster and faster now, sensing that everything is about to become incredibly messed up.

The highly provocative proximity of the words "balaclava" and "baklava"—the sheer fuck-you impudence of it—is a deliberate and unambiguous signal that **XOXO** is decisively

ratcheting up his sabotage of the epic. And **Vance** under-
stands, on a completely intuitive level, that the faster he spins
the BMX wheel, the faster the epic might reach its conclusion
(i.e., the masochistic, hyperviolent death of **Ike Karton**).

There's a ticking clock now (i.c., the spokes of the BMX
wheel against the empty soda can). **XOXO** is unraveling the
epic faster than the bards can recite it, which results in the
bards' increasingly high-pitched gibberish. The epic might
end without **Ike** dying (and on a Tuesday at 8:00 PM!) or
drag on inconclusively for an infinite number of seasons.
This is **XOXO** fucking with everyone's mind. He's denying
Ike his doom—**Ike**, so eager for a hero's martyrdom, virtually cataleptic yet perpetually flinging himself toward his
fate, "his spur caught in the bull-rope of his own inexorable
destiny."

XOXO finds it *amusing* to shit on the integrity of the epic,
to leave it in a state of suspended animation, a state of complete unfulfillment and nongratification, a form of eternal
Tie and Tease. He wants to leave *The Sugar Frosted Nutsack 2:
Crème de la Sack* with an epic case of blue balls. It's **XOXO**'s
ultimate mind-fuck.

XOXO thinks it's "cool" to just paralyze the whole looping, recursive epic, with all its excruciating redundancies,
heavy-handed, stilted tropes and wearying clichés, its overwrought angst, all its gnomic non sequiturs, all its off-putting
adolescent scatology and cringe-inducing smuttiness, all the
depraved tableaus and orgies of masturbation with all their
bulging, spurting shapes, and all the compulsive repetitions
about **Freud**'s repetition compulsion...

At this point, **XOXO** is blocking blood flow into the brains of the bards. **XOXO** is giving the bards TIAs (transient ischemic attacks) which are miniature temporary strokes and which are causing the bards to forget vast sections of the epic and simply spout high-pitched gibberish (i.e., nonlexical vocables). Of course, the fact that **XOXO** is giving the bards "ministrokes" which are causing the bards to forget vast sections of the epic and spout high-pitched gibberish is a now a crucial part of the epic, which audiences at public recitations expect the bards to "belt out like the cast of some Broadway musical." The bards are now expected to "belt out" that **XOXO** is expunging the epic in its entirety from their memories, to "belt out" that the hyperviolent death of **Ike Karton** might now be endlessly deferred.

Some bards simply start making up phrases suggested by the letters of license plates on passing cars, and attempting to pass *that* off as "the epic."

DYS:	Dad, you suck
AED:	Actress / Egg Donor
ZUP:	Zipped-up pussy
BFV:	Best fisting video
ITM:	Impeccable table manners
VNN:	Vaginas Need Nivea
JNU:	Jews Never Unite
WNN:	Welcome Nude Nigerians
CSC:	Cossack Saddle Cabbage
YWB:	You Wiggle Beautifully

CUR: Can't Understand Reality
SRL: Sadist Rapes Limbaugh
MMU: My Mom Ululates
AAJ: Anime Amputee Jamboree

A Volvo wagon (THG-87F), an old Toyota Corolla (IKR-53J), and a little blue Mazda Miata (HAH-19B) drive past.

THG: They're hot guys.
IKR: I know, right?
HAH: Hot as hell.

Two more cars: TSH-74P, SFH-19N.

TSH: They're so high.
SFH: So fuckin' high.

In response to a spate of violent crimes and growing concern that the encampments are breeding grounds for **Meir Poznak**'s extremist organization, *T.S.F.N.—General Command,* police today evacuated 1,000 vagrant, drug-addled bards in 251 caravans in southwestern France. More than 40 camps have been dismantled in the last fifteen days, and 700 vagrant, drug-addled bards are being sent back to Jersey City and the Upper Peninsula on chartered flights. Vagrant, drug-addled bards (blindfolded even though they're already blind) continuously chant *The Sugar Frosted Nutsack 2: Crème de la Sack* on their chartered flight from southwestern France to Jersey City International Airport (on West Side Avenue, at the corner of Culver).

These measures came after bards in southwestern France burned cars and a police station, following the death of a blind, blitzed-out bard who was shot by a husband whose wife had just left him for the bard at a public recitation of *The Sugar Frosted Nutsack 2: Crème de la Sack*. The jilted husband almost immediately gouged out his own eyes and became a bard. He continuously chanted *The Sugar Frosted Nutsack 2: Crème de la Sack* (including, of course, this sentence) during his arraignment until the judge threatened him with a laryngectomy.

Bards are also being recalled because of "quality-control problems" (i.e., not blind, vagrant, or drug-addled, lacking chunky chachkas, etc.). **Ken Howard**, president of the Screen Actors Guild (SAG), said that he "must reassure disappointed aficionados of the epic and persuade them to once again attend public recitations." **Howard** said that *The Sugar Frosted Nutsack 2: Crème de la Sack* owed its first responsibility to the unkempt, hairy, sweaty, heavyset, middle-aged women who'd left their husbands for vagrant, drug-addled bards. *The Sugar Frosted Nutsack 2: Crème de la Sack* has since revamped and centralized its quality-control operations, installing state-of-the-art molybdenum-steel melon ballers for double eye enucleations and a strictly enforced policy of random drug-testing of bards to ensure that they are blind and blitzed-out.

Tuesday: 9:00 PM Eastern
"Vandalizing the Denouement"

XOXO is vandalizing the epic's denouement, a denouement that's been foretold and basically guaranteed for thousands of years by blind, blitzed-out bards beating time with their chunky chachkas against jerrycans of orange soda. He's plying the denouement with drugged sherbet. He's giving the denouement an enormous military-grade ass-cheese enema.

As anyone with even the faintest familiarity with *The Sugar Frosted Nutsack 2: Crème de la Sack* knows, **Ike** is supposed to make a lewd mandala of Italian breadcrumbs for the Goddess **La Felina**, and then engage in an extended adagio with the waitress at the Miss America Diner, and write his narcocorrido, "That's Me (**Ike**'s Song)." And then he's supposed to get high with his daughter's boyfriend, **Vance**, and make a list for him called "Ten Gods I'd Fuck (T.G.I.F)," and neglect to include **Shanice**, which incurs her eternal enmity (FYI: **La Felina** was #1 on his list).

And then the scorned Goddess is supposed to wage a vindictive campaign against **Ike** that begins with her inducing the zoning board to ban Ike's latest pornographic monument to **La Felina**—"a teetering monolith of marzipan." ("Ike laughs, gathering up his notes and tapping them against the table into a tidy stack: 'Look, guys…you're fated to authorize the demolition of my pornographic monument to **La Felina**. I'm fated to die in the confrontation outside my

221

modest two-story hermitage after performing my narcocorrido with my band, **The Kartons**. So why don't we just get this over with?'")

(But, of course, **XOXO**—who fucks with your mind, who will discomfit any denouement—is preventing everyone from "just getting this over with.")

And then **Koji Mizokami** is supposed to help **Ike** shoplift an Akai MPC drum machine from a Sam Ash on Route 4 in Paramus, New Jersey, and **Bosco Hifikepunye** begins supplying **Vance** with the hallucinogenic drug Gravy to sell on the street. And **La Felina** promises **Ike** that before he martyrs himself, she'll appear to him in human form and fuck him, and she says she'll get in touch with him on his cellphone and let him know exactly when and where.

And then a God (very possibly **Bosco Hifikepunye**) is supposed to impregnate **Ike**'s teenage daughter while **Ike** is interviewing for a butcher's job at Costco. (**Ike** says to the Costco meat department manager re: his relationship with the Goddesses: "I'm just a fantasy they jerk off to." Explaining a gap in his resume, he says that during Spring Break in 1989 he was hit by a *Mister Softee* truck, but told police that it was a Hasidic ambulance in an effort to foment an apocalyptic Helter Skelter–type war between club kids and Hasids. And, in response to a question about his "availability," **Ike** tells him that he can only work for a week because he's going to be killed on Friday by Mossad sharpshooters.)

Then **Ike** is supposed to accidentally kill his father as they wrestle for **Ike**'s cellphone because **Ike**'s father is trying to change **Ike**'s ringtone from "Me So Horny" to **John**

Cage's *4'33"*—the composer's notorious "silent composition," which would almost certainly ensure that **Ike** misses **La Felina**'s call, which, for **Ike**, is "the booty-call of a lifetime."

(None of this is going to happen, of course, as anyone with even the faintest familiarity with *The Sugar Frosted Nutsack 2: Crème de la Sack* knows, because it all has to be set in motion by **Ike** making his list of *Ten Gods I'd Fuck (T.G.I.F.)*, which **XOXO** is thwarting in his effort to sabotage the epic.)

And on the morning of his father's funeral, **Ike** is supposed to wake up with an incredibly gross case of conjunctivitis, and then try to pull the pillars of the synagogue down and crush the congregation, and then his daughter is supposed to give birth to a half-divine, half-mortal infant named **Colter Dale**. ("**Colter Dale**'s teenage mom is not even pregnant for two whole days—she got pregnant on Tuesday night and gave birth on Thursday night, about forty hours later. Even hamsters and marsupial cats have longer gestation periods! This preternaturally truncated pregnancy could simply be the result of the exceedingly clever way that episodic reality is edited (see TLC's *I Didn't Know I Was Pregnant* and MTV's *Teen Mom*), or it could point to a wider trend that experts are noticing in which very young mothers, after preternaturally truncated pregnancies, are giving birth to precociously mature infants who almost immediately get pregnant or father children themselves, each generation a miniature version of that which preceded them. This is being called *The Russian Nesting Doll* or *Matryoshka Doll Phenomenon*. Shorter and shorter gestation periods for pregnant teens who are giving birth to precociously mature infants may not be the result of endocrine-disrupting chemicals like polybrominated biphenyls or phthalates or high-fructose corn syrup or smartphone radiation, as experts have previously proposed, but may actually be caused by military-grade ass-cheese and Gravy leaching into the water supply.")

And soon after that, the **The Kartons** are supposed to begin their "Last Concert" (which is also their *first* concert). **Ike**, who has refused to suspend work on his banned monument, his "teetering monolith of marzipan," wears an impenetrable, bulletproof protective groin cup, fashioned for him by **Bosco Hifikepunye**, the God of Miscellany (Fibromyalgia, Chicken Tenders, Sports Memorabilia, SteamVac Carpet Cleaners, etc.), at the behest of **La Felina**. "This is the first single from our new album, *Folie à Famille*," **Ike** says in his raspy, almost inaudible whisper. "We call it a 'narcocorrido' because it's about mortal men who traffic in Gravy." **Ike**'s daughter plays her bass guitar tuned to cello standard tuning, in intervals of fifths (C–G–D–A) using a banjo string for the high A. She's recently been seen using a five-string setup, tuned to C–G–D–A–E, with banjo strings for the A and E.

After the performance of the narcocorrido, **Ike** is supposed to retreat back into his hermitage. Rocking **Colter Dale**'s cradle as canisters of nebulized military-grade ass-cheese and 3-Methylfentanyl (the aerosolized fentanyl derivative that Russian Spetsnaz forces used against Chechen separatists in the 2002 Moscow theater hostage crisis) shatter the living room window, he taps his ring on the tabletop, and, blind from the gas, begins chanting *The Sugar Frosted Nutsack 2: Crème de la Sack* to the infant, in its entirety, from the very beginning: "There was never *nothing*. But before the debut of the Gods, about fourteen billion years ago, things happened without any discernable context. There were no recognizable patterns. It was all incoherent. Isolated, disjointed events would take place, only to be engulfed by an opaque black void, their relative meaning, their *significance*, annulled by the eons of entropic silence that estranged one from the next. A terrarium containing three tiny teenage girls mouthing a lot of high-pitched gibberish (like **Mothra**'s fairies, except for their wasted pallors, acne, big tits, and T-shirts that read "I Don't Do White Guys") would inexplicably materialize, and then, just as inexplicably, disappear...." And using his distinctive periodontal curette, the God **XOXO** engraves the epic into the smooth tabula rasa of **Colter Dale**'s mind.... (**Colter Dale** (half-divine) is immune to the nebulized mixture of military-grade ass-cheese and 3-Methylfentanyl that the Mossad is pumping into the hermitage.)

Ike is then supposed to go back outside, "opening the front door onto his stoop, stepping into the maddeningly bright klieg lights of the Mossad," take out his pistol, wave it—making looping figures in the air to signal all his Goddesses that his "climactic moment is nigh"—and fire wildly into the treetops.

There are supposed to be scores of Mossad sharpshooters, hundreds perhaps—they were supposed to have been abseiling onto rooftops and into the trees from black helicopters. They each aim for the hero's sugar frosted nutsack, and **Ike**, laughing, whistling the *Mister Softee* jingle ("those recursive, foretokening measures of music; that hypnotic riff") over and over and over and over again to himself, amid this fusillade of gunfire...until a sniper's coup de grace to the head....This was supposed to be **Ike Karton**'s fate—dying to an orgasmic chorus of masturbating Goddesses. This was a scene that had replayed in his mind over and over and over and over again since he was a boy. **Ike Karton**—riddled, infested, consumed, devoured by Gods.

Experts wonder if **Ike** thinks his neighbors will rise up on his behalf. ("What does he imagine? Cheering crowds? Fluttering flags?") But they don't. They shutter themselves up in their identical, brick, two-story houses and peer out from timid apertures in their drapes and blinds and watch **Ike**, the pariah, haranguing the Mossad and murmuring lascivious things to all his heavyset Goddesses, as bullets bounce off his magic groin cup, creating a mesmerizing beat...until a sniper's coup de grace to the head.

And then, years later, seated at the kitchen table, **Colter Dale** is supposed to compose his "Coda": "To Whom It May Concern: That the Gods only occur in **Ike**'s mind is not a refutation of their actuality. It is, on the contrary, irrefutable proof of their empirical existence. The Gods *choose* to only exist in **Ike**'s mind. They are real by virtue of this, their prerogative. Yours, **Colter Dale**, aka **Ahab, King of the Ants** (**Reichsführer of the Upper Peninsula**), age nine."

And none of this is going to happen, of course, as anyone with even the faintest familiarity with *The Sugar Frosted Nutsack 2: Crème de la Sack* knows, because it all has to be set in motion by **Ike** making his list of *Ten Gods I'd Fuck (T.G.I.F.)*, which **XOXO** is thwarting in his effort to sabotage the epic.

In place of this traditional sequence of events (foretold and guaranteed by blind, blitzed-out bards for thousands of years) **XOXO** nonchalantly interpolates a miscellany of spurious scenes:

- Paratroopers, in hooded leather S&M bondage outfits and armed with automatic weapons, are dropped into Jersey City one night.
- While batting flies (and imagined nano-drones) from his armpits, as the glassy-eyed **Vance** spins his BMX bike wheel, **Ike** mentions the fact, apropos of nothing, that "Hanukkah menorah" and "labia minora" rhyme.
- **Ike** goes in to see his urologist to get his prostate biopsy results. The urologist tells **Ike** that he has low-range prostate cancer with a Gleason score of 3/3 in one out of twelve cores. Hilarity ensues. When the urologist tells **Ike** that it's a slow-growing cancer ("You'll probably die of something else long before this"), **Ike** tells him, "Yes, I'm destined to be killed by Mossad sharpshooters this Friday." The urologist then advises "Active Surveillance"—a term used for a conservative treatment modality that **Ike** misinterprets as proof that the urologist *is* a Mossad agent. After threatening to sodomize the urologist and, for several side-splitting minutes, chasing him around the office, **Ike** settles for giving him a "taste of his own medicine"— an extremely rough digital exam during which **Ike** actu-

ally detects a hard nodule in the urologist's prostate. The urologist has a follow-up biopsy, which yields a Gleason of 1/5 in seven out of twelve cores, etc.

- A Goddess helps **Ike** shop for jeans. (**Ike** holds two pairs up to the sky: "Do you like these or *these*?")
- **Ike** sneezes so hard that it momentarily unfurls his rectum out his asshole like a New Year's Eve party blower.
- **La Felina**, watching **Ike** do a set of lat pulldowns, produces an orgasmic torrent of paraurethral fluid so forceful that it reminds many baby boomers of the water cannon used to disperse civil rights marchers in southern states during the 1960s.
- Three bearded, bare-chested men in cargo shorts come up to **Ike**. "We'll give you all the gold in the world in return for your daughter's firstborn baby." **Ike** kills them and bakes them into pies, which he puts on the windowsill of his hermitage to cool. When he returns from the gym, there are only two pies. "Who stole my pie?!" he thunders.
- **Ike** has a long, Pinteresque dinner with his elderly father ("like two stammering antagonists in a Pinter play"), who's wearing a red *lucha libre* mask. (It's hard to imagine **Ike**'s favorite topics of conversation—masturbating heavyset Goddesses, the interpenetration of sex and death, Ukrainian women sumo wrestlers, the demise of the Professional Women's Bowling Association, how sexy **Kim Clijsters** looks at the end of a hard-fought third-set tiebreaker, etc.—holding any interest for a man like his father.) "You don't think that being the inducer of a form of *folie à famille* makes me a more *interesting* person?" **Ike**

smiles wolfishly, an incisor gleaming in the candlelight, then bats his eyes coquettishly, trying to make his father laugh, trying to defuse the situation. **Ike** waves the fork crazily in his father's face, "I'll gouge out your eyeballs, you senile fuck." "Is that any way to speak to your father?" he replies. Waitress: "Would the schizo with the spasmodic torticollis like another whiskey?" "**Ikie** want whiskey?" parrots the father, who's brushing his teeth at the table, the senile old man in a red *lucha libre* mask. His mouth is foamy. There's an occasional squeal of feedback from his hearing aid. ("Of course **Ike** had been drinking, which clouded his thinking, and though his judgment was impaired, none of his feelings were spared...")

- **XOXO** kidnaps **Ike**'s and his father's souls and takes them to his hyperborean hermitage, where he plies them with drugged sherbet and gives their souls innumerable little hickies, like little chigger bites. **Ike** is presented with the coveted Sugar Frosted Nutsack, which is usually represented as either a military medal similar to the Croix de Guerre or the Iron Cross, or an entertainment industry award, like the Golden Globe or the People's Choice Award statuette.

- **La Felina** tells **Ike** that **Fast-Cooking Ali** is gay (a "couturier"). Only a gay man could have designed Woman's Ass. She denies ever having been sexually attracted to him. "He's too sophisticated. His mind is too agile and nuanced, his sensibility is too refined and delicate. He's too petite. Too ethereal. Too patrician."

Far from finding such scenes stupefyingly disjointed (and, as anyone with even the faintest familiarity with *The Sugar Frosted Nutsack 2: Crème de la Sack* knows, these are exactly the sort of stupefyingly disjointed scenes that **XOXO** delights in recklessly strewing throughout the epic), audiences at public recitations demand that vagrant, drug-addled bards (those dwindlingly few vagrant, drug-addled bards who have survived all the Chinean-inspired anti-bard violence) chant these very noncanonical bloopers in their entirety, demanding, in fact, that the surviving bards belt them out like the cast of some Broadway musical to the exclusion of the rest of the epic (i.e., the canonical bloopers), prompting one expert to describe this "neo-epic" (that is, this version of the epic purged of everything *but* noncanonical bloopers) as a "labyrinth of corridors invariably culminating in a flooded men's room."

Vance spins the wheel of his **BMX** bike, and in the blurred strobe of its spokes, as **Vance** spins faster and faster and faster, you can just barely discern the inchoate contours (i.e., "early drafts") of everything that's about to happen.

The mesmerizing metronomic beat of the spokes ticking against the empty Sunkist can.... They are SO high. This Gravy is super-potent. It's military-grade Gravy. Their eyes are glazed over and orange dribble runs down their chins.

Along with the humming hyperreality of being so high in the glare of a midsummer's day, there's an unmistakable overtone of impending violence and revelation.

They're SO high.

They're SO FUCKING high.

Wednesday: 8:00 PM Eastern
"A Mule with a Red Bonnet"

Three more cars go by. License plates: AGV-66N, OAM-17W, RMP-45Y.

AGV:	A grainy video
OAM:	of a man
RMP:	resembling **Meir Poznak**

A grainy video...of a man...resembling **Meir Poznak**...

A grainy video of a man resembling **Meir Poznak**, ex-bard and leader of the hard-line anti-**XOXO** paramilitary organization *T.S.F.N.—General Command,* based in Jersey City, has surfaced on the Internet in recent days and shows him announcing his retirement in favor of a mule in a red bonnet.

The man, bearded and wearing fatigues, is shown seated in a wooded area, next to a mule in a red bonnet, identified as his successor.

In December, **Poznak** was nearly assassinated by a nanny from Côte d'Ivoire pushing a stroller rigged with explosives.

A few of the dwindlingly few vagrant, drug-addled bards who have survived all the Chinean-inspired anti-bard violence are partying at a crowded club in West Hollywood (Les Deux). Throbbing dance music.

"Quiet!" one hisses to the others, covering his cellphone. "It's **Meir Poznak**!"

Poznak recites the following lines:

> *Everything that's screwed in*
> *Or glued together*
> *Is coming apart*
> *At the same time.*

The next day, **The Capo di Tutti Frutti** is found dead in the underground parking lot of his apartment complex. His hands had been bound and his head bludgeoned with a bat. His entrails had been eaten. Police suspect that a God ate his entrails because fingerprints on packets of tartar sauce found near the body were not human, and because fresh mounds of loot drops (or "God guano") had been discovered in the woods nearby.

Wednesday: 9:00 PM Eastern
"The Ascendancy of **Hmm Uh**"

Hmm Uh, who inauspiciously began her career as a gob of phlegm on the street ("some guy on the street hawks up a big gob of phlegm and spits it on the sidewalk, and **Ike** stops, and he kneels down, and he says to the gob of phlegm, 'Fräulein, my band, **The Kartons**, is giving a Final Concert later this week, and I'd be very much honored if you would attend'") and then inexplicably reappeared in the guise of a "speech disfluency" or "verbal placeholder," has suddenly (within, say, the past two minutes) become perhaps the single most influential Goddess in the history of the *Sugar Frosted Nutsack* pantheon (that "moaning menagerie"). "Impertinent with the scope of her new power, she burns with the inferiority complex of a former hawked-up gob of phlegm and speech disfluency." She's now the paramount Goddess. Elected to the post of General Secretary of the Central Committee of the Communist Party of the Goddesses, **Hmm Uh** requests several days' leave to engage in a celebratory series of drunken bisexual orgies, conducted first in one of the world's largest open-pit asbestos mines in a town in south-central Quebec called Thetford Mines, and then in a succession of squalid gas station lavatories along Interstate 19 in Arizona. The Goddess **La Felina**, "champion of the sans-culottes and scum of the earth," is said to be partying with **Hmm Uh**. Other debauched participants in the drunken bisexual orgies are said to include: creepy, unsavory looking porcelain Hummel figurines brought to life, leprechauns with disproportionately large, erect phalluses jutting out from their green breeches...and...umm... *Transformers* robots with huge, unruly tufts of fern-like pubic hair sprouting from their crotches like weird fucking Chia Pets—although, according to an updated report in *USA Today*, this is *not* true.

Hmm Uh looks half-Russian, half-Korean. She has a perpetually salacious grin on her big, round face. Big-haired, buxom, retroussé-nosed, she is simple and unlettered (and depraved).

It's amazing how prescient the Chineans were, how uncannily they anticipated the ascendancy of a Goddess like **Hmm Uh**. Yes, **Hmm Uh** is zaftig, hairy, and uninformed, but she is refreshingly young (early twenties) and much, much more cheerful than the gloomy and world-weary "chubby, sweaty, hairy, unkempt, and uneducated middle-aged women" who'd habituated the epic up until now.

Now **Hmm Uh**—patron Goddess of Inarticulation and Illegibility, of High-Pitched Gibberish, Nonlexical Vocables, and Hysterical Spastic Aphonia—is the star of her own reality show. She's the only woman on an offshore drilling rig, thirty miles out in the Kara Sea, an icebound Arctic coastal backwater north of central Russia. Total darkness engulfs the region in the winter. Hilarity and puerile boorishness ensue as **Hmm Uh** entertains fifty super-horny, frequently drunk, and stir-crazy Russian oil workers. "The waters of the Arctic are particularly perilous for drilling because of the extreme cold, long periods of darkness, dense fogs, and hurricane-strength winds. Pervasive ice cover for eight to nine months out of the year can block relief ships in case of a blowout....Until recently, Russia regarded the Kara Sea as primarily an icy dump. For years, the Soviet navy released nuclear waste into the sea, including several spent submarine reactors that were dropped overboard at undisclosed locations," according to a report in the *New York Times* by **Andrew E. Kramer** and **Clifford Krauss**.

Hmm Uh, who used to spend Spring Breaks at Novaya

Zemlya, an Arctic testing site for nuclear weapons during the Cold War, says, "Radiation isn't so bad. I think it makes men better at sex."

Wednesday: 10:00 PM Eastern
"**Meir Poznak**: Behind the Music"

Meir Poznak begins to seriously, almost obsessively, ponder the idea of "fucking with the mind of the mind-fucking God." He begins to think about whether it's somehow possible to subvert **XOXO**, the God who subverts almost everything we think. He wonders whether it might be possible to inoculate the epic *against* **XOXO** with denatured infusions *of* **XOXO**, or whether a form of mithridatism might actually be feasible (i.e., protecting the epic against the poison *of* **XOXO** by gradually administering nonlethal amounts *of* **XOXO**). Of course, he has to concede, there are myriad enemies, real and perceived. The world of *The Sugar Frosted Nutsack 2: Crème de la Sack* is a world of paranoia. There are endless provocateurs. Endless spies and traitors. Double, triple, and quadruple agents. But behind it all, pulling the strings and tying it all into knots, is **XOXO**. **Vance** and **Ruthie** and the **Daughter** (whose name is withheld because she's a minor) and her unborn son, **Colter Dale**, have all been suddenly and unceremoniously "deported" from the epic and turned into football hooligans. (**Vance** because **Mogul Magoo** bristled at the notion that a street-level Gravy dealer was thought to be a God by the Chineans. **Ruthie** and the **Daughter** for their own protection? Or because they became superfluous? There's no consensus among the experts.) **Vance** ends up in Serbia, where he joins the *Grobari* ("Gravediggers"), a gang of violent thugs associated with the Belgrade club FK Partizan. **Colter Dale**, a Liverpool Football Club fanatic, actually strangles his unborn twin brother (a Manchester United fan) to death in utero, using their mother's umbilical cord. Put a stethoscope to the **Daughter**'s pregnant belly and you can hear a drunken **Colter Dale** singing the Liverpool FC anthem, "You'll Never Walk Alone," over and over and over again ("When you walk through a storm / Keep your chin up high / Etc., etc."). **XOXO**'s "disappearing" of **Vance**, **Ruthie**, the **Daughter**, and **Colter Dale** guts the band **The Kartons**, leaving **Ike** a solo act, which, at the end of the day, is what he so quintessentially is anyway. **Meir Poznak**, as anyone with even the faintest familiarity with *The Sugar Frosted Nutsack 2: Crème de la Sack* knows, is seriously, almost obsessively, pondering all this...pondering exactly how he might fuck with the mind of the mind-fucking God.

He's skinny and fidgety and humming constantly, he's only eating fish food (the red and gold flakes). In a conversation with his brother on the morning of *Super Bowl LVI*, he says he's lost his interest in listening to music and talking to people. He says he might castrate himself (i.e., explore "nongenital sexuality"). He complains bitterly about "the whole balaclava/baklava thing" and says that **XOXO** is making everyone connected with the epic "look bad." When his brother asks what he's been doing with himself lately, he says "checking my ant traps" and "analyzing adjourned positions" (i.e., grappling with the ramifications of fucking with the mind of **XOXO**). He says that he wants to tear himself in half like **Rumpelstiltskin**. **Aaron Poznak** describes his brother as being "extremely, extremely disturbed by the proximity of the words 'balaclava' and 'baklava.'"

Later that day, an expert cadges a lone cigarette from a vacant-eyed dockworker and tentatively approaches. "**Meir Poznak** was especially upset and angry about the proximity of those words, which he said were part of a smear campaign against the epic, and he wanted to do something about it, by which I assumed he meant do something about **XOXO**," says the expert, who speaks on the condition of anonymity because of the delicacy in discussing a major mind-fucking God's mind possibly getting fucked.

During a hiatus of **Hmm Uh**'s reality show, **Meir Poznak** clandestinely rendezvouses with the Goddess of inarticulation and nonlexical vocables at her dacha in Paramus, New Jersey, and, for hours, pleasures her with his fingers and his mouth and the veiny two-headed latex toys he brings her.

The Gods (except for **Hmm Uh** and **La Felina**, who are out partying) have temporarily relocated from the top floors of the 2,717-foot, 160-story Burj Khalifa in Dubai to the bowels of the Compact Muon Solenoid, a particle detector buried in an underground cavern beneath the Large Hadron Collider in Cessy, France, just across the border from Geneva, as they await the construction of the next world's tallest building, either the 3,284-foot, 250-story Burj Mubarak al Kabir at Madinat al-Hareer (Silk

City) in Subiya, Kuwait, or the 3,200-foot, 166-story Miapolis on Watson Island in Biscayne Bay, just west of Miami Beach— whichever goes up first. The Gods and Goddesses ride the particle accelerator, like kids on the Bizarro megacoaster at Six Flags New England—over and over and over again—and each becomes a subatomic, one-dimensional oscillating string.

Thursday: 8:00 PM Eastern
"Fucking the Mind of the Mind-Fucking God"

Ike is standing on his stoop, staring off into space, thinking about which heavyset, hairy Goddesses he'd like to fuck.... **Ike**—who never curdles into the comprehensible, whose willful anonymity and implacable hostility toward celebrities and desire for the bodies of women who dislike their bodies make him the favorite of **La Felina**, the patron Goddess of street scum and sans-culottes—is now exquisitely aware of the imminence of his fate. And there he stands on his stoop—alone, somber, dignified.

A distant cackling **Popeye** ("**Ike Ike Ike Ike Ike**"), the *Mister Softee* jingle, the sound of the fetus **Colter Dale** singing "You'll Never Walk Alone" from within the womb of his teenage mom...it's all speeding up now, this fucked-up caffeinated cacophony, in reverse, as **XOXO** tries to expunge the epic—with all its excruciating redundancies, heavy-handed, stilted tropes, and wearying clichés, its overwrought angst, all its gnomic non sequiturs, all its off-putting adolescent scatology and cringe-inducing smuttiness, all the depraved tableaus and orgies of masturbation with all their bulging, spurting shapes, and all the compulsive repetitions about **Freud**'s repetition compulsion—faster than the last surviving bard can recite it.

The spokes of the spinning BMX wheel hitting the empty can, that accelerating beat, the high-pitched gibberish of the horseflies (those buxom nymphs) and the transported babel of all those gasping, orgasming Goddesses...

Meir Poznak walks past the Miss America Diner, east on Culver Avenue, turns right on Towers, strides up the stairs to the stoop of the two-story brick hermitage, pulls out a semi-automatic pistol, and shoots **Ike Karton** in the face.

At that moment, war conches are sounded. **Ike** searches for his Goddesses, readjusting his gaze with three sharp, reptilian ratchets of his head, first toward the Large Hadron Collider in Cessy, France (just across the border from Geneva), then toward south-central Quebec, then a Chevron station in Nogales, Arizona. At that moment, **Meir Poznak**, first-person shooter, pupils dilated, trained by Russian Spetsnaz forces, a guy who is determined to fuck with the mind of the mind-fucking God, a guy who, after a clandestine tête-à-tête with **Hmm Uh**—the Goddess of Inarticulation and Nonlexical Vocables—fully commits himself to consummating his love for **Ike Karton**, strides up the stairs to that stoop, and shoots and kills **Ike Karton**. At that moment, the war conches are sounded, and the high-pitched gibberish of tiny iridescent-winged nymphs and nano-drones and swarms of bold-faced notables (with their rising chorus of nonlexical vocables) is like a hissing crescendo of white noise.

The Ballad of the Last of the Severed Bard-Heads

Oh fuck, **Ike Karton** *est mort!*
Pa rum pum pum pum, rum pa pum pum.
Got shot point-blank with a Glock 34!
It's all about the dum dum de da dum dum!
Ike Karton *is dead.*
Schlemiel schlimazel! Hong Kong ping-pong!
The 9 mm round entered his eye and exited out the back of his head.
Ding a ding a dang a dong dong ding dong!
Ding a ding a dang a ding dang dong!

Highest Rated Comments

I had a threesome to this song.

> Svetlana Stalin 1 month ago

Wow...Even though it uses nonlexical vocables, it's REALLY moving...I'm actually crying. Takes me back in time to better days. Thanks for posting this.

> Mark McGuire 10 months ago

Lick my legs, I'm on fire.

> PJ Harvey 19 years ago

Where are my shoes? I've got to see the Captain.

> Harvey Cheyne Jr. (played by Freddie Bartholomew)
> in *Captains Courageous* 75 years ago

Kill the white man, and take his women.

> Dr. Fu Manchu (played by Boris Karloff)
> in *The Mask of Fu Manchu* 80 years ago

Friday: 10:00 AM Eastern
"**Ike**'s Funeral: Live Coverage"

A small group of mourners attends **Ike**'s funeral: **Hadassah Lieberman**, **Barry Bonds**, SAG president **Ken Howard**, **Andrew Cuomo**...

Several eulogists wistfully remind the thin trickle of mourners (basically **Lieberman**, **Bonds**, SAG president **Ken Howard**, and **Cuomo**) that **Ike** "never congealed into the comprehensible" and "liked the bodies of women who didn't like their bodies" and was "perpetually flinging himself toward his fate."

And they reminisce about how **Ike** used to sit at the kitchen table in the early morning, not writing letters or composing narcocorridos, but making lists—lists of which celebrities he thought should be guillotined, which should go to the gulag, which should be rehabilitated, etc. This was also called **Ike** "going into the forest to gather wild garlic," **Ike** "soaking in his own marinade" or **Ike** "drinking his own bath water."

Excerpts from the Eulogies

"**Ike** is on a bus headed uncannily for the abyss—such is his largesse, his desire to share his death wish with others, i.e., his brothers, who dig his maudlin quest for martyrdom and queue up to join him literally loin-to-loin in stardom, his weary one-way ride to his last stop, his long-awaited suicide-by-cop, much ballyhooed in Bollywood and headed straight for the vicinity of infinity."

"**Ike**'s eyes roll back in his head as he's ravaged—the conquistador as comestible, like Magellan devoured by cannibals and savages."

"Those moaning, self-flagellated phantasms, having all their apocalyptic orgasms, those marathon sessions of seizures, those deathless, mirthless masturbators, so provocatively posed in their marble pantyhose."

"This was just the aristocratic, autoerotic attitude of those whose hot buttocks were the pure products of the imagination of the God who'd invented the platitude."

"**Ike**—marionette, umbilicated to his Goddesses, murmuring in a language garnished with umlauts."

"His birth as an object of divine desire, and his death— the Goddesses sated—supine and on fire, hated by his neighbors."

"This shit's retarded. It's *The Ballad of the Last of the Severed Bard-Heads*. 'It's not toasted, it's Pop-Tarted,' **Ike** boasted to all his drug-addled, big-dick bards (the Ultra-Penis Committee) from the Upper Peninsula and Jersey City. *Denken und Dichtung,* that high-pitched drone. 'It is a far, far better rest that I go to than

I have ever known,' he says, quoting **Dickens**, quieting down **Colter Dale**, quaffing Dewars, getting tight, looking radiant in night-vision goggles and a 'tight T-shirt'—'TTS' on the Missouri license plate, which has a light-blue gradient and says 'Show-Me State.' He hates celebrities and all their wealth, and he flexes his biceps and he flagellates himself. He secretly ate flanken, like an Inquisitor and a Marrano both wrapped into one, which is why it says that 'suicide-by-cop sounds fun.'"

"The quintessential heroic visionary, quiet and quick to violence, brainstorming with mice and swans in Paranoid Park, near a man-made hill. 'Remember,' he says, without moving his lips, even keeping his Adam's apple still, 'when all the old, decrepit waiters at **XOXO**'s Dantean *Hooters* were summarily shot to death by Mossad sharpshooters?' And some weird little guy whom one of the mice glimpses out of the corner of his eye—some fat little spy on a bicycle path, snapping photos—hunches over to laugh like **Quasimodo** getting a Gatorade bath on the sideline. And **Ike**, like stone, like a scrimshaw statue honed out of white whale bone, cataleptic but analytic, and incredulous at his own indigenous Jersey City perspicacity, thinks to himself, Once I get all my guillotines deployed and rendezvous with my producer, **Fast-Cooking Ali**, let's see who calls me paranoid and the inducer of a folie à famille."

"**Ike** dreams of surprising **La Felina** in a Korean sauna, or the subproletarian wife of some bard, or coming upon any matronly lady marbled with lard, sweating in a place that's sweltering, any place where there's no tradition of air-conditioning or adequate ventilation, where there's a draconian prohibition on deodorant and showering, like a women's penal colony on a former coffee plantation, where the rich aroma of large, self-pleasuring women is overpowering and intoxicates Mossad sharpshooters in guard towers, and where even a hydrocephalic moron can get a hypertrophic hard-on lasting more than four hours."

"The jubilant blaze of masochistic martyrdom and orgasm, like some fabulous hissing centripetal fireball of molten marble, forms a high-pitched, accelerating vortex of seizures and spasms that pulls this clique of masturbating Goddesses from the Large Hadron Collider into **Ike**'s sugar frosted nutsack, like a highly concentrated, coruscating cascade of hypothetical particles, these Goddesses who are masturbating to naked photos of **Ike**, even though they say they're just reading the articles, into **Ike**'s sugar frosted nutsack, where, like an interlooping troupe of parasitic worms or writhing embroidered runes, they agree to synchronize the oscillations of their original orgasms, so as to produce ever more seizures and more spasms."

* * *

This final section the mourners chant backward, in memory of **Ike** having "continuously pulled himself out of his own ass, inside-out":

*Smsaps erom dna seruzies erom reve ecudorp ot sa os, smsagro lanigiro rieht fo snoitallicso eht ezinorhcnys ot eerga yeht, senur derediorbme gnihtirw ro smrow citisarap fo epuort gnipoolretni na ekil, erehw, kcastun detsorf ragus S'**eki** otni . . .*

In an interview after the funeral, **Hmm Uh**, the Goddess born of hawked-up phlegm and risen from the lowest-of-the-low to become the single most influential Goddess in the pantheon ("that moaning menagerie"), is asked whether **Ike Karton** and **Meir Poznak** (seemingly so different— **Ike** austere, taciturn, inscrutable; **Meir** flamboyant, loquacious, explicit) could, in a sense, be considered one and the same person (since they abet each other's fates with such uncanny reciprocity). The divine celebutante answers, "Hmm . . . uh . . . kinda, I guess."

Experts were abuzz recently over a video that was posted online purportedly showing **Ike Karton** and **Meir Poznak** as teenagers at the Newport Mall in Jersey City: both boys were wearing black pants, identical padded and oversize cargo coats, and matching brown fur hats. The date of the video is unknown, although judging from the horses tied to posts and the honky-tonk piano version of "The Ballad of the Last of the Severed Bard-Heads" that's audible every time the doors of the saloon swing open, it appears to have been shot in the late 1870s.

Saturday: 3:00 AM Eastern
"The Sugar Frosted Nutsack 3: **Hmm Uh** (Rig Diva): The Fitted Cap"

The most enduring legacy of *The Sugar Frosted Nutsack 3: Hmm Uh (Rig Diva)*—which is what most experts now consider to be the authentic title of the epic—may well be the fitted cap.

This unique, custom-fitted cap (95% wool, 5% cotton) features a gleaming "textured" white crown and visor— a *trompe l'oeil* corrugation (think super-close-up of a Frosted Mini-Wheat, abstracted into a scrotal topography). Embroidered (raised) over this glittering, puckered white dome (signifying, of course, "the sugar frosted nutsack")—and foregrounded in such glaring contradistinction that they seem to float over it, like 3-D—are the words "*The Sugar Frosted Nutsack 3*" in a shade of dazzlingly vivid, preternatural blue (think Gatorade Frost Glacier Freeze or Frost Cascade Crash or Pine-Sol Sparkling Wave). Embroidered below, in an equally vivid, man-made shade of red or pink (think Ajax Ruby Red Grapefruit Dish Liquid or Pepto-Bismol), is the subtitle: *Hmm Uh (Rig Diva)*.

Beginning on the underside of the visor and continuing to concentrically wind around the circumference of the inside of the cap, inscribed in the tiny, maddeningly meticulous hand of **XOXO** himself, is the looping, recursive epic in its entirety, with all its excruciating redundancies, heavy-handed, stilted tropes, and wearying clichés, its overwrought angst, all its gnomic non sequiturs, all its off-putting adolescent scatology and cringe-inducing smuttiness, all the depraved tableaus and orgies of masturbation with all their bulging, spurting shapes, and all the compulsive repetitions about **Freud**'s repetition compulsion...

...culminating in the final words of the epic (as **Ike Karton** peers deeply into the fiery eyes of his lover/doppelgänger/killer, **Meir Poznak**, in which, of course, he sees the reflection of his own fiery eyes, in which are reflected the fiery eyes of his lover/doppelgänger/killer, **Meir Poznak**, which again, of course, reflect his own fiery eyes, etc., etc., etc....two fiery orbs becoming smaller and smaller and smaller with each mirrored iteration...receding into the infinite depths of this *mise en abyme*...of course, like the red taillights of a bus receding into the farthest-flung depths of a fathomless distance...disappearing into the scintillating somethingness of the nothingness that never was...), **Ike Karton**'s cryptic dying words, which are, of course, "One size...fits all."

ABOUT THE AUTHOR

Mark Leyner is the author of the novels *My Cousin, My Gastroenterologist; Et Tu, Babe;* and *The Tetherballs of Bougainville.* His nonfiction includes the #1 *New York Times* bestseller *Why Do Men Have Nipples?* He cowrote the movie *War, Inc.* and lives in Hoboken, New Jersey.